FORCE OF NATURE

A RILEY THOMPSON THRILLER

ROBIN MAHLE

HARP HOUSE PUBLISHING, LLC.

Published by HARP House Publishing
June, 2018 (2nd edition)
*Formally titled, *Inherent Clarity*

Cover design: CoverMint Designs

Editor: Hercules Editing and Consulting Services

[1]

The water pipes clattered in the walls, a familiar yet unwelcome sound that signaled the start of another school day for young Riley Thompson. She rolled her eyes at the noise the shower produced minutes before her alarm mandated her awakening. Dillon, the eldest of the Thompson kids, was the originator of the disturbance. In a room down the hall from the family facilities, Riley lay in her bed. As a grayish light emerged through the window, she looked to her sister, Gracie, in the neighboring twin bed. The girl of six seemed unaffected by both the daybreak and the clamor. Possibly, it was that she had grown accustomed to the sounds that infiltrated their neglected house.

Riley swung her legs over the edge of the bed and her feet thumped onto the floor. "Gracie, it's time to get up."

The girls were separated by only a small nightstand that had been repainted several times over. The pink shade had begun to peel away, revealing the former blue color beneath. It had been Dillon's before he outgrew it. One of the many repurposed items in the home.

Dillon was a teenager now, fourteen to be exact, and had become somewhat removed from the rest of the family. A likely result of teenaged angst, but it was hastened by a growing necessity for self-preservation.

Riley stood, raising her puffy arms over her head and pushed up on her tiptoes in a deep stretch. The ensuing moan brought Gracie to laughter. She pulled her pajama top back down over her slightly rounded belly, which her mom insisted was just baby fat. Riley thought maybe that was true, but the ten-year-old remained self-conscious about it nonetheless.

"Come on, Gracie; you have to get up and get ready for school."

"Okay, okay. I'm up." Gracie rubbed her brown eyes and finally sat up in bed, tossing the covers away in a huff.

Riley shook her head at her little sister before turning to the closet. Hands at her hips, the long stare across the sparse choice of clothing from which she had to choose began. Ultimately, she decided on the blue long-sleeve sweater paired with black leggings. It would be warm enough to see her through the day. In fact, it seemed as though the afternoon temperatures had been on the rise as of late, a sure sign that spring was just around the corner.

"I'm going downstairs for breakfast. You'd better hurry and get dressed. If Daddy sees you up here much longer, you'll be in for it." This final warning served to light a fire under Gracie as the girl seemed to take heed.

Riley stepped lightly down the stairs, trying to avoid the inevitable comparison her father would make between her feet and a herd of elephants. She grasped the wood spindles to steady herself and made her way down. As she reached the bottom and moved toward the kitchen, she spotted her mother, Ellen, standing in front of the stove.

The sizzling of bacon sounded in her ears as the smell reached her nose. It was a delightful smell that usually only arose on weekends, or on mornings after one of her father's episodes. The growing frequency of these "episodes," as her mother so politely deemed them, was part of the reason Riley ensured a quick departure from her bed this morning, complying with the household rules to avoid any instigation on her part. As her mother remained with her back turned to Riley, the sense that Ellen hadn't fared well last night struck her hard. That was usually what happened first, perceiving the pain or anger or whatever it was the person was feeling at the moment. Then, the visions would come. They would force Riley to be witness to whatever it was that had brought about those feelings. And when Ellen turned to her, it only served as confirmation of the images she'd seen. Riley looked away.

"Good morning, sweetheart," Ellen began. "Sit down and I'll get you a plate." Ellen pulled open the white cabinet door that creaked against rusting hinges and retrieved a plastic plate for Riley.

"Mom, that's a baby plate. Can I just use a regular plate, please?" Riley asked, ignoring what had become too common lately. Much like Ellen did.

"Sorry. Of course you can." Ellen grabbed a ceramic plate from another cabinet and placed three strips of bacon and a scoop of scrambled eggs on it.

Before she could thank her mother, Jack appeared from

upstairs and made his way into the kitchen. “Christ, Ellen, why don’t you make her even chubbier than she already is?”

Riley looked to her dad and back at the plate again, removing a piece of bacon. “Here you go, Mom. I’m not that hungry anyway.” She looked to Ellen and the two exchanged a familiar look, and the girl had seen behind her mother’s eyes, behind the fresh lump of red, swollen skin beneath the right side. The previous night’s episode was as clear to Riley as if it had happened to her.

Pinpointing the exact moment in time this ability in Riley presented itself was easy to recall. It had been at her grandfather’s funeral five years ago. Although she hadn’t recognized it at the time, Riley had been the recipient of a gift from which she could see no good purpose derived.

The theory that the eyes were the window into the soul might have been true, but if that was the case, Riley wished she hadn’t been the one who could see through that window. She tried to keep to herself as much as possible so as not to observe more than was necessary. Fortunately, her best friend Kaitlyn understood. She was the only one who did. Of course, she was the only one Riley ever told.

Jack proceeded to pour the coffee into his thermos as he prepared to leave for work, snatching the extra piece of bacon Ellen still held in her hands.

“I can make some toast for you too, if you’d like,” Ellen said to him.

“No time. I’m late as it is.” Jack wrapped his arm around Ellen. “You know I’m sorry about that, don’t you?” he whispered, and planted a gentle kiss on her cheek, careful to avoid the mark for which he had apologized.

She nodded and turned away from Riley’s watchful glare.

"You might want to put some makeup on that if you plan on leaving the house today." Jack's hushed tone returned to normal again. "And maybe hold off on that bacon yourself. Don't want you ending up like this one here, little girl." He smiled at Riley while patting Ellen's plump backside.

When she was sure Jack was gone, Ellen began, "Don't listen to your father, Riley. You know he doesn't mean any harm."

"I know, Mom." Riley took a few more bites of scrambled egg, then pushed away her plate. "I'd better get Gracie. We won't make the bus if she doesn't get down here soon."

Riley stood at the bottom step and cast her gaze upwards. "Gracie! You'd better get down here or I'm gonna get on that bus without you."

"I'm comin', I'm comin'." Gracie appeared on the upper landing, her light brown hair still slightly disheveled.

Behind her was Dillon. "Go on; hurry up," he said, standing inches away, towering over her tiny frame. He might have only been fourteen, but he stood nearly six feet tall. No one was quite sure how the boy ended up with so much height. Jack was five foot ten on a good day and Ellen barely reached five foot four. His height served him well, as he was just a freshman at Owensville High School. The small town of the same name inside Clay County, Indiana was where they called home.

Dillon gently nudged Gracie, following her down the steps. "I'm gonna have breakfast at school, Mom," he shouted as he reached for his backpack, which hung on the banister of the staircase. "Bye, Riley." He kissed the top of her head. "Bye, Gracie. Be good."

Riley held the front door open and watched Dillon hop on his bike and head down the path to the street that fronted their home.

As he turned parallel to the house, he glanced sideways at her, shaking away the strands of black hair that had fallen into this eyes, and unveiled a rueful smile. She knew he hadn't the stomach to look at his mother and so avoided the need. The fact that he couldn't bring himself to help her when Jack was in a foul mood was tearing him away from the family and Riley could see it happening as he peddled faster.

The only upside to this day so far, was that the sky was clear and Riley was glad for that small miracle. She and Gracie would have to walk the quarter of a mile to get to the bus stop and she preferred if it remained dry. Although, as she stood in front of the opened door, a chill passed through her. Still cold enough for a light jacket, but in this part of central Indiana, it could be much worse. Early March brought slightly warmer temperatures, but a lot of rain, so today was a nice change of pace. Riley began to think that it might even be a good day to play at the park after school with Kaitlyn, assuming Kaitlyn's parents would allow it, of course. She wouldn't question her own mother's acceptance of the idea. In fact, Ellen often preferred Riley and her siblings to be away from the house as much as possible these days.

She closed the door and turned to the coat rack to pull on her fleece. Gracie was finishing her bowl of cereal, not yet appreciating the splendor of bacon and eggs, then they would head out for the bus.

"Don't forget your lunches, girls." Ellen placed their lunch boxes on the counter.

Gracie looked at her mother with that same inquisitive stare she always had when Ellen's face was marked. They didn't talk about it. Ever. Instead, Gracie would be left with the unsettling feeling that something bad had happened and Riley never elaborated. It was hard enough for her to understand, let alone her six-year-old sister.

"Thank you, Mommy." Gracie said, taking hold of her lunchbox.

"I made your favorite. Peanut butter and grape jelly!" Ellen bent down to kiss Gracie on the cheek.

Riley picked up her own lunchbox, noticing how light it was. Maybe a piece of fruit, an apple or a pear, might be accompanying the sandwich, but probably nothing else. At least she could get a free milk from the cafeteria. She didn't know why they let her have milk, but not a meal, although she took what was allowed and told Gracie to do the same. "Thanks, Mom." Riley hugged her mom tightly, but couldn't look her in the eyes. She'd seen enough pain in her today.

"Me and Kaitlyn might go to the park after school, if that's okay?"

"Sure, honey, but let Gracie come with you." Ellen's fingers glided through Riley's long blonde hair. It was stick straight and not at all like her sister's, whose hair was thick and wavy, like their mother's. Instead, Riley had her dad's hair.

She cast a look to Gracie, noticing her pleading eyes. Of course she could come along. "Okay, Mom."

The girls headed toward the door, Ellen following closely behind. Still dressed in her nightshirt and robe, she stood behind the opened door as the two filed out. "Have a good day, babies."

Riley looked back at her mom and examined the woman's pear-shaped figure. Her face was still slender and still very pretty for her age. Although Riley was unsure of what constituted "old," she was pretty confident Ellen wasn't in that category. At thirty-four, most might believe her to be much older.

"You too, Mom." Riley turned back and jogged to catch up with Gracie, who was already at the end of the drive. "Wait up!"

Sprigs were already returning to the great big oak trees that lined either side of the street, a sure sign of warmer days to come. As they continued to walk to the end of the narrow lane, she spotted Kaitlyn standing on her front porch. They were only five houses apart, but it might as well have been a mile.

The only reason they even lived in the same neighborhood was because Riley's house used to be her grandma's and grandpa's before they died and left it to her dad. She hardly remembered the place they lived before, except that it had been smaller than this one. Either way, she was glad because that house was just about the only thing they could call their own.

Jack drove an old Chevy truck. It was silver, but was dirty most of the time, so was hard to decipher the exact color. Her mom had to take a bus into town, or she could walk, but it was more than a couple of miles to the main part of town. The old bus system worked just fine as far as Jack was concerned, not that they could afford another car anyway.

Riley waved to Kaitlyn, who immediately smiled and took to running toward her. As much as she loved Gracie, she couldn't imagine her life without her best friend. There had been a time, long ago, when the families were best friends. Then something happened, and although the girls still spent most of their free time together, their parents barely acknowledged one another when they passed on the street.

"Did you finish your homework?" Riley asked as the three girls started walking again.

"Yeah. Did you?" Kaitlyn asked.

"Yeah, I was up pretty late doing it, though, and then I had a hard time getting to sleep." Riley only needed to look at Kaitlyn and Kaitlyn knew what it was that had happened. Once in a while, she and Kaitlyn would talk about the way things were at her house, but Riley didn't like to burden her friend.

"Well, I'm glad you got it done. Mrs. Downey would give you that look and make you stay after class or something stupid like that."

"I know! Then we wouldn't be able to go to the park today after school. Do you wanna go?"

"Let me text my mom." Kaitlyn retrieved a cell phone from her backpack and began thumbing the screen while they continued on to the bus stop. "Okay. Yeah, I can go, but I have to be home by five."

"Okay, cool." Riley gazed longingly at Kaitlyn's phone. She'd been asking for one for the past six months, but only Dillon had a cell phone, and her parents always replied by telling her she was too young and didn't need one. The more likely reason was that they couldn't afford it, but Riley wished her mom was here right now to point out this perfect example of its necessity.

The girls reached the corner where a few kids stood waiting, appearing unmoved by their arrival. They acknowledged one another with a quick hello, followed by a nod. Gracie started to talk to the only other first grader in the group, but at least she had someone.

Owensville had a population of about a thousand people. That was down quite a bit from the days when the Caterpillar plant was running at full capacity. It had shut down six years ago and moved forty miles away to a bigger city. Riley's dad worked there until it closed. Now, he was working at an aluminum plant in the next town over, a job he only recently acquired.

She could remember when there were lots of kids waiting at this bus stop, but over the past couple of years, their numbers had been dwindling. Some of the houses on her street were now vacant too. She'd seen Dillon hanging out with his friends at one of them. The windows had been boarded up, but it seemed the teenagers had found a way in. Riley never ratted him out, though, knowing it would only cause trouble for him at home.

"I see the bus!" Gracie pointed down to the end of the road where the bright yellow bus was slowly approaching.

The kids shuffled to the edge of the broken curb and haphazardly formed in a line. The bus rolled to a stop and the driver pulled the lever to open the doors. It was the final stop before heading to the only elementary school in town. Kindergarten through eighth grade. No middle school here. Not enough kids to support one. So from there, Riley would go straight to the only high school in town, where Dillon attended.

The bus was almost full, but a few seats remained near the front. No one ever wanted to sit up front, but since they were at the last stop, Riley and Kaitlyn usually got the honors. Gracie and her friend almost always sat across from them. Sometimes, the bus driver would save those seats for the troublemakers, but it seemed that wasn't the case today.

Kaitlyn opened her backpack and pulled out a couple of breakfast bars. "Want one?" She held one out for Riley.

"Sure. Thanks." Riley smiled and unwrapped the foil-covered treat. She was still hungry, regardless of what Jack would have said about it.

The bus quickly filled with sounds of children laughing and talking as it pulled away and, the further it drove from home, the better Riley began to feel.

[2]

T**he Indiana Hoosiers** were playing against Penn State in a basketball game that Carl Boyd had been waiting for all day. The reception was coming in shoddy and his frustration had grown as a result.

Carl didn't have much to look forward to nowadays, but Indiana basketball was one of them and with March Madness quickly approaching, he began to curse his satellite TV provider. He opened the door of his mobile home and looked at the dish mounted on the top. The late afternoon sun was shining in his eyes, but by all accounts, the dish appeared to be secured.

"Damn it!" Carl went back inside, the narrow screen door slamming against its metal frame. The satellite dish was the only luxury he could afford, and what was the point in paying for it if he couldn't enjoy a couple of hours watching a much-anticipated game? He decided on a beer to cool his temper.

The kitchen was small and cramped and only five feet away

from the living room. Carl lived in a small beat-up trailer in a park on the edge of town. The twelve by sixty foot, white mobile home with faded blue trim suited his needs, even if it wasn't the nicest place to live. What did he care? He didn't have anyone to share it with and that was fine by him.

Carl pushed back the few strands of white hair that remained on his head before opening the refrigerator door to pull out a cold one. By the looks of the contents inside, a trip to the grocery store in town might be required sooner rather than later. Come to think of it, it would have to be later because his Social Security check wasn't due to arrive until early next week. Might mean another trip to St. Vincent's this weekend. Not that he minded too much. They usually served pretty decent food there.

Carl popped open the can of Keystone Light and took a swig before returning to his chair in front of the TV. It looked like the reception was improving and that made him happy.

A few hours passed before Carl realized he must have fallen asleep in the chair. The sound of a neighbor's car pulling onto the dirt road between the units startled him awake. He peered through the blinds from where he sat and spotted Helen across the way walking into her trailer, slamming the car door behind her.

The shadows that bounced from the window caused him to consider the time. Upon glancing at the clock mounted on the paneled wall, he noticed the hour. "I'm never gonna sleep tonight now."

It was practically dinnertime and now he regretted having that beer. It was rare that he enjoyed drinking at all because of all the damn pills that doctor at the VA had him on. Said it would help his "condition." What did he know? He was just some punk kid who'd never been in a war, never knew what it was like to have the nightmares and the flashbacks. Didn't matter that it was damn near forty-five years ago. No one forgets that sort of thing.

The doctor told him not to drink alcohol with the pills and Carl usually did pretty well with those instructions, except that he really wanted one today. Too late now. He was going to be up all night.

Carl pushed himself off the recliner, grunting and groaning along the way. He was a man of sixty-seven, after all, and things didn't work the same as they used to. Shuffling into the bathroom to do his business, Carl now stood at the sink and splashed some water onto his face. One of the light bulbs in the fixture over the mirror was burnt out and so, as he looked at himself, the dim light made him appear even older. "Jesus, I look like hell!" Carl shook his head as his eyes dropped to the rest of his body that reflected back at him.

His shoulders were much narrower than they used to be, like there was no meat left on them to hold up his arms. The thin white t-shirt he was wearing was short-sleeved and protruding out of those sleeves were what looked like twigs, nothing like the guns he used to have when he was in the Marine Corp, but that was a long time ago.

Carl raised his right hand and laid it over the tattoo on his left arm, just below the shoulder. He remembered getting that tattoo as if it had happened yesterday. He was about to deploy for his second tour and was headed out to the Quang Nam province. "Swift, Silent, Deadly," he began. "Not so much."

RILEY AND GRACIE WAVED GOODBYE TO KAITLYN BEFORE

continuing toward home after spending the afternoon at the park. Riley checked her watch and noticed they had only five minutes to spare before their mom might consider them "late." She didn't like to be late.

They slowed their approach when the girls appeared to simultaneously spot their father's truck already in the drive. It was too early for him to be home from work. This wasn't a good sign.

Riley jutted her arm in front of Gracie, bringing the girl to a stop just in front of their house. She looked at her little sister.

"We have to go in, Riley. We can't stand out here all night."

For a moment, Riley considered running back to Kaitlyn's house, dragging Gracie along with her, but in the end, she knew it would only make matters worse. Whatever had happened while they were away at school, whatever was going to happen now, couldn't be changed. "I know, I know." She inhaled a deep breath of the cold evening air. "Better just get it over with."

Standing now on the front porch, Riley gently nudged Gracie to get behind her. She turned the door handle and pushed, opening the door to the sound of the blaring television in the living room and clattering dishes in the kitchen. She wondered for a moment if Dillon had returned home from practice. He spent most of his time in his room, so it was too difficult to know for sure if he was there.

Riley began to feel relief at the normal, everyday happenings inside her home. She even turned to Gracie and smiled. Gracie seemed relieved too and the two walked into the kitchen where their mother was preparing for dinner.

"Hi, Mom," Riley said, dropping her backpack onto the kitchen table. But when Ellen turned to her, Riley took a step back. "What's wrong, Mom?" Her guard suddenly returned to its usual place. Of course, as the words escaped her lips, she was already envisioning it. Jack and Ellen standing in the living room, arguing over his lost job. Jack insisting he'd been laid off, but Ellen knowing better. Riley shut her eyes for a moment and inhaled through her nose, working to shed the images. She had no control over her visions, but had come to understand that this sometimes helped.

It was evident that Ellen had been crying for some time, but she managed a thin smile at the sight of her daughters. "Nothing; everything's fine, sweetheart," Ellen whispered. "How was your day? Did you enjoy the park?"

Riley had heard the "everything's fine" line a million times and needed not to inquire further anyway. "It was a good day, Mom. Me and Gracie had fun at the park. I'm going to go put my stuff away now." Not much point in saying anything else. She was powerless to offer the kind of help Ellen needed.

"Be sure to keep quiet. Your father's watching television and doesn't want to be disturbed."

"Okay, Mommy, but why is Daddy home so early?" Gracie asked.

On hearing this, Riley stood on the second step and cringed.

"Oh, honey. He had some problems at work today, that's all."

The girls walked quietly up the stairs, careful not to disturb Jack. As Riley traded her school shoes for slippers and her black leggings for a pair of ratty sweatpants, she heard the front door. Dillon was home. Riley rushed to the landing in time to catch a glimpse of him setting his gym bag at the bottom of the stairs and removing his jacket.

"I need to talk to you, son."

Riley heard Jack's voice carry into the entryway. She watched as Dillon rolled his eyes and dragged his lanky body into the living room, disappearing from view. The sound of their voices hadn't reached her ears, so she carefully padded down the staircase, standing on the third step from the bottom to listen in on the conversation.

"I'm gonna need you to step up, you hear me?" Jack said.

"But, Dad, that'll mean I won't be able to play basketball this season. It'll ruin my chances to make varsity next year."

"You think I give two shits about that, son?"

Riley flinched at her father's raised tone.

"This family is what's important here and I just lost my goddam job! You're old enough to get part time work at the grocery store so you can help keep food on the damn table."

"I thought that was your job." Dillon muttered.

Riley's heart leapt into her throat as she backed up a step, fearing she might be seen listening in.

Jack rose quickly from his chair. "What'd you say to me?" He was now inches from Dillon's face.

Riley could just see them standing toe to toe near the passageway. *Please don't hurt him, please don't hurt him.*

Dillon's shoulders straightened up and he raised his head. "I said I thought that was your job." He waved away the stench of alcohol on Jack's breath. "Maybe if you didn't drink so much, you might still have a job!"

Ellen emerged from the kitchen and caught sight of Riley standing on the steps. "Get upstairs!" she whispered and pointed a stern finger.

Riley rushed back to her room where Gracie sat on her bed, brushing the hair of one of her Barbie dolls.

"What's going on down there?"

"Dillon's talking back to Dad. I think Mom's trying to calm him down."

"Why does he do it, Riley? Why does Dillon always make Daddy mad?"

"I don't know, Gracie." She closed the door, deciding she'd heard enough. It was only a matter of time before Dillon would race up to his room and slam his door shut. She worried so much about her brother. He always pushed Jack to the breaking point, which wasn't that hard to do, especially if he'd been drinking.

By the time dinner was on the table, it seemed Jack had calmed down and so had Dillon. All that could be heard was the sound of forks and knives scraping along plates. Riley glanced up at the faces of her family. They weren't much for talking, that was for sure. Not like at Kaitlyn's house. It seemed they were always laughing and joking around. Sometimes, she wished she was a part of their family.

"I'm sorry about earlier, son." Jack began.

Ellen raised her head in pleasant surprise.

"You're right. I'll find something else soon. No need for you to stop playing ball. It might be your only chance to get out of this God forsaken town."

Once in a while, Riley could see the man her father used to be. Back when he had a good job in town, but that was a long time ago, when Gracie was just a baby. It seemed the harder it got for Jack to find work, the more he drank. And of course, the more he drank, the harder it became for him to keep a job.

Mrs. Downey had her back turned, writing the day's

assignment on the white board. The kids wasted no time in taking advantage of the teacher's watchful eye having been cast momentarily elsewhere.

"What are you going to do this weekend, Riley?" Jacob whispered, blowing away the hair that had fallen in his eyes. It was possible he was going for a Justin Bieber look, but had missed the mark just a bit.

"I don't know yet. Why? What are you doing?" She always felt a little flustered when Jacob talked to her. He was kind of a geeky kid – at least everyone else seemed to think so – but she thought he was cute.

"My mom said we're going up to Indianapolis to see my uncle and cousins. We're leaving right after school."

"That sounds exciting. I've never been there." Riley's eyes lit up at the idea of traveling to the big city. She'd never even been outside of Owensville.

"Yeah. It's been a long time since I've been there. It's pretty fun." Jacob immediately turned back to the front of the class as Mrs. Downey cleared her throat. He shifted back for just a quick moment to smile at Riley.

"For those of you who are interested," Mrs. Downey began, "we'll be volunteering at St. Vincent's on Saturday, helping out with serving the food and doing some cleaning up after the lunch service. I'm going to be handing out extra credit to the students who would like to volunteer their time."

Riley tossed a glance to Kaitlyn, as if to say, "Are you in?" Kaitlyn shrugged her shoulders. Riley took that to mean yes and so she quickly raised her hand. "Me and Kaitlyn would like to go."

"Wonderful!" Mrs. Downey replied. "I'll leave a sign-up sheet on my desk. Remember, it could make a difference to those students who are looking to bring up their grades. And, of course, it'll mean a great deal to those less fortunate."

Riley immediately thought of her own family and how if her dad couldn't find another job, they might find themselves standing in line in the same soup kitchen. She wished things were like they used to be, but that wasn't likely to happen anytime soon.

The school bell rang for lunch and the kids quickly marched out; some with their packed lunches and some who ate a hot lunch from the cafeteria. Half the kids in her class alone got free lunches, but she didn't. That might change, but for now, Ellen packed her lunch. When she opened it, she pulled out the peanut butter and jelly sandwich and the apple. She smiled at the unexpected sight of a Tootsie Roll.

Jacob approached Riley and Kaitlyn with his lunch tray. "Can I sit down?"

Riley looked to her friend for approval, but instead answered before Kaitlyn could roll her eyes at the request. "Sure!"

The boy set his tray down and sat next to her. "So you guys are gonna help feed the homeless at the shelter?"

"They're not all homeless," Riley began. "Some just need a meal because they can't afford their groceries."

"My dad says people who go to those places are all drunks and losers who can't hold a job," Jacob said as he tucked into food that appeared to resemble a cheeseburger.

"Well, that's not very nice," Riley was quick to reply. "Some people really do need the help, you know. My dad says there aren't any good jobs out there."

"I don't know. I guess it's a nice thing for you guys to do anyway." Jacob raised the carton of milk to his lips and took a sip.

"Yeah. It is," Kaitlyn replied.

[3]

The dim lights in the bar masked the precise time of day, but as Carl Boyd, Jr. sat on the barstool, nursing a bottle of domestic beer, he figured it must have been about five o'clock. The place was starting to pick up as happy hour appeared to have begun. And since it was a Friday, it should be jumping in another hour or so.

But CJ, as he was called, wasn't there to get drunk and hit on the local talent. He was there to meet up with Johnny and Bennett and the brothers were late.

"You want another?"

The young woman who was tending bar was nice to look at, even if she was a little on the scrawny side. CJ took a quick glance down at the modest cleavage she'd exposed while leaning over the bar to ask the question. She must've noticed because she raised up almost immediately, straightening the custom-made neckline of her vintage Journey concert t-shirt. CJ figured she was probably too young to even remember their music. "Yeah, I'll take another. Thanks."

He'd met Johnny and Bennett a couple of years ago when he moved to Ohio. CJ hadn't really found a place he'd wanted to call home since leaving Indiana, but it seemed his dad, Carl Sr., had had enough of his freeloading and finally kicked him out. Just as well, though; his dad's illness wasn't getting any better and it scared him sometimes. The old man would jump out of bed, screaming and running out toward him where he slept on the couch. He'd have to shake his dad to pull him out of it. It seemed that Vietnam had screwed him up pretty badly. Of course, he'd only ever known his dad post-war. He was born in seventy-seven.

The brothers had convinced CJ to take up roots from Columbus and head down south a little to the hick town in which he now found himself, near Lancaster. They were good enough guys, he supposed, except maybe for the fact that they were involved in one of those militia-type groups. The kind that wanted to take up arms against the government or something like that.

CJ didn't really care about government one way or the other and so he never thought much about what those two did in their spare time. But that had changed a few months ago when he'd needed a job and one of the members of the group told Johnny he could help out with that. It seemed CJ had become indebted to that man and his involvement with the group had grown in recent weeks.

So CJ was now waiting for the two of them to show up and take him to the meeting that was supposed to start in half an hour. He didn't know where it was taking place; sort of an initiation-type thing, he guessed.

The hard slap against CJ's back nearly caused him to spit out the swig of beer he'd just swished around in his mouth.

Johnny laughed as he watched CJ cough, his brother joining in soon after.

"What the hell, man!" CJ said as he wiped his chin. "You scared the shit out me. Where the hell you been?"

"Bennett had to take a shit. Took him an hour!" Johnny's laughter bordered on the obnoxious.

"Shut the fuck up, man. It did not!" Bennett pulled out a stool and sat down next to CJ.

"All right, all right. Doesn't matter. Are we gonna get out of here or not?" CJ wasn't sure how he felt about the impending meeting. He didn't know what would go down, but didn't have a choice. He'd been given a halfway decent job and didn't want to screw it up.

"Yeah, okay. Let's get the hell out of here. Come on, Bennett; stop looking at the pretty bartender."

"What? Don't we have time for a beer?"

"No! Now let's go," Johnny said.

Bennett returned to his feet, leering at the girl behind the bar. It seemed that she hardly took notice. Like it'd happened to her plenty of times and she was used to it. CJ watched her reaction and kind of liked the fact that she could obviously handle herself. Maybe a trip back here once this meeting was done would be in order. Maybe she wouldn't care that he probably had a good ten plus years on her.

CJ dropped a twenty on the bar. "Keep the change." His tab was only ten bucks, but he figured the big tip might help him out later. At least he hoped it would. His job wasn't the sort that accommodated such discretionary spending.

Johnny drove an old Ford Gran Torino and not the lovingly restored version. This 1970s beast was thrashed all to hell, but then, CJ didn't think Johnny cared much about that. The engine roared and the tires squealed as they pulled out onto the main road.

"So where we headed?" CJ asked, sliding around on the vinyl seat in the back.

"Can't tell ya or else I'd have to kill ya!" Bennett roared with laughter at his own clichéd joke.

Johnny glared at his brother, then raised his eyes to the rear view mirror. "About ten miles north of here. That's where we hold our meetings."

"So if I go to this meeting, does it mean that I'm part of the group?"

"Well, as you've made it this far, I'd say yes. Pretty sure ol' Raymond wouldn't have invited you if that weren't the case."

He felt Johnny's gaze linger a little too long and began to wonder if he was trying to work out if CJ was afraid. Of course he wasn't. Why would he be? He just had to sit and listen to a bunch of good ol' boys talk about how things used to be when they were young and how they couldn't stand what was happening to their beloved country.

Maybe they had a point, but there were better ways, he thought, to deal with such matters. Wanting to take up arms against the government might not be the right answer. Still, he'd do what he had to do to get through the night, then go back and see the pretty barmaid.

About twenty yards ahead was a large building. CJ thought it could have been a barn or stable at one time, but it had clearly been neglected over the years. It was the only building as far as he could see. It was definitely secluded and he felt just a little nervous about it now.

"Is that it?"

"That's it," Johnny replied, driving onto the gravel lot. "I see most everyone's here already. Good."

Half a dozen or so cars were already in the parking lot as Johnny pulled into a spot, kicking up dust in the process; enough that it practically obscured the entrance.

"Well, let's do this." Bennett opened the car door, hiking up his baggy jeans as he stood.

CJ and Johnny emerged and the three men stood around for a moment while the dust settled.

"I'm not gonna have to do some crazy shit like shoot a dog or something, am I?" CJ asked, feeling more than just a little unsettled.

"What the hell do you think we do here, CJ? We're not animals. We just sit around and shoot the shit and down a few beers. Then we go home to our families, screw our wives, and go to bed, just like everyone else," Johnny replied.

"You ain't got no wife, Johnny; just your left hand." Bennett broke out into hysterics again, although neither of the other two joined in.

"Just get the hell inside." Johnny swung his arm toward the entrance.

CJ walked inside behind the two brothers. The first thing he noticed was the giant Confederate flag hanging from the rafters. He wondered for a moment if he'd just been transported from Ohio to the backwoods of Mississippi or someplace like that. He leaned toward Johnny's ear. "These guys aren't part of the Klan, are they?"

Johnny cocked his head, squinting hard as if he had just heard something highly offensive. "What? No, man. Jesus, what the hell's wrong with you? You take me for someone like that? Or the brothers I choose to associate with?"

"No. I'm sorry, man. Course not. It's just, you know, the flag."

Johnny kept walking until he reached the table where Raymond McAllister sat, beer in hand, arm around the back of the chair next to him. "Ray, good to see you, brother." Johnny shook his hand.

Raymond ascended from the chair. "Johnny Denton, good to see you too, brother. And I see you brought our friend Carl Boyd." Raymond turned toward CJ and extended his hand. "How the hell are ya?"

"Doing well, sir. Thanks for asking. It's a pleasure to meet you and, please, call me CJ."

"Oh hell, son, don't call me 'sir.' It's Ray and of course you already know Doug."

"Good to see you, Doug." It seemed as though CJ's boss was the number two guy in the room. At least, it appeared that way, since he was sitting next to Raymond.

"How long's this man been working for you now, Doug? A few months?" Ray asked.

"Something like that. Maybe closer to four or five months," Doug replied. "And he's doing a hell of a good job."

"Thanks, Doug. That's kind of you to say." It had probably been the longest CJ had been employed anywhere. It was a shitty job in a mom and pop hardware store, but it paid the bills.

CJ was staring down the barrel to forty and he knew he had to get his shit together. He'd screwed around with his life long enough. This job wasn't the answer, but it was a start.

Standing here now, he wondered what the hell it was these people did. Calling themselves militiamen was all well and good, he supposed, but did they actually do anything to further their cause or were they just posers? CJ had hoped the former wasn't the case. He didn't want trouble, but these men looked like the type to either cause it or to go looking for it.

"So, what'd you think?" Johnny asked as they drove down the single-lane country road. Bennett appeared eager for an answer as well.

"Yeah, it was all right, I guess. I don't know. They all seem like good guys." CJ stared out of the rear passenger window at nothing but blackness. They were way out in the country and about to cross over a tributary that led out to the Ohio River, onto one of the old iron and steel truss bridges that had been built before World War II. Not many of them remained, but it seemed this one had recently been reinforced with concrete on the roadbed. The sound of the tires as they rolled along grew louder.

"What's that?" Bennett asked, turning around to CJ.

"Nothing. I was just saying that those guys seem all right." He returned his gaze to the window only, this time, shadowy trees passed by in a blur.

They arrived back at the bar where CJ's car sat virtually alone in the parking lot. He hadn't realized how much time had passed and wondered if the place was still open. But as he glanced at the front door, he saw a couple of staggering bodies emerge. It was still open.

"Thanks, guys. Appreciate the ride," CJ said as he began to step out.

"No problem. So, I'll catch up with you tomorrow?" Johnny asked.

"Sure. Sounds good." He rapped his knuckles on the hood of the car and nodded. "Thanks again."

Johnny and Bennett Denton were gone.

CJ walked inside, noticing the place had nearly emptied out. It was almost midnight and, around these parts, if no one was buying, they'd likely shut it down for the night. He approached the bar once again and there she was, looking a little more tired than she did earlier in the evening, but still, not looking too bad.

"Oh, you're back. It's last call. What can I get you?" she asked.

He was a little surprised she remembered him. Of course, he had been in this bar more than a few times, although he'd seen her only once before and that was just briefly because her shift was ending. "I'll take another Bud."

"Coming right up." Her smile was bright, even at the late hour and her shoulder-length black hair swayed as she moved toward the back of the bar.

He waited patiently for her return and began to think about the meeting. He hadn't wanted to say anything to the brothers, but he didn't feel at all good about joining their little club. They had made it fairly clear that they wanted things a certain way and would do what it took to make them happen.

CJ had spotted more than a few guns and rifles around the room, against the back walls. He was all for the right to bear arms, but looking at those seemingly disgruntled people around guns made him nervous. It was too late now. He was in with them and doubted that they took kindly to people leaving.

"Here you go." The bartender placed the bottle in front of him.

"Thanks." CJ looked up at the girl. "So what's your name?"

"Melissa." A warm smile played on her lips.

Maybe the big tip had worked. "Melissa. That's a nice name." CJ looked down, trying to be coy, but unsure if he was pulling it off. "I'm Carl, but my friends call me CJ. You gonna be finished here soon? Maybe you wanna grab a coffee for something?"

"Or something—maybe," she said.

[4]

The branches of the tree outside Riley's bedroom window tapped against the glass as the wind continued to howl. The sun hadn't broken through the clouds and it looked as though a cold day was on order. As Kaitlyn's dad honked the horn of his car, she reached for her coat, which lay on her bed, before rushing downstairs.

"I'll be back around four o'clock, Mom," she said, making her way to the front door.

"Okay, honey. Have fun."

It was still early on this Saturday morning and Gracie remained in her pajamas, watching cartoons in the living room. Dillon was known to sleep until twelve, if he was allowed to, but he had a game later this morning and so Ellen would have to get him up soon. She would leave Jack to wake on his own, as it was highly unlikely that he would go to Dillon's game anyway, claiming work needed to be done around the house or some other made up excuse.

Riley opened the door, almost losing her grip on it with the force of the heavy winds. She raced to the end of the path, her hair whipping around her face, and pulled open the rear passenger door, sliding in next to Kaitlyn. "It's really windy!" Riley brushed her hair away. "Thank you for picking me up, Mr. Ross."

"My pleasure, Riley. I think it's a good thing what you two girls are doing." He continued along the road.

Riley smiled at her friend, who didn't appear as enthusiastic as Riley was. The drive to the shelter wouldn't be long; in fact, it was near the old warehouse that had been a furniture store until closing recently, just a few miles from the main street.

"How are your folks?" he asked, glancing into the rear view mirror.

"Fine." What else could she say? He knew better than most what kind of people the Thompsons were. What kind of person Jack was. After all, the two used to be as close as brothers.

"Glad to hear it."

He said nothing more, thankfully, and Riley looked on, taking notice of the swaying traffic lights and the occasional debris, newspapers and such, that drifted by.

"Okay, looks like we're here. Now, Kaitlyn, you're going to call me when you're ready to leave, is that right?" Mr. Ross asked.

"Yeah. We're supposed to be done by four o'clock, I think, but I'll check with Mrs. Downey. Just come back at four, okay?"

"All right. You two have fun."

The girls slid out of the back seat, waving goodbye to Mr. Ross, then raced each other to the entrance of the building. Kaitlyn turned a final time to her dad, signaling it was okay for him to leave.

Inside didn't look much different to Riley from her own school cafeteria. There was a long buffet-style counter and a bunch of tables lined up, just like in her lunchroom. She searched for Mrs. Downey, finally spotting her appear from behind the double doors of the kitchen. "I see her. Come on." Riley took hold of Kaitlyn's hand and walked toward her teacher.

"Good morning, girls. Glad you could make it," Mrs. Downey said.

A few of their other classmates were also there, but not Jacob. Riley knew he was in the city this weekend and didn't expect to see him, but felt mild disappointment nonetheless.

"Okay, let's get to our stations. Here are your aprons and hair-nets for the girls." Mrs. Downey handed out the items and proceeded to instruct the children on their respective duties. "Riley, I'd like you to serve the potatoes and Kaitlyn can work next to you, handing out the rolls."

The girls giggled with excitement upon hearing that they'd get to work side by side. They went to their stations and prepared for the breakfast service. Riley was nervous and unsure of how to behave around those who were either homeless or just plain down and out. Her family wasn't much better off, but they never came to one of these places.

As the doors opened for the morning service, Riley watched the people trail in. They were just normal, everyday people that could have easily been one of her neighbors. Families, single people; they all looked just like everyone else.

Her nerves began to settle a little at this discovery and, as one of the young children approached her, she asked, "Would you like some hash browns?"

The little girl didn't answer, only nodded. The girl's mother stood beside her. "Say, 'yes, please.'"

"Yes, please," the little girl repeated.

Riley dished out a large spoonful of the golden hash browns and set them on her plate. "There you go. I hope you like it." That was all it took. The little girl smiled back at her and Riley felt much better. She looked to Kaitlyn. "This was a good idea."

The morning turned into day as the girls prepared for the lunch service. Mrs. Downey checked on them to be sure the kids weren't too tired and could continue on. "After this, you can help clean up and then head home. I'm so proud of both of you." The teacher smiled and patted the girls on the back.

It wasn't often that Riley heard those words. In fact, if she did, it was usually from Mrs. Downey. Jack had grown too critical of her in recent months and her mother did little to stave off the mild but noticeable denigration. This was a much-needed bolster to her confidence.

The trays had been placed in their warmers and the smell of cheeseburgers and chili drifted through the air. Riley could feel her own stomach growl when the scent reached her nose and wondered if she might be able to eat after everyone else had been served.

"Ready?" Kaitlyn asked.

"Yep." Riley tucked her hair inside the net and tied her apron. "I hope there's leftovers. I'm starving."

A similar, but much smaller group of people entered the dining hall. Riley put on her friendliest smile as they began their approach. She handed out the cornbread while Kaitlyn got to dish out the chili. She recognized a few of the faces this time.

From the local grocery store, one of the cashiers had come in. Riley wondered why he would need such help. He had a job. Of course, what she hadn't known was that the man only worked part-time and for less money than he earned while doing the same job last year, making this a necessary trip. She handed him some corn-bread and he thanked her.

Riley began to feel lightheaded and started to sway a little. Must have been the hunger, except that this was somehow different.

"Are you okay?" Kaitlyn asked. "You don't look too good, Riley."

"I'm okay. I think I'm just getting hungry."

"Do I need to get Mrs. Downey?"

"No. I'll be fine." Riley looked up and spotted the man who now stood in front of her, waiting to be served. She blinked hard, but images began flashing in her mind, like a movie that was only visible to her. A sense of...dread came over her.

"Corporal Boyd," a man in an olive-colored t-shirt with some sort of chain hanging around his neck shouted from the front of the dining hall. "Jackson, Mills, Nelson." He held out envelopes and waited for the owners of the various names he'd just called out to come and collect them.

The man who was called Corporal Boyd approached.

"Staff Sergeant Combs wants to see you."

Boyd, as it stated on his uniform, didn't question as to why, but only proceeded out of the hall and headed toward the offices of the Staff Sergeant.

On arrival, he saluted and then stood at attention in front of the officer.

"Corporal Boyd, please take a seat."

"Yes, sir."

"I received this a few hours ago. I apologize for not bringing this to your attention sooner, but I'm afraid I have some upsetting news." The man held out an envelope that had already been opened.

The words "Western Union" were scrolled at the top. Below, in typed letters, it began:

"From: Mr. and Mrs. Wilhelm, Indianapolis, Indiana

USMC Corporal Carl Boyd,

I'm sorry to inform you that on the morning of October 17, 1973, your wife, Rosalyn Boyd, and daughter Mary were killed in an automobile accident. The accident occurred while Rosalyn was entering an intersection. Another vehicle approached simultaneously, and they collided with one another.

Please know that neither suffered any pain as God took them instantly after the collision. My deepest regrets and sympathies.

Mr. Wilhelm."

Boyd dropped the telegram and plunged his head into his hands.

"Riley?" Kaitlyn asked again, sounding more urgent this time.

Riley finally steadied herself. "I'm sorry, sir." She handed him a piece of cornbread.

The man had been standing in front of her for a while. It seemed Riley's expression had turned completely blank for a time.

"You sure you're okay, there, young lady?" the man asked.

Riley blinked a few times to help clear her vision. "Yes, sir. I'm very sorry, Mr. Boyd."

Carl creased his brow at her reply. "How did you know my name?"

"I—uh, I'm sure I've seen you around town before, Mr. Boyd. Would you like another piece?"

"No...thank you." Carl moved on down the line, casting suspicious glances back at Riley.

"What was that all about?" Kaitlyn asked.

"Nothing. I'm fine."

Riley couldn't help but keep an occasional eye on Mr. Boyd. He sat alone and looked off in the distance as though preoccupied and was eating in a perfunctory manner. She didn't know what her vision meant, except that the man had lost his wife and daughter in a car accident a long time ago. It hurt when he read the message and it was a pain that still lingered, much as she suspected it probably had lingered inside Carl Boyd too.

She recognized that the uniforms were military and that it had been around 1973, at least, according to the telegram. He had looked much younger. In fact, if it weren't for his eyes, she wouldn't have been sure it was the same man. The blue eyes, sad and lonely, they were what made her confident that the Mr. Boyd that had stood in front of her had been the same man in the uniform.

She had grown used to the visions, as well as anyone could, but this was so unfamiliar to her. Most had stemmed from her own family or friends. So to have this one of a complete stranger caught Riley off guard. She would need to hold herself together for a while longer, until it was time to leave, but it rattled her a great deal.

Carl began to approach and Riley stood up straight, as if she needed to be at attention. He walked past her to return his tray and proceeded to leave the dining area. Riley noticed the mark on his arm. It was only partially visible beneath his t-shirt, but she realized it had been a tattoo. Whatever it was about Carl Boyd, Riley was drawn to him in a manner she'd never experienced before and was pretty sure she hadn't wanted to experience again.

At the end of the lunch service, the girls wiped down the tables and returned to the kitchen to get the final word from Mrs. Downey that they had permission to leave.

"You all were a tremendous help here today and I couldn't be more proud of each and every one of you. I'm sure your parents are waiting for you out front, so I'll walk out with you all."

They appeared triumphant in their accomplishments as the four kids in Mrs. Downey's fifth grade class exited the building. Kaitlyn seemed impatient as Riley stayed behind to talk to Mrs. Downey.

"Mrs. Downey, do you know who that man was that came in at lunch? The one with the tattoo?"

"I'm sorry, Riley, but I'm not sure who you're talking about."

"He's old, kinda bald, and was wearing an Indiana Pacers t-shirt."

Mrs. Downey seemed to search her memory for any sign that she had seen this "old man" Riley was asking about. "Do you mean Carl Boyd?"

"Yes, I think so. I think he might have been in the army or something." Riley continued as Kaitlyn's frustration grew.

"Yes. That's Mr. Boyd. He's a Vietnam veteran and a very nice man. Did he say something to you?"

"No, not really. I—I just wanted, well, I saw the tattoo and it looked like an army symbol or something and I wanted to ask. That's all."

"He keeps to himself most of the time. I've seen him at the clinic and the drugstore occasionally, but I'm afraid I don't know him well."

"Okay. Thanks, Mrs. Downey." Riley signaled her goodbye and the two girls skipped out to the front, disappearing beyond the exit doors.

RILEY DECIDED TO WALK THE DISTANCE BACK TO HER HOME from Kaitlyn's, insisting Mr. Ross need not drive her down. The skies had mostly cleared and the threat of rain had evaporated. She wanted a moment to herself, unable to shake the feeling that Carl Boyd would need help and soon, in what way she didn't yet know, but it was a strange and frightening sensation. It had come upon her as he left the kitchen. An intangible warning. However, she knew so little about him. What could a ten-year-old girl possibly offer as help?

The wind had picked up again and Riley pulled her jacket closed as she approached her home. It was anyone's guess as to what the mood of the house would be on entry. Riley had almost wished for Kaitlyn to suggest that she have a sleepover, but tomorrow was Sunday and she would have to go to church early.

Riley walked in, shedding her coat inside the warmed entryway. The radiator worked especially well in this part of the house. "I'm home."

It was nearing the dinner hour and Ellen emerged from the kitchen, wiping her hands with a dishtowel. "How'd it go? You girls have fun?"

"Oh, Mom, it was amazing. The people were so nice and so grateful just to eat a hot meal."

"Yeah, I'm sure they're all there just looking for a free handout." Jack appeared from the small powder room in the corridor, hiking up his carpenter-styled jeans.

"Oh, Jack, don't say things like that. People are having a hard time right now, and we're not that far from standing in those lines ourselves," Ellen replied.

"Yeah, well, maybe you should get off your ass and find a job then."

Ellen ignored him and instead returned her attention to Riley. "Why don't you go on upstairs and see Gracie. She's been asking when you'd be home."

"Okay, Mom." Riley took to the stairs, but stopped, turning back to her father. "Dad, what is a Vietnam veteran?"

Jack was of the age where it was likely he would've served in the Gulf War, but he hadn't. His own father had been stationed in Korea, although after that war. In fact, he didn't know anyone who had served in Vietnam. "It's a person who fought in the Vietnam War and it happened in the 1960s and 70s. I don't know much about it. Why don't you look it up?"

Riley shrugged and continued upstairs.

[5]

The poorly insulated trailer was losing heat by the minute. The damn heating system was acting up again and Carl would have to plug in the portable appliance if he hoped to keep from freezing in the night. It was expected to get below twenty degrees and now that the sun had lowered, those temperatures were dropping right along with it.

He retrieved the space heater from the bedroom closet and plugged it in, setting it directly in front of his recliner. At least his feet would stay warm.

As Carl settled back down again with a full belly and sipping on his instant coffee, his thoughts turned to the girl. It was the way she'd looked at him; it made him feel uneasy. Just standing there, holding out that piece of cornbread. Her eyes were empty, like she wasn't even there.

Carl shuddered but wasn't sure if it was his mind envisioning her again or if it was just the cold. Another sip of coffee would help, certainly.

It only took a few more minutes before he decided to hoist himself off the worn-in recliner and head to his bedroom. On the top of his closet was a box filled with pictures and trinkets. It was pretty much all Carl had left of his past. He didn't know why, but he felt compelled to sift through that box. It was something he hadn't done in years and the box was coated in dust.

Carl walked back to his favorite chair and started flipping through the pictures, one by one. They had all been taken so long ago. He was a different man then. That was before they knew what was wrong with him, but it had been too late to offer salvation to his struggling marriage.

After his second wife left him, he moved back home to Indiana. Back to the Podunk town he'd sworn off long ago. He shuffled the pictures, glancing at a few, while intently studying others.

What was it about that girl he had seen today? Not in at least the past five years had Carl even had an inkling to take a look at these pictures. They brought up memories of the past and he mostly preferred to forget about that. No sooner had he looked in that girl's eyes did he begin to recall Rosalyn and Mary. Damn if he didn't hate thinking about them, but there they were, right up at the forefront of his mind with their smiling faces and contagious laughter.

That was when everything had changed for Carl. That moment when his staff sergeant gave him the news. He wasn't allowed to go home for the funeral. They were about to execute the operation and too much was at stake. In a former life, Carl had quite the skillset. There wasn't much call for that sort of thing back home, away from the jungles of Vietnam.

He'd returned to a country that didn't want him, but Carl made his way in the world, what was left of it anyway. He'd met a woman. A kind-hearted woman who gave him a son. She put up with him for damn near fifteen years before she just couldn't handle the episodes anymore. Vicky took their son, CJ, and moved to Wisconsin. It was then that Carl figured he ought to try and get some help. He knew lots of vets who'd had problems when they got back. Some took their own lives as a result, but Carl didn't believe he was that bad off. He thought he could control it and that he'd eventually recover, but it didn't end up happening that way.

According to the VA, Carl had PTSD and suffered from paranoia. Well, who wouldn't? After all the shit he'd seen over there, it was no wonder. They said he'd probably had the paranoia long before the war and that Vietnam only made him worse. Well, wasn't that a kick in the pants? He'd survived that God-forsaken jungle only to come home believing people were after him, or were keeping tabs on him.

Carl placed the lid back onto the box. That was enough for tonight. But as he slid the box back onto the shelf of his closet, it came to him – the reason for this unexpected nostalgia. It was the girl. She had to have been about the same age. Yes, that little girl reminded him of Mary. Long, stringy blonde hair, round face, and great big brown eyes. That was his Mary. The one he lost along with the love of his life.

CJ OPENED HIS EYES TO SEE THAT THE PRETTY BARMAID HE'D gone home with last night was, fortunately, still pretty this morning. It was reassuring that he hadn't just been wearing beer goggles.

He rolled away, attempting to leave quietly, but it seemed he'd disturbed her anyway. "I'm sorry. I didn't mean to wake you. It's just, well, I need to get back home."

"That's all right. Can I make you some breakfast? I've got some frozen waffles, I think." She rubbed her eyes and further smeared the makeup she'd forgotten to remove before falling asleep last night.

"Thanks, but I'll grab a coffee at a drive-through on the way home. I had a really good time last night. Thank you." This part was always the most awkward. Thanking someone for sex. It didn't seem right, like he should maybe leave a fifty on the nightstand or something.

"Okay, well you can come on by the bar anytime. I usually work nights and most weekends. Maybe we can hook up again soon?"

It was a slim possibility. This was a small town that didn't have a deep well from which to dip his bucket, but she was much too young for him. By the looks of her, she probably hadn't had her heart broken yet and he didn't want to be the one to do it. He never stuck around for long and could at least admit that to himself. So, the idea of seeing her again, while appealing, wasn't very realistic.

"I'm sure we can." CJ pulled on his jeans, the rise fitting perfectly over his firm backside. He turned to face her again and began buttoning the blue and grey plaid shirt over his well-toned stomach. She seemed to watch in admiration. This wasn't new to CJ. He was considered, by all accounts, an attractive man; rugged, sharp cheekbones and strong chin. Not the pretty-boy, Hollywood type.

But this girl didn't know anything about him and CJ was reluctant to reveal himself. If his dad taught him anything, it was how to avoid getting close to people. "I'll stop by the bar sometime." He leaned in to kiss her. "Goodbye."

As he drove away from the modest house Melissa shared with a friend, he recalled the tenderness of her skin against his and the heat their bodies generated together. His head rested against the back of the driver's seat and his cheeks raised in a smile. She was something else.

But that would have to be pushed to the back of his mind as he set off home, alone, once again. CJ heard his cell phone vibrate in the center console of his quarter-ton truck. Sometimes, his job required that he pick up tools and such from various locations, so the truck suited him well for that purpose, although it was worn with age and he often wondered how long it might last.

He raised the cell phone to take a look at the incoming text message. What the hell did Johnny want at this hour? Never mind that it was a Saturday, and CJ figured the guy would be nursing a hangover, as was so often the case.

As he glanced at the message, his first inclination was to call Johnny up and ask him why he had to be there. But instead, he typed a quick reply, simply stating "*OK.*"

This was what he had hoped wouldn't happen. Getting dragged into another group meeting with those people wasn't exactly on his list of priorities. He'd planned on parking it in front of his TV to catch the college basketball. Hell, it was his day off. Didn't he deserve a break? Instead, he'd get to watch an hour or so, then head back out to that giant shack in the middle of nowhere for what? What did they need him there for anyway?

THE DENTON BROTHERS WERE STANDING OUTSIDE THE BARN. Johnny was leaning against his car with a cigarette burning between his fingers; his dark, scraggly hair tucked behind his oversized ears. Bennett had his hands shoved deep in his pockets, trying to protect himself from the cold; his chunky frame doing little to aid his warmth.

CJ continued toward them, eventually parking next to Johnny's old beater and shut down the truck's engine. He stepped outside and the cold immediately struck him, so he reached into the back seat where he kept a denim jacket. It would do for now. "You mind telling me why I gotta be here tonight, Johnny?" he said, pushing his arms through the sleeves of the jacket.

"I'm sorry, CJ. It's just that I got a call from Doug. He and Raymond thought you ought to be here for this. That's all."

"So, what's going on? Is it another meeting or something?" he replied, still irritated.

"I guess. I don't know, man. I just do what I'm told. Let's get the hell inside; it's cold as shit out here. Come on, Bennett." Johnny dropped his cigarette butt to the ground, smashing it into the dirt with his boot.

He opened the door and waited for CJ and Bennett to walk inside. There weren't as many people this time around. Maybe only a dozen or so. Hardly enough to fill two of the tables.

CJ wasn't sure if they were just early, or if this was it, no one else was coming. He saw his boss, Doug, and next to him, of course, was Ray and a few others he couldn't remember by name. He'd only met them last night. This wasn't what he'd signed on for. Being at their beck and call wasn't part of the deal and he hoped this wouldn't be the normal course of business.

"CJ!" Raymond took to his feet. He was a large man; tall with white hair and flushed cheeks. He reminded CJ of a beardless Santa Claus.

"Nice to see you again, Ray. Didn't think we'd be meeting up again so soon."

"Well, you know, things do come up and I really wanted you to be in on this one."

This one?

"Johnny, Bennett, why don't you two have a seat and we can get started," Doug said.

CJ and the brothers sat down, having absolutely no idea why this little gathering had been summoned.

"We got some information," Raymond began, "about this new crew in town. Sounds like they're wanting to meet up, work something out so as to be amicable for all involved."

What the hell is he talking about? CJ started to shift in his seat and brushed a finger under his nose as if he had the sniffles. What the hell were these people up to and who was this other crew? He looked at Johnny, but he had that same stupid look on his face as always. The kind that suggested he was just along for the ride.

"So I invited them over tonight. Last thing we want is for these guys to think we don't play nice with others," Ray continued.

"I'm sorry guys, but I'm new here. What is it that we're talking about?" CJ had to step up and say something, even if Johnny's look warned he ought to keep quiet.

"Didn't these boys tell you anything?" Doug asked.

CJ looked to the Denton brothers. "Afraid not."

Johnny seemed to perk up now that all eyes were on him. "I thought it best he learn it from you all. I mean, he works for you, Doug. I figured he'd already talked to you."

"Rather than us sitting here wasting time on who said what, let's just give the man a chance to hear us out," Ray insisted. "CJ, I brought you in because you've proven to Doug that you can be trusted. He says you come in on time every day, you're pleasant to the customers, and you don't try to skim off the till. To me, that makes you a stand-up guy. So, I thought you might like an opportunity to make a little extra cash, fill your coffers, as it were."

Now this was what he wanted to hear, presuming it was, of course, on the up and up. "Hell, yeah. Any chance I can get to do that, I'm all in." Perhaps he was under the assumption that he'd had some sort of choice in the matter.

"Glad to hear it," Raymond continued. "So, as I was saying, these folks will be here soon and I just wanna make sure we got our ducks in a row. Understand?"

The men appeared to be in agreement.

CJ listened as Raymond began to explain that they'd have to share territory with these new guys if they wanted to keep the peace. That they'd moved in from up north, near Cleveland, and had a much larger presence than they did. So they'd have to play nice if they wanted to keep their share of the pie.

What pie? He still didn't know what the hell this was about, until Raymond continued.

"I say, when those boys get here, we agree to the percentage split. I know it's gonna be low, but we'll suck it up. For a while. Once we get in their good graces, we'll find out who their suppliers are and go from there."

A sinking feeling in the bottom of CJ's stomach made him the slightest bit queasy. He wasn't sure where Ray was going with this, but he figured it was something along the lines of guns or drugs, or both. This was no militia group; this was a goddam patriot mafia.

A knock on the door echoed inside. CJ flinched at the sound.

"Our guests have arrived." Raymond nodded his head to Doug.

The unspoken command brought Doug to his feet and took him to the entrance. He pulled open the door where three men stood. "Fellas, come on in." Doug stepped aside and in walked one very large man and two men of average build. They were toting guns.

CJ swallowed the lump in his throat and tried to keep his composure, but if he was being honest with himself, he'd admit to being scared shitless right about now. This was nothing like he'd expected. These guys were just supposed to be like a kind of National Guard. Meeting up on occasion and maybe doing some military-style training. Nothing harmful; just offering up security for local events, or helping out in the community when it was needed. He'd heard that they'd helped with rescue efforts during the flood last spring. But maybe this was how they afforded training and equipment. He wondered if it was just this handful involved, or was it the whole group. Maybe he'd been chosen because he was fit and could easily handle just about any weapon.

CJ had done a fair bit of hunting with his dad in his early years, before his mom decided Carl Sr. was too dangerous for him to be around. So, he knew how to handle a rifle and other small firearms. It wasn't a skill he'd used for any other purpose but to hunt on his own occasionally. And that was just small animals. He wondered what it was these people hunted.

"Thanks for the invite, Raymond." The large man greeted Raymond with a firm handshake. These were big boys, and their ham hands locked together for what seemed a little too long.

"Of course. Call me Ray. It's Dennis, right? Why don't you boys take a seat and we can get started."

CJ listened as they began discussing routes and local law enforcement, but it wasn't until they brought up the tractor-trailers and how to disguise shipments that he finally figured what it was they were transporting.

These guys were running guns. Lots of them.

[6]

The stifled voices of Jack and Ellen had risen to the point that they had roused Riley from her sleep. The walls were too thin to squelch the sound and she knew the arguing stemmed from the fact that Jack had just gotten home and it was almost two o'clock in the morning. No doubt, he'd had a fair few drinks under his belt and that this was driving the quarrel.

Riley took in a deep breath; the air was cool since Jack had refused to keep the heat on at night, insisting it was too damned expensive. But she had enough blankets to keep herself warm. In a few more hours, she would have to get up for school and so she curled up on her side, pulling the pillow over her head to block out the noise, praying for sleep to find her again.

There wasn't much point in trying to stop it. She'd watched Dillon intervene before and it never turned out well for him. Nothing he did ever seemed to help and, in fact, it often only provoked Jack further. It seemed they all had to pretend it wasn't happening. Riley often wondered, though, what Dillon's breaking point would be. How much would he watch his mother endure before attempting to lash out against Jack? She wondered who would survive if that day ever came.

It was a great deal for a girl of ten to withstand, not that she saw herself as a child. Riley behaved too much like an adult, taking it upon herself to care for Gracie, shielding her from the troubles her family faced. As she looked across the bedroom, Gracie still lay quietly sleeping through all the noise. The girl could probably sleep through a tornado.

Riley wasted no time getting out of the house on this chilly Monday morning. School was a far better option than sitting at home, witnessing the train wreck that was her parents' marriage. Gracie wasn't the least bit happy about the big rush, but did as her sister asked.

On their way downstairs, Riley noticed Dillon standing in the foyer, his chest rising and falling quickly. His grip on the wall of the living room archway was turning his knuckles white and he shot a look to his sisters as they descended.

Riley knew in an instant that he had caught sight of Ellen and was now working up the nerve to confront Jack about it. She held his gaze, shaking her head at him. "Don't do it." Riley moved her lips, but no sound materialized. A burning sensation grew in her chest and the heat rose up to her neck. She could feel his anger and see through his eyes at the one to whom it had been directed.

This was it; the moment had come and she could do nothing to stop it, except plead with her eyes to return Dillon to calm. He continued to hold her stare. His face reddened by the second, threatening to spill over with uncontrollable rage.

Riley pleaded in silence as she worked to cool the escalating heat. Although she hadn't seen Ellen, Dillon clearly had and knew when enough was enough. It was difficult to control the anger she felt coming from him. It was as if she was becoming angry too, but she had to convince him to stop.

Dillon wiped his watery eyes with the back of his hand, hard and in a determined manner as though he was acknowledging her request, but with great reluctance.

"Come on, Riley. I thought we were leaving," Gracie said, alerting Jack to their presence.

"What are you doing there, Dillon?" Jack said.

Riley waited for his response as she continued to hold his gaze.

"Nothing. Just leaving for school." Dillon yanked his coat off the wall and slung his backpack over his shoulder. He didn't bother closing the door behind him.

"Goodbye, Dad," Riley said as she walked into the kitchen. "Bye, Mom."

Ellen was facing the kitchen window and didn't turn around. "Goodbye, sweetheart. You have a good day at school. Goodbye, Gracie."

Riley knew why her mom didn't turn around and that was fine by her. She was angry and didn't know if it was a residual feeling or her own. All she knew was that she wanted get to the bus stop and see her friend, forgetting all about this place.

The lunchboxes sat on the edge of the kitchen counter and Riley picked up both of them. "Let's go, Gracie."

KAITLYN WAITED AT THE BUS STOP ALONG WITH THE OTHER kids. The girls had made it just in time as the school bus approached.

"You okay, Riley?" Kaitlyn asked.

"Sure. I'm fine. Just a little tired, that's all." Riley stepped up onto the bus and reached for Gracie's hand to help her.

As the girls slid into the green bench seat, Kaitlyn began, "Riley, you gotta tell someone; please."

"They'll take me and Gracie away. You know that, right? Is that what you want? Besides, it'll get better once Dad gets another job." Her voice cracked as she spoke, knowing her words were nothing but lies.

The bus rolled along the crumbling street and out onto the secondary road, which was only in moderately better condition. Riley turned her head to look out the window, knowing Kaitlyn would get the hint and let her have a moment to herself.

She noticed the old trailer park at the end of the road that ran perpendicular to the one she was on now. Shady Acres Mobile Home Park. In that moment, the thought of Carl Boyd burst into her head. Her eyes squinted as she tried to get a better look at the derelict place, but the bus passed by too quickly. "I think I might stay after class for a few minutes to talk to Mrs. Downey. Do you think you could make sure Gracie gets off the bus with you after school?"

"Sure, but what about?" Kaitlyn asked.

"Maybe you're right; maybe I should talk to someone—just to get some things off my chest." This was far from the truth, but it would be enough to keep Kaitlyn satisfied and give Riley a chance to talk to Mrs. Downey about Carl Boyd. She believed or rather felt that he might live in that trailer park.

Riley watched with anticipation as the time on the big wall clock was about to strike three. She counted down the seconds until the other students would quickly escape, leaving her alone with Mrs. Downey.

It was uncertain if her teacher could offer any help on the matter, but Riley would need to ask. Something about Carl Boyd pulled her to him and she needed to know what that was.

The kids shouted and cried out with laughter as the bell rang. Riley stood up at her desk, waiting for the room to clear.

"I'll make sure Gracie gets home. Don't worry about it. Okay?" Kaitlyn tossed her arm over Riley's shoulder.

"Thanks, Kaitlyn. I won't be long and, if Gracie asks, just tell her I needed to ask Mrs. Downey about a homework assignment or something."

"See you tomorrow." Kaitlyn smiled and departed with the other students.

The teacher was standing at the white board, erasing the day's lessons when Riley approached.

"Mrs. Downey?" she asked.

She turned to see the small, pudgy girl standing in front of her. "Riley. What is it, honey?"

"Um, I was just wondering, um, do you remember that man at St. Vincent's on Saturday afternoon?"

"There were lots of men there, Riley. Could you be more specific?" Mrs. Downey set the dry eraser down and folded her arms in front of her.

She was a kind woman and a good teacher. Sometimes, Riley wished her mom was more like Mrs. Downey; attentive and caring. She supposed her mother exhibited those qualities, but not to the degree Mrs. Downey did. Her own children were already grown and out of the house, and Riley figured she was so good to her students because she didn't have to deal with kids at home too. Either way, Riley was very glad to have her for a teacher.

"He was old, like a grandpa. Skinny, and he had a tattoo, I think, on his arm. I think you said his name was Carl Boyd. At least, when we talked on Saturday about it."

"That's right. Yes. What about him, sweetheart?"

"Well, I—I wanted to know if he was homeless." Riley couldn't figure out exactly how to ask what she wanted to know without Mrs. Downey raising an eyebrow, so this was the best she could do.

"I don't think so, Riley. I think he lives here in town somewhere. I'm afraid I don't know that much about him. Why do you ask?"

"I don't know. I just thought he could use help; that's all. Like maybe I could bring him a meal or something. I feel kinda bad for him."

"Well, that's very kind, but I'm sure Mr. Boyd is all right. And if he needs help, he knows where to go. You're a very caring little girl, Riley. I hope your parents know that."

Riley shrugged her shoulders. "Thanks, Mrs. Downey. I'll see you tomorrow." She moved toward the exit, but before leaving, the teacher stopped her.

"Everything all right at home, Riley? You know you can talk to me whenever you want."

"Everything's fine, Mrs. Downey. Thank you. Bye." Riley headed into the now empty school halls. Mrs. Downey probably suspected what was going on at home. She figured a lot of people probably did.

Making her way out of the school halls, Riley couldn't help but think about Carl Boyd and the Shady Acres trailer park. It seemed an almost certainty that he lived there. The digital wristwatch that had been a birthday present showed 3:20. With meticulous calculation, she contemplated the time it would take to make the journey and know for sure. She decided it would add at least twenty minutes to an already fifteen-minute walk home.

Would her mom notice her absence? Maybe, but with Jack home and Gracie likely playing around the house, she would probably not be missed until closer to four thirty, maybe even five o'clock. They'd all assume she was at Kaitlyn's, although Ellen wouldn't dare call her house unless the hour grew later than five.

Riley's conclusion was that it would be a safe bet to take the walk and that she'd be home in plenty of time. The nagging feeling that Mr. Boyd would need help, her help, pushed her to this decision and she had to understand why.

With weary legs, her gross underestimation of distance to the Shady Acres mobile home park became a glaring reality, but Riley drew closer until finally she stood next to the green-lettered sign. There wasn't much time remaining to figure out if Carl Boyd was a resident because, glancing at her watch once again, she realized it would take her a good half an hour to get back home and it was already four o'clock.

The dirt lot encompassed maybe fifteen or so trailers. Most were in an advanced state of disrepair. Some of the homes had makeshift metal overhangs with cars parked beneath whose operating capacity could be in serious question. A few lawn chairs dotted the perimeter of the single-wides, along with several propane tanks stationed at the front of them.

An uneasy feeling settled in her gut and the idea of sprinting home had crossed her mind, but Riley pushed through the fear and she continued down the narrow path that made its way through the middle of the park. She glanced left, then right, then left again as she walked slowly past each one, her shoes leaving a trail of footprints in the damp soil behind her.

The idea that it would strike her when she reached proximity to his trailer seemed reasonable, although it hadn't happened just yet and she was almost half way along. A moment later and a creaky screen door opened at a trailer on her left and the sound startled her. It was an old woman staring at Riley with suspicious eyes. Maybe they didn't see many kids around here or maybe the ones they did seemed to cause them trouble. Whatever the reason for the mistrustful glance, Riley rethought her earlier plan.

It only took a few more steps, and a wave of recognition soared in her mind. There it was. The trailer on the right, dingy white with blue trim. How she became aware of this precise location was unclear, but there was little doubt in her mind that Carl Boyd lived right there. So what was the next step of her brilliant plan? To knock on his door and ask if he needed help? In that instant, it became obvious that she hadn't planned that far ahead.

Riley lingered in front of his home for a moment longer and then began to turn away, fearing what would come of this plan of hers. Would the old man be angry with her? She didn't know him at all, really. Maybe in his old age, he'd grown to dislike kids and he'd come out wielding a cane, yelling at her to get off his property. She considered this to be viable assumption and began to take a few steps back, but it was too late. She spotted the thin metal blinds on one of the windows part in the middle. It was him and he'd seen her.

Her mouth dropped and she remained frozen. The legs beneath her wanted to dart away, but the recollection of why she was there kept her still. The blinds closed again and, a moment later, the front door opened.

"Are you lost or something?" Carl asked. Leaning outside, his eyes narrowed at the unexpected sight of this little girl whose acquaintance he seemed to immediately recall.

"Um, no, sir. I was—I was just looking for you, actually." Riley couldn't bring herself to approach him. Instead, she shoved her hands into the pockets of her pink fleece jacket, blowing away the wispy hairs that had landed on her face.

"Looking for me? Whatever for, young lady? I saw you at the dining hall on Saturday, didn't I? You kept looking at me funny, isn't that right?"

"Um, yes, sir. I'm sorry about that, sir." Riley dropped her gaze.

"Do your parents know where you are, missy?"

"No, sir. I—I was just on my way home from school."

"Well, I guess you'd better come inside, if you want. I won't bite ya and stop calling me 'sir.' It's Carl."

A hint of a smile danced on Riley's face as she finally found the courage to move her feet forward. Something told her Carl Boyd was harmless and wouldn't hurt a fly. Of course, her mother would have a heart attack if she knew, but what she didn't know, wouldn't hurt her, or some crazy thing like that adults always said.

"Have a seat. You're awful far from the—elementary school, is it?" Carl motioned to the small loveseat placed underneath the window that she'd seen him peer through.

"Yes, sir. I'm in the fifth grade. My name is Riley Thompson." She waited for Carl to position himself into his recliner and then sat down, folding her hands neatly in her lap and crossing her feet at the ankles, just like her mother taught her to do.

"You want some water or something?" Carl asked.

"No thank you."

"Okay. Well, then, why don't you tell me what it is you're doing here? How did you know where I live?"

That would be a tough one to explain. No one other than Kaitlyn knew of her abilities to read people, or rather have the unique perspective to see things as they did; their emotions, feelings of apprehension, fear, things like that. And, she could see as clear as day both the worst moments and the best moments of their lives. It was that sense of apprehension that brought her to Mr. Boyd today. Her own, not his, and that was something new for Riley.

"I felt it."

"I'm sorry. You what?" Carl's raised a brow with what appeared to be both suspicion and interest.

"I can sense things. I don't know how else to say it. I just can and I sensed that you lived here." She would have to reveal her knowledge of his past if she stood any hope of helping him in the future. "Sir, I know this is gonna sound crazy and I hope it doesn't upset you, but I know about your wife and daughter." Riley's shoulders raised up as if ready to take her lumps.

Carl's face turned devoid of emotion. "Who told you that? Someone at the dining hall? Was that why you were looking at me like I was some kind of alien?"

"No, sir. Please don't get mad. I just know. I saw it inside you when you were standing in front of me. I saw you talking to some man in a uniform and you were wearing one too, like an army uniform or something, I don't know. He gave you a piece of paper." She pleaded her case, praying he would believe her.

"Enough!" Carl rose from his chair. "I don't know who told you that, little girl, but it's very rude of you to bring up such a thing. Now, I think it's best if you just go on home." He moved to the front door and pulled it open, waiting for her to leave.

"I'm sorry, Mr. Boyd. I didn't mean to hurt your feelings, I promise." Riley began to walk out, but stopped on the top step just outside the door. "It's just that, sir, I think you might be in trouble and I think I might be able to help."

[7]

The **blankets converged** in a heap at the end of the bed and the elder Carl Boyd lay in a pool of sweat shrouded in darkness. The heat had kicked off and the temperature hovered around the fifty-degree mark inside the small bedroom, but he sweltered nonetheless.

It was the girl and she'd triggered the dream. As Carl stared at the shadowed ceiling, he endeavored to slow his breathing to something along the lines of normal. Why had she done this to him, bringing back such painful memories?

He rolled out of bed and made his way into the bathroom, tugging on the chain that led to the fixture above the mirror. The light stung his eyes and when he regained focus, Carl hardly recognized the face that reflected back at him. Pale skin, gaunt cheeks, colorless lips. What had become of the man he once was? The robust man who had pulled several American soldiers from the hole in the ground in which they'd been kept prisoner? Who was this frail old man looking back at him?

And the girl had gotten to him. He allowed her to bring back those memories. What the hell did she know of any of it? Someone must have said something to her and this little girl thought she knew about him, what he'd been through. She knew nothing and neither did anyone else in this damn town!

Carl smashed the mirror with the side of his fist, shattering it on impact. The pieces fell into the sink, chiming against the porcelain. Some bounced out and fell to the ground. He turned his hand to see what he'd done. Streams of blood quickly oozed from the gash he'd produced. Carl's lips began to quiver, not from the pain, but from the memories and the anger they brought with them. He dropped his head and sobbed harder than he had in years.

The punishment Riley received for returning home so late after school without anyone's knowledge of her whereabouts was to be sent to bed without dinner. By the time she'd reached home, her mother was nearly ready to call the police. She counted her blessings that Jack had still been at the bar on her return. If he'd been home, the absence of a meal would have been the least of her concerns. He'd never struck her before, but that didn't mean he wouldn't start if she gave him cause.

Now that it was late and the house was quiet, Riley decided to sneak out of bed and head downstairs to settle her rumbling tummy. The floorboards creaked under her weight and she stopped dead at the noise, wondering if it would cause Gracie to stir. It didn't, and so Riley continued on, opening their bedroom door and tiptoeing down the hall to the landing. She reached for the stair rail in the darkness and carefully took her first step down. As she grew more confident and her eyes adjusted to the scant light that filtered in from the burning lamppost outside, she proceeded down to the bottom. A few final creaks of the nails against the wood of the treads and she'd made it.

Upon entering the kitchen, Riley noticed Jack sitting at the small dining table. It seemed they both caught sight of one another at the same time. She halted in place, fearing he would be angry and tell her to go back to bed, but he only stared at her. And there was something very strange about him, something she couldn't recall seeing in him before. Sorrow.

Jack wiped his teary eyes. "What are you doing up?" His tone was hushed.

Riley noticed the half-empty bottle of booze that sat on the table in front of him. She was well versed in the many different varieties her father consumed. It seemed tonight it was a bourbon. She'd recognized the label. Jack appeared weak, with swollen eyes and breath that was heavy with the stench of liquor. She decided that it was safe to approach, sensing a profusion of regret drowning inside him. Riley couldn't recall ever seeing him cry before, not even at her grandfather's funeral. She continued and sat down next to him.

"What's wrong, Daddy?" It was rare that she felt any emotion coming from her father except for the occasional rise of anger. He simply wasn't around enough for her to notice much of anything about him. Perhaps it had been better that way.

Jack cleared his throat. "Nothing. I'm fine. Why are you awake?"

"I was thirsty." Riley dared not tell him she had wanted food.

"Okay, then. Go and get yourself a drink of water, then go back upstairs and get to sleep." Jack's manner was declining in its assertion.

"Are you okay, Dad?" Riley touched his shoulder and flinched at the outpouring of sorrow that filled her senses. It was so strong and full of grief.

Jack broke down as if it had been the first time his daughter had ever touched him. "I'm so sorry, baby. I'm so sorry for everything I've done. To you kids, to your mom. I don't mean any of it, I swear. I don't know what's wrong with me." Jack pulled Riley's hand to his cheek, pressing it firmly as the tears fell against it.

"I know that, Daddy. It's okay. Everything will be okay once you get another job. I know it will." Riley wanted to believe him, wanted to believe that things really would get better.

Jack raised his eyes to meet hers and, for a moment, she saw the man he used to be. The loving father who used to take them all to the county fair and buy her cotton candy. But Riley's gift wouldn't allow that memory to flourish. Instead, it was quickly extinguished, replaced by the realization that Jack was not a well man and that his head was swayed by the alcohol in which it bathed. It was then that she knew things would not get better, not for a long time.

"We'll be all right. I know." Jack placed his hand on top of Riley's. "I love you so much, sweetheart. I hope someday you'll forgive me." He took a deep breath and cleared his throat. "Go on and get that drink now. You've got school in the morning and you need your rest."

"Okay, Daddy." Riley walked to the cabinet for a glass and

filled it with tap water. She was so hungry, but didn't want to ask for food. Instead, she gulped the entire glass to help fill her belly.

"Goodnight, Daddy." She leaned in to kiss his cheek and he held her head gently as she did.

"Goodnight, baby."

As Riley reached the foyer, she turned to see Jack raise the bottle of bourbon to his lips.

Riley and Gracie stepped onto the bus, taking their usual seats, and as it approached the crossroads, she glanced to the end of the road at the Shady Acres sign. She had upset Mr. Boyd. It wasn't intentional, but he was angry with her and she didn't know what to do about it. Whatever it was about him had triggered something inside her that no one else had. He needed help. She didn't know why, when, or how, but her feelings had not betrayed her yet and she would need to convince him of it before it was too late.

The bus pulled up alongside the school and the children filed out, scattering in every direction, but all eventually heading to the playground before the first bell.

Riley was preoccupied with thoughts of Mr. Boyd and so she hardly noticed when she nearly bumped into Jacob. "Oh, sorry. I didn't see you there."

"That's okay," he said, smiling at her. "I meant to ask you yesterday, but how did it go with the volunteering on Saturday? Did you and Kaitlyn have fun?"

She was glad to set her mind on another topic, even if only for a moment, but the fact that it was a moment with Jacob made it all the better. Riley's cheeks flushed just a little. "It was good. We had fun." There was no chance she'd mention Carl Boyd or visiting him yesterday. She hadn't even told Kaitlyn and she was her best friend.

The sound of first bell echoed around the school building.

"Guess we'd better get to class," Jacob said, slinging his backpack over his shoulder.

Kaitlyn ran toward Riley. "Why didn't you come out to the swings? I've been waiting for you." She looked to Jacob. "Oh. Well, we need to get to class anyway." She put her arm around Riley and turned away from the boy. "Let's go."

Mrs. Downey proceeded to write the day's homework assignments on the board. It was almost time for the final bell.

Riley had difficulty focusing on class and wondered if she'd make it through the homework as a result. Her thoughts had been bordering on the obsessive regarding Carl Boyd. The images of him and his past, his family; it all kept flashing before her as though she was flipping through a photo album of his life.

The bell chimed and the sound of screeching chairs on the linoleum floor made the hairs on Riley's arm stand on end. The kids were funneling out of the classroom faster than the speed of light, it seemed. She would do as her mother instructed and get on the bus, ensuring she and Gracie were home at their appointed time.

As she followed Kaitlyn's lead and headed toward the exit,

Mrs. Downey called her name. Riley turned to Kaitlyn. "I'll catch up with you." She proceeded toward the teacher's desk.

"I understand you made a visit to Mr. Boyd yesterday afternoon, Riley."

How did she know that? Riley worried trouble was coming.

"I um, I was just—I just wanted to talk to him."

"Riley, why on earth would you walk by yourself to go and see that man? I got a call from one of the administrators at St. Vincent's. Seems Mr. Boyd paid him a visit and wasn't very happy that you showed up at his home. He accused them of giving out his address."

"But—I..."

"Riley, I don't know how you figured out where Mr. Boyd lives, but you should never have gone there, let alone by yourself. Do you know what could have happened to you, young lady?" The teacher shook her head. "Just leave the poor man be. I honestly don't understand why you would go there in the first place." Mrs. Downey folded her arms in front of her chest.

"I don't know. I guess I felt bad for him. I thought I could help and see if he needed anything." Riley dropped her shoulders.

"Well, you upset the man a great deal. He's very private and prefers to keep to himself. Now, do I need to call your mother about all this?"

This was, of course, the last thing Riley would want. If Ellen found out, that would be it. Grounded for a month, at least. Maybe longer if her dad got involved. "No, ma'am. It won't happen again. I promise."

"It better not. Now you go on before you miss the bus. Goodbye, Riley."

"Goodbye, Mrs. Downey." Riley slunk out into the hall and

took to a jog to catch the bus, arriving just in time before it pulled away without her. She sat down next to Kaitlyn.

"What was that about? Didn't you talk to her yesterday? Is she gonna tell your parents you said something?"

It was the first time that Kaitlyn had asked Riley about yesterday. "No. Not really. It's okay now. I just want to get home."

The hardware store had virtually emptied out for the night. CJ was just about to close up shop when two men whom he immediately recognized pushed open the door, the little bell at the top ringing as a signal that a customer had entered. Only these men were no customers.

These were two of the men from the meeting the other night. The other "crew," Ray had called them. The first man to enter was called Dennis. CJ didn't know his last name and didn't really care to know it. The other night he'd been toting a .38 caliber handgun, although CJ cast his eyes toward the man's waist and didn't see one strapped there today. That put him a little at ease.

Dennis wasn't quite as tall as CJ. Maybe only five feet eleven inches to CJ's six feet one, but the man had girth. He continued to size him up as the two approached the checkout counter where he was closing out the register.

The other was almost the same height, shaving an inch or so off. Both had short, military-style hair that didn't quite seem to complement the Harley Davidson long-sleeved t-shirt Dennis was wearing and the Metallica t-shirt the shorter man wore. They looked a little like undercover cops, if CJ was a betting man.

"Where's your boss—Doug?" Dennis asked as he stepped up to the counter.

"He already left for the day. I think he had an appointment or something like that. Is there anything I can do you for?" CJ replied, taking notice of the other man scanning the shop as though he wanted to rob the place.

"You was at the meeting the other day, isn't that right?" Dennis asked.

"I was, yes."

"Good. Give this to Doug. He'll know what it's about." Dennis slid a flash drive across the counter. "You be sure he gets this, now."

"Will do." CJ picked it up. "You two have a nice evening."

They didn't reply, only continued walking toward the door, and eventually left.

CJ exhaled the breath he'd been holding in and immediately moved toward the door to lock it. He flipped the sign to show "Closed."

On his return to the counter, he examined the flash drive, turning the small stick over in his hands as if that alone would tell him what it contained. He began to recall the conversation at that smaller meeting, the one he'd wished he hadn't attended.

They'd been somewhat vague, but from what CJ could glean, the men had been wanting to familiarize themselves with a warehouse about twenty miles away. It was in a complex that was still under construction and all had seemed interested in knowing its layout. He didn't think too much about it at the time, because, well, they didn't really say much. But as he stared at the drive, his curiosity was getting the better of him.

CJ looked around the store and out toward the front to see if anyone was coming near. The skies had already turned to dusk and so most people in this town were probably bellying up to the dinner table right about now. He looked toward the backroom, where Doug usually stayed, unless someone needed help that CJ couldn't take care of himself.

He began to walk toward the room. Inside was a desk, piled high with receipts and a desktop computer that was switched off. CJ knew the password, of course. Doug had trusted him enough to share that information. Hell, he'd trusted him enough to drag him into his little group of militia boys who played with guns and drank too much beer, and God knows what else.

CJ glanced around again as if he was about to watch a dirty movie and he wanted to be sure no one else was nearby. Once he was confident of his solitude, he powered up the computer and pulled out the chair for a seat.

After a very long wait, the machine was ready and CJ inserted the flash drive. He clicked on the file icon and a window popped up with several file names inside it. He thought he'd try the first one, because, well, why not? He had no idea what any of them contained and so he decided to start at the top. The file was named "Warehouse B."

It seemed to take days for it to load – the file must have been large – although he hadn't paid much attention when he'd clicked on it. When it finally opened, CJ studied the image that appeared. His mind worked to figure out exactly what it was that he was looking at.

It took a moment or two and CJ was no engineer, but he soon realized what it was. These were schematics; a blueprint of the building, Warehouse B.

"What the...?" He moved the mouse around the drawing,

along the electrical lines, the ventilation lines, all of it, but couldn't make any sense of it. Why would they have building blueprints? What the hell were these guys planning and would CJ be forced to take part?

[8]

The waitress approached Carl as he sat alone, staring out of the window from his booth. "Good morning Carl. Are you ready to order?"

He turned his attention to the woman named Anne. She and her husband had been running the diner since before he left Owensville the first time. He'd frequented the place almost every Sunday morning since his return, after the divorce, unless funds were short, which usually happened when he was in between his Social Security checks. He'd finally received it on Friday and Carl thought a decent breakfast was in order.

He looked at Anne and wondered how she managed to keep a smile on her face, seemingly at all times. He knew that the dwindling number of residents in this little town had to be taking a toll on their business. It certainly had with several other proprietors who'd already shut down and moved out. Small town America was a dying breed.

Still, there was Anne with her ever-present smile. The years had left their mark on her, but Carl could still see the young woman whom he'd met so long ago. He might've even had a crush on her at one time, but he respected the fact that she was married. Never once did he consider her to be anything more than a friendly face who served him eggs, sunny side up, with two slices of bacon on just about every Sunday for the past several years.

"The usual, please, Anne. Thank you."

"I'll have that right up for you, Carl." Anne walked away with a little extra something in her step. Maybe she'd had a little crush on him too, back in the day.

As he sipped on his coffee, black, no sugar, Carl noticed several people heading into the diner. He checked his watch, realizing church had probably just let out.

The last time Carl stepped inside a church was the day he wore a powder-blue tuxedo, standing at an altar and about to marry CJ's mother. He had to chuckle at the memory. Those were the days when he still had a headful of black hair and wore it long enough to touch his shoulders. Beards were in fashion too, or so Carl believed. So the image of him standing in that ridiculous suit with long hair and a beard brought a smile to his face.

His hair was much thinner now and had crept back so far that it was hard to tell where his forehead ended and his scalp began, although he treasured the fact that he'd still had some hair, even if it was mostly salt, no pepper.

The door of the restaurant opened up and in walked several people dressed in their Sunday best. Carl had lived in Indianapolis for a while and he knew that there was something special about small towns like Owensville. People here still dressed up for church, had local carnivals, and chili bake-offs. It was good for an old man like Carl, but not so good for the younger ones, the families with young kids trying to find and keep good jobs.

He would enjoy it for as long as he could, figuring he wasn't due much more time on this planet anyway. It seemed to get a little harder for him each year. The winters seemed to be colder and the money seemed to last less and less.

"Here you go, Carl. Enjoy." Anne set the plate of food down in front of him and refilled his coffee cup.

"Perfectly cooked as always, Anne. My compliments to the chef," Carl replied.

"I'll be sure and let him know."

Carl watched as Anne walked to another booth, smiling in her usual way, ready to take another order as the diner grew busy.

He crunched down on the crispy bacon and caught sight of a woman walking in with her three kids. He recognized one of them immediately. The teenaged boy slid first into the booth, a small girl sliding in after him. On the opposite side, the mother and the girl he knew to be Riley took their respective positions.

Carl cast a watchful eye on the family. His heart sank a little at the sight of the woman. Her face appeared older far beyond what he believed her years to be. She was pale, whitewashed with too much makeup. Only it didn't conceal the bruises well enough. The purplish hue was still visible beneath her eye.

No man followed behind, no man sat in the booth with them, which left Carl to assume a man, perhaps the children's father, was the one who'd marked what had once been an attractive woman. His disgrace seemed to keep him away from the church where the family had likely been.

Most of the people in this town knew one another, although since Carl kept to himself most days, he didn't know them. But looking at the girl called Riley, he knew the family. They were the Thompsons and Riley could only be the granddaughter of Leonard Thompson.

He suspected as much when he'd seen the girl last week at the shelter, although he hadn't taken notice at the time. He'd been more concerned that the girl had frozen up on him, holding a piece of cornbread in her small hand. And when she came to see him earlier in the week, Carl was going to ask her then, but of course, he'd lost his temper and shooed the girl away.

Now, it was clear. Leonard and Fiona Thompson lived in the house on Orchard Lane. He'd grown up with Leonard, but after what happened when he was in Vietnam, Carl didn't see the point in reestablishing any kind of friendship they might have had. Even on his return to Owensville fifteen years ago, Carl refused to see Leo, although it had been one of Leo's requests before the end. Leonard passed some years ago, Carl recalled; five or six? He'd lost track, but remembered that it had been shortly after the man's wife died. Now, as he observed the family in the adjacent booth, he wondered if they occupied that old house.

Seeing the mother bearing the marks of an irate husband, he wondered if the children suffered the same. Carl began to feel guilty about getting so upset at the girl. She had reminded him of Mary. They had the same chipmunk cheeks and huge brown eyes. But her words frightened him. How did she know those things? Why would she have come to see him, insisting he was in need of help?

Carl's hand trembled. The coffee splashed over the rim of his cup and ran down to his fingers, but he could feel nothing. His mind had retreated to a place where he felt nothing but fear.

"Get down, get down, sir!"

Carl's head was pushed hard into the bottom of the trench by a fellow soldier. The grenade he'd just thrown over the side was about to explode and would annihilate the North Vietnamese soldiers who were charging over the hill about twenty yards out.

He raised his hands to shield himself as the explosion rumbled the ground. The man next to him, PFC Brooks, raised up again to fire on the approaching enemy that remained.

Carl reached for his gun, which was propped up against the wall of the trench and began firing alongside the man who might as well have been Carl's brother. But Charlie kept coming, from the trees and other small hills that surrounded them, so many that Carl couldn't keep count.

"Get the RTO. It's hot, it's hot. We need CAS!"

PFC Brooks yelled for radio support. Another round of fire whistled over their heads. The enemy was drawing near. Others in the trench tried to hold the line, but they needed air support now!

"Carl? Carl, are you all right?" Anne reached out for his arm and gently pushed it down so that the coffee cup landed on the table without further spilling. "You're okay. Come on now; you're scaring everybody."

Carl whipped his head around to see the concerned look on Anne's face, suddenly returning to the present. In fact, as he cast his gaze around the restaurant, everyone seemed to have their eyes trained on him, including Riley Thompson. He stared at the girl. She seemed afraid for him. "I'm fine." He yanked his arm away. "I'm fine. I'm sorry, Anne." Carl slid out of the booth, grabbed his coat, and walked out of the diner as quickly as he could, refusing to acknowledge the stares.

Riley watched him march across the street to his car. Carl Boyd scanned the area as though he was being followed. He stepped inside the car and revved the engine hard, pulling out of the parking spot, the tires of his old Ford Taurus squealing on the asphalt.

The moment he began to tremble, Riley could feel her own hands doing the same. The rest of her family, unaware, tucked into their breakfasts, but she watched as his eyes turned blank and his stare focused just above her head. She felt it. His fear. Riley knew what was happening; she could see everything. The smoke in the air, the filthy ground he was sitting on, and the sandbags around him. The smell of gunpowder, burning bodies, and humid air still surrounded her.

Her heart still pounded just as his had, and she'd lost all appetite from the lingering odor. Riley wanted to run after him, tell him that he needed help, that he was in danger. But what did she really know? It was merely a feeling, a sense that something was going to happen to him. Riley had to pull herself together. It was the first time she'd experienced another's feelings in such a powerful manner and it frightened her. The stares of the people who were witness to it frightened her as well. She wondered how he must have felt.

Carl ran inside his trailer; angry, humiliated, and out of breath. How could this have happened? He'd taken his pills, just like the doctor said. It'd been so long since he'd had a flashback like that and especially in public.

It had taken him years to get the people in this town to see him as someone other than the man ruined by a terrible war. He'd gone to the VA. They were supposed to help him. They gave him these damn pills and told him they would stop the paranoia, dial down the flashbacks. And they had, up until now.

Carl paced the small trailer, his footsteps echoing against the tin frame of this crappy place he called home. What the hell was happening to him? He walked to the refrigerator and pulled out a pitcher of water, pouring it into a cup that had sat dirty on the counter for two days.

Gulping the water down, he tried to swallow the rage and the fear that those visions brought back with a vengeance.

He yelled a great, deep, sorrowful yell that all in the park would be able hear. Carl slammed the glass into the sink, shards splitting and falling into the drain. It was too much to endure. He moved to his chair and slumped down into it, breathing deeply to try to bring calm.

First, he'd been forced to recall the moment he'd heard the news of his family, now he was suffering from the flashbacks again. Why? Why now?

He raised his head, using his sleeve to wipe his eyes and nose. "That girl. It's that girl. Goddammit! Why?" His chest still heaved as he searched for an explanation. "Why does she think I'm in trouble? Carl was beginning to sink into that familiar place. The one the pills were supposed to stop him from going. "Who's after me?" He darted his eyes around the room. "What do they want from me?"

Carl stood and moved toward the window, parting the

venetian blinds to peek outside. He stared out at the empty lot. No one was around, no one was outside pulling weeds or sitting in their chairs, soaking up the warmth of the sun.

"I've got to see her. I've got to go see Mary."

The hardware store had been busy all day. Weekends were usually when all the men with the "honey do" lists showed up, looking forlorn and having no real idea how they were supposed to fix the damn kitchen sink in the first place. But they couldn't let their wives know that. Calling the plumber wasn't an option for these men.

As the hours passed, the store quieted down and CJ was ready to finish his shift. Doug had been helping out in addition to the high school kid who worked there on the weekends. The only problem, now that the day was almost over, was the prospect of another meeting. CJ still hadn't figured out what they were planning. He'd copied the contents of the flash drive to his own computer the night Dennis and his lackey came in, just as a precaution.

Doug said little the next day when CJ handed him the drive. A quick "thanks" and that was all he got. Over the past few days, however, Carl took to reviewing those files, studying them with every bit of energy he had. He'd never read a set of blueprints in his life, but he figured he had gotten a pretty good grasp of Warehouse B.

"I'm gonna run home and get changed." Doug appeared from the backroom. "You coming alone tonight or with those Denton brothers?"

"I'll hitch a ride from them. We're probably gonna meet up beforehand and grab a beer," CJ replied.

"Okay, then. I'll see you at eight. I sent Ricky home already, so you'll lock up on your own."

"Will do, Doug. See ya later."

THE NIGHT SKIES WERE CLEARER THAN THEY'D BEEN IN A while as CJ cast his gaze up toward the stars. Standing outside of the bar, he could hear the muffled sound of the band playing inside. He hadn't gone in, anxious because he knew Melissa was working tonight, having recognized her car in the lot. CJ hadn't bothered to call her all week and so he knew he'd be on the receiving end of a nasty look if she'd caught sight of him.

He felt cowardly standing outside in the cold, pulling his jacket closed around him, but he was never much for getting close to people. See, the problem with people was that they'd always let him down and so he'd learned not to bother with them much anymore. And as he checked the time on his phone, it seemed the Denton boys were about to let him down too. It was already pushing seven forty-five and they should have been there. Yet another example.

Just as he was about to give Johnny a call, he heard the growl of the guy's car engine that was in desperate need of a tune-up. A moment later, headlights appeared in the distance. "Finally."

CJ moved a few steps forward and raised his arm, waving for their attention. Johnny pulled up alongside him and rolled down the window.

"Sorry we're late, man. Hop in."

CJ scowled and walked around to the passenger side, glaring inside the entire time. "What the hell, man? Where you two dipshits been?" he asked as he opened the door.

Bennett grabbed the front seat and pulled himself forward. "Lost track of time, dude." He held out a burning joint. "Want some?"

CJ shook his head and sneered at the man, climbing into the back. "Seriously? Do either one of you know what the hell is going on here?"

Johnny pushed his foot to the floor and the car spun its tires. He regained control and pulled back out onto the main road. "Just relax, CJ. This is a good thing for us—all of us."

"So you know what's going on?"

Johnny looked at CJ. "Just take my word for it."

There was something in that look that set CJ's nerves on end. He'd never been in any real trouble with the law and wasn't looking to be now. "Johnny, you gotta tell me. What are these guys into and what've they got planned? Come on, man. Look, you and me go way back. You gotta give it to me straight. Is this shit gonna get us locked up?"

Johnny boomed with laughter, the back of his head hitting the headrest. Bennett soon joined in, but CJ wasn't laughing. "Look, we own this town. There's no danger of any of us getting busted, all right? Just slow your roll. I don't know all the details. I'm not that high up on the food chain, but what I can tell you is that your little gig at Doug's hardware store, well, let's just say that I'm guessing your role there is gonna be somewhat more involved from this point forward."

What the hell did that mean? CJ began to wonder if Johnny actually knew anything. He already figured these guys were involved in illegal activities, he just didn't know to what extent and was a little afraid to find out.

"You're gonna be paid well, my friend. Take my word for it," Johnny said.

CJ met Bennett's eyes in the reflection of the passenger side view mirror. It was as if Bennett immediately lost his high and a concerned look crossed his face. This didn't help CJ's already unsettled feeling that had nestled in the pit of his stomach. Still, he was already along for the ride and would stay to see what this payoff would be, as if he had a choice.

[9]

Sunday lunch was something to which Riley always looked forward. The smell of roast beef in the oven, boiling potatoes on the stove, and rolls sitting on the cookie sheet, the last to go into the oven. She didn't mind the vegetables either, so long as they were smothered in gravy.

Jack was in the living room, watching whatever sport happened to be on at that moment. It seemed whatever had transpired the other night between him and Riley had evaporated, returning to exactly the way things always had been, and that meant no interruption of his sports. Dillon had gone off with a friend, as usual. And so it was just Riley and Gracie left in the house with their parents.

This morning's incident was still fresh in her mind. Riley didn't reveal any of this to Ellen. There had been a time, early on, when she'd discovered what was happening to her, that she tried to bring it up with Ellen, but it never came out right and only served to confuse her mom. In the end, she'd opted to deal with this on her own, but that was before Carl Boyd.

Now she was forced to deal with this aftermath; the random images that would flash before her. The leftovers, she called them. Riley sometimes felt like a leftover, a forgotten remnant of an ill-conceived idea. The idea that she could be a part of a normal and happy family. In fact, they were all remnants of happier days.

She wanted so badly to help Mr. Boyd, but how? How could a ten-year-old do anything that mattered? Not to mention that she had no clue what kind of help he needed. This was what was frustrating. Would it just come to her at some point in time? Would it then be too late to do anything about it?

As Riley stood at the bottom of the steps, casting a glance toward the kitchen, where her mother stayed buried, and then looked to the spot where her father had not moved since they'd returned this morning, she began to wonder why this had been laid on her shoulders. Life was hard enough and now what had seemed to be nothing more than a benign insight into people was turning into something worse. It was turning into a nightmare.

Riley swallowed a rising swell of animosity that seemed to come from deep inside. Her heart had begun to beat faster, but the reason was elusive. Resentment like she'd never known was now just on the other side of the front door.

She gripped the finial of the bannister, her head growing lighter by the moment. Riley wanted to call out to her mom, but couldn't find her voice. *What's happening to me?*

The front door sounded with a great boom. Riley turned toward it, squinting to find focus. Again the noise came. "He's here."

"Who the hell's pounding on our goddamn door?" Jack pushed

up hard from his chair and stepped firmly toward the entrance. "Riley? What the hell are you doing just standing there?"

Ellen rushed out and locked eyes with Jack for a moment, then turned her attention to Riley. "Are you okay, honey?" She moved toward her daughter, whose face had begun to glisten with sweat.

The pounding sounded again. "Just a damn minute." He pulled the door open. "What in God's name are you doing beating down my door like that? Who the hell are you?"

Riley recognized the man instantly and so did Ellen.

"Sir, what are you doing here?" Ellen stepped toward the door, revealing only a part of herself as she stood behind Jack.

"You know this man?"

"I need to see Mary. Let me talk to Mary!" Carl Boyd stood on the porch, where the sun's fading glow had been shaded.

"Who the hell is Mary? Are you drunk?" Jack was becoming annoyed by the disruption.

"Mr. Boyd." Riley pulled her hand away from the support of the stair rails and rushed to the front door.

"Get back, Riley." Jack thrust his arm to halt her approach. "Look, I don't know who the hell you are, but you got the wrong house, buddy."

"Mary," Carl began as he looked to Riley. "Mary, you look so beautiful. I'm so sorry I couldn't protect you." His arms outstretched.

"Hey! I'm gonna call the cops if you don't leave!" Jack seemed to stare Carl down. "Look, I told you, you got the wrong house. There's no Mary here! This is my daughter. Now leave before I kick your ass all the way down the street!"

"Calm down, Jack. This man needs help." Ellen reached for Jack's arm. "We saw him at the diner this morning."

"Sir, it's me, Riley Thompson. Remember? I came to your house the other day? I'm not Mary, sir. I'm sorry, but she's dead, Mr. Boyd."

Jack and Ellen quickly turned their attention to Riley.

"What the hell are you talking about?" Jack looked at her with searing anger. "Why were you at this man's house?" He turned back to Carl. "You messing around with my daughter, you sick son of a bitch? Ellen, get the cops over here now!"

"No, Daddy. Please, it's not like that. I met Mr. Boyd at the shelter last week. I went to see him 'cause I thought he needed help. Please, Daddy. He needs help. He thinks I'm his daughter who died a long time ago."

For a moment, Riley thought her father's eyes softened just a little at this revelation.

Carl gripped the doorframe to steady himself. He hunched over as if he'd lost the air in his lungs.

"The police will be here soon." Ellen returned from the kitchen.

"Oh no, Mom." Riley lowered her head. "This is all my fault."

Carl seemed to catch his breath and rose up again. He looked at Jack as if this was the first time he'd ever seen the man. "What's happening? Where am I?"

"You're standing on the front porch of my goddamn house, calling my goddamn daughter 'Mary.' I don't know what the hell kinda drugs you're on, but the police are on their way and they'll sort this out one way or another."

"Daddy, please." Riley stepped toward him.

"Get on upstairs!" Jack shouted.

She looked to Carl, her eyes pleading forgiveness, although she had done nothing wrong. Riley turned away and did as she was told, slowly climbing the stairs while her father continued to argue with Mr. Boyd.

Upstairs in her room, Riley waited in silence, her ear plastered against the door, trying to hear what was happening. She was afraid for Mr. Boyd, fearing her father might hurt the man who was clearly not in a sensible frame of mind. She knew the name Mary, and it confused her that Mr. Boyd seemed to think she was his daughter.

And why had she turned so angry herself? Her heart had filled with near-rage just before the man pounded on their door. With so many questions swirling in her head, all she could do was wait in utter confusion. She had no one to talk to and now Mr. Boyd was about to be taken away by the authorities.

"What's going on downstairs? Why is everyone yelling?" Gracie asked.

"Nothing. It's nothing. Just go back to playing with your dolls."

"How come no one ever tells me what's going on around here? Everyone thinks I'm just a baby." Gracie stomped away in a huff.

She watched her sister for a moment, sympathetic to her frustration. She felt it too, but for very different reasons, and it was unsettling. The last thing she wanted to do was make Gracie feel as confused and upset as she was. "Look, a man who needs help came to the door and now Mom and Dad are trying to help him."

That wasn't exactly the truth, but it was better than shutting Gracie out altogether.

A distant siren had grown louder and was drawing near. Riley rushed to her bedroom window and pulled back the curtain. Her eyes squinted for a moment as the lowering sun shined directly into her face. "Oh no."

A patrol car with the words "Owensville Police" fixed to the driver's side door rolled up alongside their front yard. She watched as the officer stepped out, his brown uniform making him look more like a UPS man than a policeman. He yanked up his pants and proceeded toward the front porch.

Riley pushed her head up against the window, looking down as best she could, but the roof overhang blocked her view of the happenings below. "I have to find out what's going on." She rushed toward the door. "You stay here!" she said to Gracie.

"You can't go down there. You'll get in trouble."

"No I won't. Not if they don't see me." Riley quietly opened her door and stepped softly into the hall. She tiptoed all the way to the top of the stairs and peeked just around the corner near the landing to get a better look below.

"I'm Officer Ward," he began. "What seems to be the problem here?"

Carl was back on his feet and seemed to be steadying himself. "I'm sorry, officer. I believe I've made a mistake."

"You're damn right you made a mistake!" Jack said.

"Just hold on," the officer began. "Can I have your name, please, sir?"

"It's Carl Boyd."

"And you're the Thompsons?" He turned to face Jack.

"Yes. Jack and Ellen Thompson. Look, officer, this man came banging on my door, insisting that my daughter is someone he knows. Scared the hell out of her, I tell you what."

"Jack." Ellen's soft tone hardly reached his ears as he seemed to completely ignore her.

Officer Ward looked to Ellen. His expression shifted at the sight of the fading marks on her face. She pulled her hair over her ears, an involuntary response Ellen had picked up.

"Mr. Thompson, I'm sure this was just some misunderstanding. I'll see to it that Mr. Boyd is taken home. Mr. Boyd, if you'll come with me."

"Thank you, officer. Crazy son of a bitch scaring the hell out of my little girl like that."

Riley leaned around the corner and caught the officer's eyes, briefly, but it was enough to get his attention.

"Is that your daughter up there, sir?" He pointed to Riley.

"Yes, that's Riley."

"Do you suppose I could have a quick word with her, just to see if I can straighten all this out?"

Jack appeared put out by the request. "I guess so. I don't know why, but I guess." He turned his eyes up to the top of the stairs. "Riley, come on down here now. This policeman would like to have a word with you."

She took a reluctant first step, then another.

"Come on now; hurry it up, girl," Jack said.

Officer Ward seemed to watch Riley carefully. She felt his eyes on her. She felt all their eyes on her. Quickening her pace, she managed to make it down the stairs without further demand. "Yes, sir."

The man in the uniform bent over, placing his hands on his knees. "Hi there, Riley. I understand this man frightened you. Is that right?"

She cast a timid look to Jack, then proceeded. "Um, not exactly, sir. See, I know Mr. Boyd. I met him at the shelter last week." Riley was hesitant to mention that she'd gone to his house and was pretty sure Jack wasn't going to say anything. That would open up a whole new can of worms and it seemed he just wanted this to be over with so he could get back to his sports.

"I see. And did you tell this man that you lived here?"

"No, sir. I—I um..."

"I knew where the girl lived, Officer," Carl interjected. "I knew the child's grandparents and this used to be their house."

Jack suddenly appeared interested again.

"I'm afraid I forgot to take my pills today and I seemed to have gotten confused. If I could just go on and leave this family be. I'm so sorry, Riley, if I frightened you at all."

He hadn't, of course, but what else was there to say? Jack needed some kind of closure here and she picked up on that. Even Ellen seemed confused by the entire situation, although she knew the man from this morning, and what had happened.

"It's okay, Mr. Boyd. I understand. I'm sorry about Mary. I really am." She held Carl's gaze, hoping he would see that she knew—everything. Maybe then he would be convinced that he needed to be mindful of her warning. Even if she didn't know what that warning meant. The most frightening part for her was that she could literally *feel* all of his hurt and resentment as he approached, before she knew it was him at the door. It was the first time something like that had ever happened. Riley didn't care for it and hoped it would be the last.

"Thank you, Riley." Carl turned to the officer. "I'm sorry I caused all this fuss. If I could just go home now. I don't feel well."

"Yeah, whatever drugs they got you on aren't working, old man. You should go home and stay there where you can't scare anyone else." Jack's words were growing more vile by the moment. It was as if he'd felt vindicated and wanted to flaunt his victory.

"Sir, I think the man's sorry for the trouble." Officer Ward glanced again at Ellen, pursing his lips, fully aware of her situation. He then looked to Riley, searching for any visible evidence of the same.

"I'll make sure Mr. Boyd gets home." He turned to Jack, staring for a length of time that quickly became uncomfortable for everyone.

Riley had seen that look before. Like the officer wanted to punch Jack right in the face. The last time she recalled such a look on someone's face was the last time Kaitlyn's family had been to her house. That was four years ago and Riley remembered it well.

Jack had had too much to drink. Nothing new there, except in those days, it hadn't been nearly as frequent as it was today.

What had started out as an innocent disagreement between friends turned into something ugly and mean. Jack lashed out at his friend, Mr. Ross—Mike, she'd heard her dad call him. They were talking about why the plant had closed. Mr. Ross said it was because the unions cost too much. Jack didn't seem to agree.

"Unions are what keep us middle-class folk in decent houses and allow us to save for retirement," He'd said.

"They're robbing everybody. Don't you see that, Jack? Sure, the retirement's nice, but what company could sustain those types of payouts? There simply isn't enough going into the pot for everyone to get their share. And what about the dues? They keep raising 'em, and for what?"

Unfortunately, Ellen had come in between the men, trying to calm the situation. Jack wasn't happy about that. He'd swung wide and struck her right across the mouth, drawing a little blood too.

Mike Ross jumped from his seat and well, that was all Riley knew because both her mom and Kaitlyn's mom rushed all the kids upstairs. She remembered the yelling and slamming of doors. And that was it. That was the last time the Rosses came over or vice versa.

So there it was again, that same look that Officer Ward was conveying to her dad right now. He finally broke away, nodding his head to Ellen and Riley.

"Come on, Mr. Boyd. Let's get you home." He helped Carl down the steps of the porch and to his car. The patrol car followed Mr. Boyd's down the street and disappeared.

Jack pushed the door closed hard enough to make Riley jump. "That dinner sure as hell better not be ruined. Ellen, you better go check on it. Riley, get back upstairs." Jack started to walk back to the living room, mumbling under his breath, "God damn crazy son of a bitch."

Ellen stopped Riley before she started up the stairs. "Riley?" She tossed her head in the direction of the kitchen. Riley followed.

"What was that all about, young lady?" Ellen asked. "Did it have something to do with what happened in the diner this morning?"

"I don't know—I think so. Mom, Mr. Boyd isn't well. He needs help."

"Well, I can see that. He clearly needs a lot of help, but you're not the one who can do it, understand? He needs medical attention, that's all." Ellen opened the oven door and a waft of beef billowed out. "At least the roast isn't burnt."

"It's more than that, Mom. I can feel what he's going through." Riley needed her to understand. She had to say something.

"What do you mean, you can feel it?" Ellen folded her arms.

"Mom. You know there's things about me that you don't like to think about; I know that." Riley watched as Ellen's face masked in guilt, because of course she knew; she just chose to ignore it. "I saw what he saw this morning, in the diner. He was in some war, Mom, and he was afraid. I don't know why this is happening to me, but I can feel all of his feelings. And, I know that he's in trouble."

"What kind of trouble?"

"I wish I knew, but I can help him. I just need to talk to him so we can figure it out together. Will you help me? Please, Mom?"

Ellen looked at Riley's pleading young face. "If your father finds out, there'll be hell to pay. You know that, right?"

"Dad won't know, I promise. This will just be between us."

The front door opened again and Dillon walked inside. Dusk had settled in and that was usually his cue to come home.

"Your brother's home. We'll talk about this later, okay?"

"Okay, Mom." Riley's heart sank in disappointment. Maybe her mom would help, but it wasn't likely. She didn't want to admit that whatever it was Riley possessed scared her. She wasn't the only one.

[10]

The assignments had been divvied amongst the men and they were ready to head out. CJ realized that this was something dangerous and that if he'd had the nerve, he'd leave right now and head straight for the authorities. But they'd promised him a great sum of money. Enough that he'd be able to pack up and leave town before they'd take any notice.

The deal was, they were going to Warehouse B in the next town over. They were going to take the crates and load them up into the moving truck that Johnny would be driving.

During the course of the meeting, CJ discovered what was inside those crates and why they'd wanted them. Guns. Ammunition. RPGs. Enough to blow up the entire town, he suspected. These guys weren't screwing around. The plan was to take back the territory Dennis and his bosses were muscling in on. Raymond wasn't about to let those sons of bitches ruin everything. He'd made that perfectly clear in the moments leading up to this.

While CJ was terrified at the prospect, it seemed a well-laid-out plan. One that would see them all in and out safely in a matter of minutes. Less than half an hour. So he would go along and take his ten percent. Then, he'd be out of there quicker than anything.

"You're coming with me," Johnny said, waving CJ over.

The two hopped into the truck. It looked like it had been a U-Haul that'd been painted white.

"How long till we get there?" CJ asked as Johnny started up the engine.

"About half an hour, I'm guessing. Then, once we get there, just stick to the plan. Ray and Dougie got it all worked out. Just do your part and don't worry about it. We'll be fine."

The convoy of five cars and the truck started down the darkened highway. It was approaching ten thirty. By all accounts, they'd be there by eleven.

"You done this kind of stuff before?" CJ asked, hanging on to the handle above the passenger door.

"Not like this exactly, but something like it." Johnny turned to him. "Look, I know this caught you off guard. I'm sorry about that, I really am. It's just that's how these guys operate. We needed another man for this job. It's been in the works for a while, and both me and Doug thought you'd be the best guy to do it. You're honest and loyal. You're the kind of guy we need to help pull this off." He turned back toward the road. "Besides, you'll like the money. It's a good deal all the way around; trust me on this one."

"All right. If you say so. I trust ya." CJ revealed a reluctant smile, understanding that the man had said "trust me" a few too many times. He looked ahead, watching the headlights illuminate the road in front of them. In the side mirror, he spotted the other cars behind them.

The two remained silent for the duration, until a dim light appeared in the distance. CJ began to feel his heart beat a little faster in his chest. He glanced again into the side view mirror; the others were still behind them.

The industrial complex up ahead was still under construction. He figured they must be over in Ashland, another small town just outside of the one they just ditched. CJ had heard there'd been some recent improvements over there, construction jobs. In fact, he almost took up shelter there instead of following the Denton brothers to his current residence.

Johnny turned off the headlights and shifted into a lower gear, practically crawling into the parking lot of the large structure CJ had recognized as Warehouse B. He'd studied those plans for the better part of a week and knew the place inside and out. He recognized the building to the left, a partially constructed office with a warehouse at the back. And the building to the right. A larger front office with double the space behind it.

"This is it." Johnny pulled around the back of the building and waited.

Two others joined them. "Where're the other cars?" CJ asked.

"Probably taking up more strategic locations. We don't want everyone to be parked out front. Might look odd were anyone to drive by."

It was eleven o'clock on a Sunday night and they were sitting in a construction site. It wasn't likely that they'd see anyone driving by.

"So what now?" CJ was beginning to feel impatient and just wanted to get this over with and go back home.

"We wait for the word." Johnny turned his attention to CJ. "The boys need to get inside first. They'll have a look around, make sure all is okay, then give us the word. We'll jump out, roll up the trailer door, and go inside to help them get us loaded up. My guess is that we've got four, maybe five pallets to get out. Shouldn't take more than twenty minutes from start to finish."

CJ looked at his watch, waiting in silence and thinking about the pretty bartender whom he hadn't seen in a while. He might pay her a visit after this, knowing he'd need some kind of distraction. Whether or not she would want to see him remained to be seen.

Several minutes passed and, until he heard the noise, he hadn't realized just how many. Checking his watch again, he saw that it had been nearly half an hour they'd been waiting. But it seemed the boys were ready to load up.

Johnny opened the driver's door. "It's time. Let's go." He disappeared outside.

CJ moved quickly, hopping out of his seat and running around to the back of the truck where Johnny waited. "What now?" he whispered.

Johnny simply raised his index finger to his lips, suggesting the need for silence. The rolling door of Warehouse B raised high. "Come on."

He followed Johnny inside where he spotted the others scrambling to move the pallets. Doug was working the forklift, guided by Bennett to the nearest pallet. On top of each pallet were three wooden crates.

As CJ walked inside, he noticed that this building was still just a shell. Inside was nothing more than a concrete floor with masonry walls and a few metal support beams dotted around the huge open space. With the exception of the pallets and a few pieces of equipment, the place was empty.

He noticed Raymond standing near the metal rolling door, his eyes shifting back and forth as he held his phone to his ear. CJ wondered who he was talking to at a time like this.

"CJ, git over here. I need some help!" Johnny raised his voice just above a whisper, but it was apparent he'd gotten agitated by CJ's wandering eye. They couldn't be there all night and time had already ticked away too quickly.

"We gotta get outta here now, boys!" Raymond stepped with purpose toward the forklift.

They'd only succeeded in loading up one of the five pallets. Doug turned his attention to Ray. "What's going on? We're not finished yet."

"They're coming. They know we're here. Now get the hell off that forklift!"

"Did he just say they're coming?" CJ felt the panic rising in him. Johnny looked almost as surprised as he had. "Let's get the fuck out of here."

Johnny ignored him. Instead, he ran to Ray's side and the two huddled for a moment. It was all CJ could do to keep from bolting out of there without him. He spotted Bennett ripping one of the crates open and yanking out rifles, as many as he could carry. "Stupid son of a bitch."

CJ began walking toward Doug. "What the hell's going on, man? Why aren't we leaving?"

Doug had already jumped off the forklift and was waiting for instructions. "Shit, I don't know." He began to jog toward Ray.

Carl stood in the middle of the warehouse while everyone seemed to be trying to figure out what to do. He had no idea how much time they had before "they" got there, whoever "they" were, although he suspected he already knew.

In that moment, the men raced toward the loading dock outside. Everyone was heading out, except him. "Son of a bitch." CJ took to running out after them. "Johnny! Johnny, hold the fuck up!"

The cars roared to life and as CJ caught up to Johnny inside of Doug's truck, he realized what was happening. He jiggled the rear passenger door handle, slapping the roof of the truck. "Let me in! Open the fucking door!" But Johnny only looked at him.

CJ came to the sudden realization that he wasn't going anywhere. Johnny had the keys to the hauler and he and those backstabbing sons of bitches were leaving him there to face them, the men who presumably had ownership of those guns.

Johnny looked at him through the passenger side window. "I'm sorry, CJ, but it has to be this way."

Doug shifted his pick-up into gear and squealed out of the parking lot along with the others. CJ stood in the middle of the now empty lot. His heart pounded hard against his chest and adrenaline coursed through his body, but he was paralyzed with fear.

Ahead of him was the main road; behind him was undeveloped land, with undulating hills and trees. He didn't know what lay behind that swath of ground. The complex was large, perhaps large enough in which to take cover. CJ had only seconds to make a decision. The idea that he could talk his way out of it had occurred to him. Lay blame on the men who were setting him up to take the fall for this botched robbery. But would they believe him? He'd seen the man called Dennis and questioned if he'd had even one sympathetic bone in his body.

He could call the cops. He had his cell phone, but how would he explain his own involvement? He'd had a few misdemeanors on his record, but nothing like this. CJ raised his hands to his face and grunted, trying desperately to find a solution to this dubious situation in which he'd now found himself.

In the distance, he heard tires rolling fast along the road and it was coming from more than one vehicle. Whatever he was going to do, it had to be done now.

CJ darted toward Warehouse A. It hadn't been as far along in the construction process as B had. He felt relief at the sight of a window frame opening. Not all of the windows had been installed yet and he thanked God for that.

He jumped inside and scanned the area. It was pitch black, no hint of any source of light. But CJ figured it had to be similar to B and so he stepped quickly but carefully through the darkness toward the north side of the building. That was where the ventilation units would be housed and if they hadn't yet been installed, he stood a fairly good chance of hiding out inside that small room.

Light pushed inside and quickly caught CJ's attention. They were headlights. He backed flat up against the wall as if a spotlight was searching for him. Instead, they faded from view. His heart started again and he continued on toward the room.

His hands felt along the wall until he found the door. It was definitely the right place. The metal door had louvers over a portion of it to allow the system to expel air, keeping the pressure down. He turned the handle and it opened with ease.

CJ believed it safe enough now that he could retrieve his cell phone and turn on its light so that he could confirm his location. The small room lit up just enough so that he could be assured he was in the right spot and it appeared that he was. One of the units had been installed, but there was enough space for him to hide behind it. He had no idea if they would search all of the buildings, but he couldn't take the chance of being out in the open in any event.

These men were not going to be happy and CJ suspected they were in Warehouse B right now, searching through their crates of presumably stolen or black market guns and ammunition. How the hell could he have allowed himself to get involved in this? He'd prided himself on being a loner, someone who didn't have many friends and kept to himself. All this had started out that way, except that he took Johnny's word that it would all work out. *"Trust me."* CJ guessed he was wrong about that the same way he was wrong about Johnny.

His eyes widened at the sudden noise. CJ stood still behind the big metal box, listening for it again. It was the sound of footsteps—several of them. "Shit, shit, shit." They were inside and they were looking for him. Whatever breath he'd had in his lungs waited with nowhere to go. He couldn't move and he couldn't breathe.

The steps were coming closer and he could hear men whispering. He figured three, maybe four of them. It could have been one or a hundred; either way, CJ was screwed if they found him. He had no weapon, no way to defend himself in any manner.

"We just got word that it was one of McAllister's boys. Stupid som' bitch found out where we were keeping the supply and decided to take it upon his self to take whatever he wanted. We're going back to meet up with 'em and sort through all this. They say they're gonna find him and hand him over."

The footsteps started again, only now they were heading in the opposite direction. CJ shook his head, disbelieving what he'd just heard. They were pinning it all on him. Saving their own asses and letting him, the new guy, take the fall.

Several more minutes passed by before he began to hear the vehicles pulling away, the headlights once again shining through and disappearing just as quickly. CJ looked at his phone. It was almost one o'clock in the morning.

He couldn't go home, not that he had any way to get there. Some of his acquaintances knew how to hotwire vehicles, but it wasn't a skill he had possessed, so taking off in the U-Haul truck wasn't an option. Besides, they'd likely be on the lookout for it.

"What the hell have I gotten myself into?" His head rested against the ventilation unit as he considered his next move.

He had some buddies up in Columbus, but thought they'd be reluctant to help him out of this particular situation. A few were already on parole, so they were out of the question. Another friend was married and so CJ was pretty sure his wife wouldn't let him drive for two hours to pick him up. So who was left?

CJ began to realize he really had no one in this world on whom he could depend. Here he was, a man of thirty-eight. No wife, no kids, hopping around from job to job. He was as worthless as his dad always told him. But then, looking around this tiny room in which he had found himself confined, maybe his dad had been right. He might have been crazy, but he was dead on about that.

There was one person he thought maybe, just maybe, might come help him out of this jam. CJ opened his phone and pressed the contact button.

"Hey, it's me, CJ. I'm sorry it's so late. You just getting off work?"

There was silence on the other end. It was to be expected. After all, he hadn't bothered calling her in the last week, so why would she want to hear from him now? Still, the fact that she remained on the line gave him some hope.

"I'm in some trouble and I could really use a lift."

CJ STOOD JUST OUTSIDE OF THE BUILDING, SHADOWED FROM any light. She would be there in a few minutes, or so he hoped. She could have always changed her mind.

Up ahead about thirty yards, he could see a car slowing. It almost stopped before turning into the lot. It was dark and the entrance was difficult to see, but he knew it had to be her. He stepped out of the shadow and flashed the light from his phone in the direction of the car. It turned and headed toward him.

The old compact car stopped just a few feet before him. CJ walked around to the passenger side. She rolled down the window.

"You're lucky I came for you, CJ." She looked around, shaking her head.

"I know that. I'm very lucky and very grateful that you're here Melissa."

"Well, get in then."

[11]

The faint sounds of chatter among the children on the bus had little effect on Riley. Tired from a restless sleep, she absentmindedly watched the scenery pass her by on their way to school. The better part of the previous night had consisted of worrisome thoughts of an unknown threat she felt powerless to do anything about. The notion that her ability had become stronger also weighed heavily on her mind.

It seemed nothing had changed when she stood ready to leave this morning, Ellen ignoring any mention of the night before when Carl Boyd had disrupted their evening. It occurred to Riley then that she was alone in the matter.

Kaitlyn tried to get her attention, but eventually, she gave up. There wasn't much point in getting her involved. Now, a new school week was beginning and things would go back to the way they were, as if the old man had never shown up at the Thompson's door.

"So Carl, I hear you had some trouble with the police last night. Care to fill me in on what happened?" Dr. Lucy Elliot sat behind her desk, elbows placed on each armrest, her hands clasped together just beneath her chin.

"I don't know. I don't remember." Carl was sitting on the other side, an unwilling participant in the conversation, but it was the only way Officer Ward would let him off. Carl had to agree to see his doctor and get checked out, and make sure his medication didn't need any adjustments.

"Well, according to the officer, you showed up at the home of Mr. and Mrs. Thompson, insisting that you talk to your daughter. Carl, you remember what happened to your daughter, don't you?"

It was hard to ignore her condescension, but he knew she was only trying to get to the bottom of the situation. Dr. Elliot was the VA's choice to treat Carl. The VA hospital was all the way up in Indianapolis and Carl didn't have the money to travel the two and half hours once a month for a checkup. They outsourced when distance to a facility was an issue. Still, what could he say? That he'd had a flashback, a long forgotten memory of that dreadful war? That, somehow, the little girl knew all about his family? She wouldn't buy it and neither would he, if it hadn't happened to him directly.

"Yes, I—I went there. I'm not sure why, exactly. There've been some triggers lately and I think maybe I just didn't handle it well. I sort of lost track of where I was and ended up at their home."

"From what Officer Ward indicated, you knew the Thompsons' daughter. How do you know her, Carl, and how did you know she lived there?"

Carl shifted in his seat. "Look, I don't know what that cop told you, but I got lost, plain and simple. I ended up at their house and I was confused. Hell, I don't know; maybe you need to up my meds."

"And you've been taking them regularly, is that right?" the doctor asked.

"Yes, ma'am, I have."

She seemed to study him for an awkward length of time. "You mentioned flashbacks. How many have you had recently?"

"Not many. One or two, that's all." It was only one and that was because that girl was there. She triggered it somehow. He knew it was her doing, but wasn't about to further muddy the waters.

"Okay, well, perhaps we've only experienced a small setback then. I think we ought to up our appointments to every week for a while, at least until I'm confident these episodes are finished."

"Fine. If that'll make you happy."

"I'm not doing this to make me happy, Carl. I want to be sure we aren't going to have any more issues of this nature."

He pushed up from the chair. "I understand. Thank you for your time, Dr. Elliot. I'll set the appointment with your receptionist up front. Good day."

"Good bye, Carl. I'll be sure to inform Officer Ward of our solution."

He didn't turn back in acknowledgment, only rolled his eyes and left the room.

Carl sat in his car in front of the school. He wanted

to apologize to Riley for upsetting her and her family last night. Maybe that would help to smooth over the situation with both the cops and Jack Thompson. But if he was being honest, he'd admit why he was really there.

He checked the time, assuming that school let out around three o'clock. That was usually when he noticed all the buses driving around. The problem would be in getting her attention. Even in this small town, a strange old man trying to talk to a little girl outside of school would have negative implications. He had to figure a way to at least lock eyes with her. To somehow get across the idea that he was ready to listen to what she had to say. And, he felt bad for the girl. After seeing the children with their mother in the diner yesterday morning and then again last night, it was pretty clear Jack Thompson was a man with serious anger management issues. This was surprising because Carl had known Jack's father and, although things had transpired between the two, he knew the man to be decent.

Carl had come across that type plenty of times and some of the Marines he'd served with were no exception. He'd been witness to many men, good soldiers, who'd changed because of the imminent threat of death that loomed over their heads every single day when they were in that jungle. It was pressure that some just couldn't handle and they'd take it out on the weak. Although he didn't figure Jack Thompson was the sort to risk his life for his country; just the sort who couldn't handle being a man.

The school bell struck at exactly three o'clock. Carl stepped out of his car and walked toward the front, careful not to get too close. There were several cars with parents waiting inside and plenty more standing, waiting for their children to emerge. He wasn't sure he'd even spot her among all the young people. It had been so long since he'd been around kids. A smile formed on his lips as he thought about CJ, recalling a time when he'd been at his school, picking him up and taking him to baseball practice, but that was so very long ago.

Carl retrieved his glasses to try to get a clearer look at the blissful faces that had rushed out of the building. "Oh hell, I'm never gonna pick her out of that crowd." But he watched and waited. He knew she took the bus, so he strolled near the large yellow vehicles, thinking she might be headed that way. But he didn't have to spot her. Instead, she spotted him.

Out of the sea of children appeared a short, slightly tubby girl with long, stringy blonde hair. It was Riley. Carl hesitantly raised a hand to shoulder level, not wanting to draw anyone else's attention. She'd seen him.

He watched as she turned to another girl, saying something he couldn't interpret. Riley began to walk toward him. Carl looked around, confirming no one seemed concerned by this. It wasn't like he was holding out a lollipop or anything. He looked like he could be her grandpa, after all. Besides, he figured if he stayed in plain sight, the less suspicious the other parents would be.

"Mr. Boyd. What are you doing here?" Riley asked on approach, stopping a good ten feet away from him.

"I'm sorry about last night, Riley. I honestly don't know why or how I ended up at your home. I hope you'll forgive me."

"It's okay, Mr. Boyd. You came here just to apologize?"

"Well, no, actually. See, I got to thinking about what you said the other day at my house and I thought maybe we could meet up again sometime soon? You could bring your mother, of course. I'm sure she'd prefer that."

Riley turned at the sound of her name. Kaitlyn was waving her back over to the bus. "I'll ask my mom when I get home. Maybe we can meet you at the diner tomorrow after school?" She turned back again, ensuring the bus hadn't left. "I have to go, Mr. Boyd. Tomorrow after school at the diner, okay? Bye, Mr. Boyd!"

Carl walked back to his car, turning to be sure Riley made it to her bus in time. He wasn't sure if her mother would agree, but he'd be there at the diner tomorrow, just like she asked. The old man was wise enough to recognize that when certain people were placed in your path, it was probably for a damn good reason.

The calls kept coming in on his cell phone, but CJ wasn't about to answer any of them. Johnny had called at least five times since this morning. Doug called three or four times. Maybe they wanted to help him, tell him that they'd offer protection against these other men. But then, he recalled the look in Johnny's eyes and thought they just wanted to know where he was, track him down, and hand him over as some sort of gesture of good faith. Like admitting they'd been wrong about him and were sorry for the trouble he'd caused. "So here you go; do what you want with him!"

Well, CJ wasn't going to have any of that. Melissa had taken him back to her place. No one would know he was there. He was safe, for the time being, but needed to figure out his next step. Where could he go? Who could he trust?

As he watched Melissa sleeping next to him in her double bed, he was grateful she had forgiven him for brushing her off like he had. If she hadn't come, he'd probably still be there, sleeping on the concrete floor of that ventilation room, or maybe hitchhiking his way to God knows where, praying he wouldn't be found. All he had were the clothes on his back. He couldn't go home. No chance in hell he could go to work. Doug had proven himself to be a back-stabbing son of a bitch just like Johnny.

CJ believed he could possibly get to the bank first thing this morning and withdraw all the money he had, which wasn't much. Maybe six hundred bucks and that was only because he'd gotten a paycheck on Friday and hadn't paid his bills yet. He'd be broke otherwise.

The last thing he would want would be for Melissa to get into any danger, and so further involvement on her end probably wasn't a good idea. He felt guilty for the way he'd treated her. It was most likely the first time he'd ever felt guilty about anything, especially his treatment of a woman. He'd been pretty much a shit for most of his life, but after what she'd done for him, he couldn't help but regret his earlier actions.

The time showed eight a.m. He was going to have to make a decision. Either get up and get out before she awakened, or ask her to help him out one more time. But then, that would be it. Just get him to the bank and he could manage the rest of the way.

"Melissa? Are you awake?" he whispered, stroking her arm gently.

"I am now."

He smiled at her wry sense of humor. "I'm sorry to wake you, but do you think you could give me a ride to the bank when they open at nine? I'll get out of your hair after that, I promise."

Melissa rubbed her eyes and pulled the sheet up over her exposed breasts. "What are you going to do after that, CJ? It seems like you're in a precarious situation here. Don't you think the police might be able to help you out?"

The idea had occurred to him, going to the cops, but he was afraid it would backfire. He was a willing participant, up to a point. How was he going to explain his presence at the warehouse? Then, of course, assuming he could get around that little problem, he'd have to stay in town, meaning he'd be exposed. He didn't think Raymond McAllister was the type of man that liked loose ends.

"I don't know, Melissa. I mean, I could take them to where I work, tell them what Doug did. Maybe direct them to Johnny's place. But these guys aren't stupid and, more importantly, Raymond McAllister isn't stupid. I'm sure he's already taken the necessary precautions."

"Sounds like you're afraid."

Of course he was afraid. There were too many variables. He'd already underestimated these guys once, and he didn't want to do it again. "Maybe you're right. Maybe I am afraid. Or maybe I just don't want to take any chances that these guys will find me first and the cops won't be able to do anything about it. Look, I don't want to tell you more than I'd consider safe for you to know, but these men are into something very dangerous. I screwed up by getting involved with those assholes. Now, I just need to find a way out. Will you help get me to the bank, or should I just catch a bus?" CJ felt even worse now for jumping down her throat. She was only trying to help and he owed her a lot.

"I'll take you to the damn bank, geez." Melissa rolled out of the bed, keeping the sheet around her. "Just let me get dressed."

"I'm sorry." Carl reached out to take her hand as she walked by.

"Forget it, all right? I said I'd take you and I'll take you." She yanked her hand away and headed into the bathroom.

They arrived at the bank at exactly nine o'clock. CJ continued to ignore the calls and texts to his phone and opted to just shut it off, fearing they might have the capability of tracking him down through GPS. "I'll be back in a minute." He stepped out of the car and walked inside.

The first in line, he moved ahead to the teller with a shiny smile. "I'd like to withdrawal some money, please."

"Good morning, sir. Of course, I can certainly help you with that. What is your account number, and I'll need to see an ID as well."

CJ dug out the information she needed and waited. His nerves were frayed and he wondered if sweat would drip down his forehead at any moment. In fact, he was beginning to look like a bank robber with his shifty glances.

"Here you go, sir; here is one hundred, two hundred, three hundred..." She proceeded to count the small bills after that, but all he could do was scan the area, as if he was waiting for Johnny to pounce on him.

"And six hundred thirty-five dollars, fifty-one cents. Is there anything else I can do for you?"

"No thank you. This'll be all. Have a good day." CJ rushed toward the door, vaguely hearing the teller reply in kind.

He reached Melissa's car and stepped inside.

"Where to now?" she asked.

"Could you just drop me off at the bus station?" He folded the money and placed the wad of cash into his wallet, then tucked it away in his pants pocket.

"Where you gonna go?" She started up the car.

"I don't know yet, but you've done enough for me and I'll need to take care of this on my own from here on out."

"You don't know where you're going and you don't know what you're going to do to get yourself out of this jam? Sounds like you need me more than you think you do." Melissa reversed out of the parking lot and onto the main road.

Up ahead was a sign for the interstate. "Where to, CJ? I'm coming with you whether you want me to or not."

"But—your job... you can't. It's too dangerous."

"You'd better decide quick or I'll decide for you."

The east-west split was just ahead.

"Fine! Fine! Go east."

"What's east?"

"My dad."

[12]

The abandoned house that was located a few blocks from the Thompson home was a popular hangout for the high schoolers. It had been virtually consumed by weeds and overgrown trees. Most of the windows were boarded up, some vandalized with inappropriate spray-painted words. The eyesore was the product of a recession they said had ended.

Dillon sat on the steps of the home's front porch with a couple of the kids in his class. Any reason he devised not to go home was a good one, including hanging out with kids of whom his father would disapprove. That didn't matter much to Dillon, though. He'd stopped seeking Jack's approval long ago.

He'd been on the receiving end of Jack's drunken temper on a few occasions. In fact, the first time it'd happened was when he'd come home late after a game on a Friday night last year. The team had won and he'd gone with them to celebrate. Jack hadn't bothered to show up, but Ellen relayed the news and so Dillon didn't think anything of it after that. Until he had gotten home.

Sitting on the rotted wood of the porch steps, he pretended to laugh at one of his friend's dimwitted jokes. These guys weren't exactly Rhodes Scholars, but Dillon didn't care. What mattered was that he didn't have to be at home. He didn't have to listen to Jack bellowing orders at his mother, or watch her cower to him to avoid setting him off.

The hardest part was missing out on life with his sisters. He missed playing with them, running around in the backyard, throwing the ball around for a game of catch. The helplessness he felt when he was around his father kept him from the rest of the family. As a result, he'd begun to hang out with those less desirable. What else was there to do in this town except hang out around one of the many abandoned homes or storefronts?

"Dude, you gonna take it or what?" Matt held the joint in front of Dillon, his eyes narrowing from the effects of the schwag, which was slang for the cheap, low-grade pot he'd scored off of his older brother.

Dillon looked at what was left of the joint. "No thanks. I gotta get home soon anyway."

"Fine. More for me, then. My brother's such a cheap ass, it takes almost the entire joint just to feel a high. Oh well." Matt placed the bud between his lips and inhaled deeply.

He watched his friend take a hit. He usually gave some excuse as to why he couldn't. It wasn't his thing. Really, this kid was just an acquaintance. Dillon didn't have friends anymore, not even his teammates. It was hard to keep friends when he was ashamed to take them to his house. It seemed most everyone knew what the Thompsons were all about. Dillon wished they could move, but then, what would be the point? It'd end up being the same thing, just in another place.

"Look, I gotta go." Dillon rose from the steps, dusting off his backside. "Catch up with you tomorrow?"

"Sure, dude. Catcha later."

Dillon jumped on his bike and peddled slowly to the end of the drive and out onto the road. The sun was falling behind the tall trees on the horizon and it was growing colder by the minute. He began to pedal faster, standing up on his bike and pumping as hard as he could, begging for the cold to chill his skin so that he could feel something, anything besides resentment for the family he'd been given. It was hard enough being fourteen, let alone being fourteen in a small town where everyone knew everyone else's business.

Dillon pressed hard on his brakes, screeching to a halt outside of his front yard. The inattention to the house was beginning to show on the outside now. Peeling paint, dry rot on the porch, and dead grass on the lawn. It was coming up on spring and life should be growing, but as he looked on at the place he called home, all he could see was neglect.

He stepped off the bike and pushed it up the pathway toward the porch, leaning it against the spindles that had once been white, but were now chipping away, exposing the dry, grey wood beneath. On entry, he noticed his mother approaching.

"Hello, sweetheart." Ellen appeared from the end of the hall, near the utility room, and wrapped her arms around him as he stood in the foyer.

The scent of fabric softener lingered on her skin. Dillon inhaled the agreeable fragrance, exposing a hint of a smile as he returned her greeting. "Hi, Mom."

"Dinner will be ready in about an hour, so why don't you head upstairs and do your homework first?"

Dillon leaned in toward the living room. "Where's Dad?"

"Looks like his interview with the manufacturer in Shawnee went well today. He hasn't returned home just yet, but I expect he'll be home by dinner." Ellen patted her son on the back. "Now go and get your homework finished up before he arrives."

"Okay, Mom." Dillon peered into Ellen's eyes. They both knew exactly where Jack was, although neither wanted to admit it.

By the time he'd made it to the top of the stairs, he could hear Riley coming out of the bathroom.

"Dillon, you're home!" She threw herself around his lean, teenaged frame.

"Hey, Riley. What're you up to?"

"Oh, me and Gracie were just outside, but Mom told us to come in 'cause it's getting too cold. Where've you been?"

"Hanging out with my friends, that's all." He rubbed the top of her head, making the fine hairs stand on end with static.

"You smell funny." Riley took a step back and crinkled her nose.

Dillon reddened with embarrassment. "So Mom said Dad's job interview went well? I guess we'll all be glad when he goes back to work, assuming he can keep this job."

"Dillon, you shouldn't be like that."

"How should I be, Riley? Like Mom? Ignoring the problem?" Dillon could feel heat rising beneath his shirt. "I'm sorry. I shouldn't say things like that. It's just—"

"I know. It's okay." Riley stepped further away from him in order to meet his eyes straight on. "I need a favor."

"Yeah? What kind of favor?"

"Can you come with me after school tomorrow to go and see Carl Boyd? I'm supposed to meet him at the diner, you know, where we go to breakfast after church?"

"Yeah, I know the place, but Riley, isn't that the same guy who had that episode or whatever at breakfast on Sunday? And Mom said he came over here before I got home and stirred up some trouble. What in the world are you doing going off to meet him? Did you tell Mom this?"

"No. She would never let me go." Riley lowered her gaze. "Dillon, I feel that something very bad is going to happen to Mr. Boyd."

"What do you mean?" Dillon had long suspected Riley held some sort of special talent for reading people. He'd seen her react in certain ways on occasion, but couldn't explain it. He figured this must have been one of those times. Over the past year or so, he hadn't been much of a big brother to her or Gracie, for that matter. He couldn't let her go alone and she was probably right about not telling their mother. It was the least he could do for her.

"I just feel like he's gonna get hurt or something. Please, Dillon. I wouldn't ask if I didn't really need your help."

"I know, Riley. Okay. I'll help you. Tomorrow, after school?"

"Yeah."

Dillon bent down and pressed his lips against the top of her head. "I better get my homework done before dinner."

THE PROBLEM WITH THE PILLS WAS THAT THEY MADE CARL'S head feel fuzzy, like he couldn't think straight when he was on them. On the other hand, they did a pretty good job of keeping his demons at bay. Still, he wondered if that was a good trade off—quieting the thoughts or hardly being able to complete a thought. He supposed that depended on the day. Right now, he'd prefer to be of sound mind, if that was possible.

As he sat in his comfortably worn recliner, Carl began to get that feeling again, like he had to look over his shoulder every few minutes. He'd hadn't taken them today—since the good doctor told him he'd better get a handle on the situation. It was his small way of rebelling. He didn't like taking orders from anyone not wearing stripes.

It would be time for bed soon and that would help, provided he could see his way to sleep without peering through his window or getting up to check that his door was locked ten times in the night. Once sleep found him, though, he'd only have to suffer the effects in his dreams, which wasn't entirely bad. Sometimes, he got to see Mary, sometimes Rosalyn. Not always, but when he could remember the next day, it helped to lighten his heart, if only for a short while.

The one benefit was that he could go and grab a beer before bed. No pills meant no problem drinking. Maybe he'd stay up another half an hour or so and catch some late-night TV.

He popped open a can and pulled out the footstool of the recliner, leaning back, trying to find comfort. His mind, however, couldn't stop thinking about what tomorrow would bring. Did he really trust this girl, Riley, that she knew something about him? Something that she seemed to truly believe would bring him closer to danger?

Who the hell would want to hurt a sixty-seven-year-old veteran? He didn't owe anyone money, hadn't pissed anyone off as of late, except maybe for Riley's dad. Carl kept to himself most of the time, so the idea brought back some old familiar feelings that Carl was now trying to subdue with a little drink. But he wouldn't go back to taking the pills. Not until this whole situation was put to rest. No, he needed a clear and open mind to understand where this girl was coming from.

A distant clanging roused him from the snooze he'd been enjoying in his chair while the TV rolled the credits at the end of the Late Show. It was his front door. The rattling of the screen against the metal frame. It wasn't like an actual house with the deep sound of a knock on a real wooden door. That had always been a comforting sound to Carl. No, this was a reminder of the tin shack that was his home. Still, he wondered who the hell could be clamoring on this late at night.

Carl waited a moment longer, wanting to be sure it wasn't just part of some dream he'd been having or perhaps a side effect of coming off his meds.

The sound came again. It was definitely not his imagination this time. He pushed the lever for the footstool down and lowered his legs, heaving himself off of the chair. His bones cracked and he moaned loudly. It was hell getting old. "I'm coming. Hold your horses."

He walked toward the small window next to the door and parted the metal blinds just enough for his eyes to peer out. "What the hell?"

Outside stood a man and a woman, coats pulled tightly around their shivering bodies, looking about as if they were being watched. Of course, that could very well be the case around these parts. Tenants of this park didn't like being disrupted by the sound of a car driving along the dirt path at midnight.

Carl watched them waiting nervously at the foot of the steps, their breaths visible in the cold night air. The man was kicking his toe into the dirt and little plumes of dust floated up. He shook his head, dropping the blinds closed once again and proceeded to open the door. "What the hell are you doing here, CJ? You know it's midnight?" He didn't wait for a reply. "Get in here and bring your friend."

The two walked in as if ashamed to have arrived both at the late hour and without prior consent.

"I'm sorry to have awakened you, Dad. This is Melissa."

"Please, call me Mel." She extended her hand, waiting for a returned greeting, but none came.

Instead, Carl only nodded at the young woman and returned his attention to his son. "You in some kind of trouble?"

"Maybe we could sit down, have a coffee, and warm up a little first, Dad. It's been a long drive."

Carl eyed the woman again. She was too skinny. "Fine. Sit down and I'll put on a pot of coffee. Then you can tell me why you and your girlfriend decided to show up at my doorstep in the middle of the night."

The two exchanged what appeared to be an uncomfortable look at the term Carl had just bestowed upon Melissa, eventually finding their way to the couch and taking a seat, about a mile apart from one another.

Several minutes passed before Carl returned with a couple of mugs of coffee, skipping one for himself. It was bad enough to be awake at this hour. Coffee would only worsen the situation.

"So, you wanna tell me why you're here, CJ?"

The man turned to Melissa. "My dad doesn't like to beat around the bush."

"Yeah. I guessed that. You might want to tell him why we showed up at his doorstep."

"I like her already." Carl smirked and waited for his son to continue.

"Sorry for showing up like this, Dad. I really am. It's just—shit, I don't know. I got caught up in some kinda bad deal. I guess I'm here—*we're* here because we need a place to stay for a few days until all this blows over."

Carl began to stroke his chin, a vestige of the days when he wore a beard, and looked down at the two sad sacks who were sitting on his couch. "What kind of bad deal, CJ? The kind that'll bring the cops to my door, or the kind that'll bring the people who are generally worse than the cops?" He stared hard at his son, trying to read the boy.

CJ had been prone to trouble most of his life. Nothing too major; just enough that might prevent him from getting a good job or a loan on a car. He wasn't anything like Carl. The boy had little patience and expected things to be handed to him. Although where the hell he got that idea, Carl would never know. He sure as hell hadn't raised him that way, at least while he was around. Who knew what had happened after he left, what kind of life his mother had given him. She was a good woman for putting up with Carl for all those years, not knowing about his illness, but she did their son a disservice by the way she coddled him all the time.

"I don't know, Dad. Maybe both."

Carl rose from his chair and walked into his bedroom. It was a small trailer and so he listened as the two whispered in the other room. It was clear they thought Carl was about to toss them out on their ears, but he was still a father who loved his son, even if his son was a screw-up.

Carl carried on back toward the living room and dropped two blankets and a couple of pillows onto his chair. "Here. Why don't you two get some sleep? I'm sorry I don't have a spare bed, but the couch is fairly comfortable and, CJ, you can sleep on the recliner. It'll have to do. We'll talk more about this tomorrow." He started to turn away, back to his bedroom.

"Thanks, Dad."

"Uh-huh. Oh, and by the way, there'll be no funny business out here, you understand? I know you're full-grown adults, but I just can't be dealing with that sort of thing right now."

"Okay, Dad." CJ's cheeks flushed as his lips parted into a thin smile.

"Tomorrow, we'll sort this out one way or another. Good night."

[13]

*C**arl emerged from** the barracks under cover of darkness. The team was about to board the chopper and be dropped five klicks away from the extraction point. They believed there to be at least ten POWs being held at Mountain Camp, forty miles northwest of Hanoi. The men were scheduled to be moved to Hoa Lo for consolidation and that was the reason for the critical timing of this operation.*

He needed to focus, but the grief still struck him hard. Sometimes, bad enough that he'd have to retreat to his bunk or any place that would offer some privacy. Most of them understood. He had, after all, just lost his wife and daughter. But this was a war and they lost people every single day. Brothers. So Carl had to get his shit together.

At least the rain had stopped. The ground would still slosh beneath their feet, but they'd be able to see more than two feet in front of themselves.

The men soon arrived and were dropped inside the landing zone, taking to foot through the thick jungle. The camp was just ahead and Carl's nerves turned to steel. His brothers were depending on him and so any further thoughts of his family would have to be pushed to the back of his mind for now.

Upon arrival to the isolated camp, Carl and two others took their positions, heading south to secure the second entry point.

"Charlie." Carl pointed to the man in the low tower. He moved forward, directing the other two to flank him on either side. He reached the back of the tower, retrieving the knife from his belt.

The enemy soldier heard the footsteps, but before he could turn, Carl reached his hand around to the man's face, covering his mouth, and sliced his throat in one swift motion. The man collapsed to the ground and Carl continued to the point where the POWs were thought to be held.

Ahead, in the darkness, he and his men spotted the bamboo gates that covered the holes in the ground. "In there," Carl whispered.

Ten feet ahead. That was where they were, and Carl wasn't about to leave without them. He approached the first trap and squatted to the ground. Gunfire erupted to the north of him. The sound caught his attention for just a moment. When he turned back and looked inside the pit, Carl reeled backwards.

The eyes that were staring up at him were not that of a fellow soldier, but they were the eyes of his son.

Someone approached and grabbed Carl by the shoulders. He swung his head around, fearing it was Charlie. Instead, he saw Riley.

"It's okay. I'm going to help you."

"Dad! Dad, wake up!" CJ shook his father as he lay in bed,

yelling and thrashing around. "Jesus, Dad. Wake up. You're having a bad dream!"

Carl opened his eyes as wide as he could. He raised his arm and began to swing at CJ.

"Stop! It's me, Dad. It's CJ, okay? It was just a dream."

Carl began to register his son's words this time around and started to blink. "I—I'm sorry, son."

"It's okay. Everything's fine now. You're fine."

"Yeah, yeah. Okay." Carl raised up on one elbow and reached for his glasses on the nightstand.

"I thought you were taking pills for this sort of thing, Dad."

"Never mind. I'll be all right now. You go on back to sleep."

"You are still taking your pills, aren't you?"

It seemed Carl's expression was enough for CJ to figure out that he hadn't been. "For God's sake, why not?"

Carl noticed the time. Five a.m. "Ah shit. I'm awake. Might as well get up."

CJ raised up from the bed and headed back into the living room. "We're not done with this conversation. You know that, right?"

"Oh, son. There's lots of things we need to discuss."

Carl appeared from the hall, having splashed water on his face and hair in an attempt to tame what little there was left of it. He noticed CJ and his girlfriend perched on the edge of the couch, appearing ready to accept whatever order he was about to deliver.

"Morning." Carl pulled his robe closed. "Sorry if I woke you two up. Can I get you some coffee?"

"I'll get it, Dad. You just sit down." CJ moved to the kitchen and began making the coffee.

The room was silent, except for the sounds of the percolating pot.

CJ returned, taking a seat next to Melissa. "Dad, what's going on here? Are you still seeing your doctor?"

Carl didn't like discussing matters such as these anyway, let alone in front of someone he didn't know. "I've got it under control, CJ, so don't you worry about that." He shot a glance to Melissa. She seemed to pick up on his discomfort and didn't speak on the issue.

"I haven't seen you in more than three years, and now you and your girlfriend show up at my door. I need to know what's going on."

CJ inhaled a deep breath. "Look, I got in with this—militia group, I guess you'd call 'em, and got tangled up in some kind of territory dispute. I'm being set up, Dad, and Melissa helped me get out of town before they could find me. I've got a few bucks and the clothes on my back. That's all."

"Sir, I'm so sorry to show up like we did," Melissa began. Her tone was soft; mindful of the fact that Carl had taken them in. "I haven't known CJ for long, but what I do know of him is that he's a good man who got mixed up with the wrong people and I want to do what I can to help him out of this situation."

CJ placed his hand on her knee. "I don't know what to do now. No one knows we're here and I think we're safe, but I can't go back home and I need your help, Dad."

Carl turned his thoughts to the dream that had so abruptly transformed into a nightmare. He was often plagued with such memories; however, none that saw his family in harm's way. And there was no explanation for Riley's presence. It felt as though she was in the dream with him; not just a figment, but actually *there.*

For a moment, he wanted to rush over to the girl's house, confirm that she experienced it too, but how could she have? Carl looked to CJ again and the woman who appeared frail, but he imagined might actually be stronger than his son. The plan had been to see Riley at the diner this afternoon, but that was before these two showed up. Riley insisted Carl was in need of help. Had she seen this coming, CJ's arrival? It seemed that CJ was the one who needed help, not Carl.

Now, it was more important than ever to meet with her after school today and Carl prayed she would be there, that her mother would see to letting the girl offer help in whatever way she could. Things were happening too quickly and Carl needed to understand what exactly Riley knew, if anything. And he had to be sure he wasn't going crazy, that it had been just a dream and that she knew nothing about it.

The first thing that needed to be done, however, was that Carl had to know what they were dealing with. He would need to determine the next course of action, but a full explanation would be in order first.

"Okay. I'll help you, but you need to tell me everything. And I mean *everything*."

RILEY SHOT UP OUT OF BED, DRIPPING WITH SWEAT, HER heart racing in her chest. She looked at Gracie, still sound asleep. Her head turned to the window. Dawn was beginning to emerge through the lightweight curtains. A final confirmation that she was, in fact, awake, was the time on her clock. It was five a.m. A full hour before she needed to be up for school.

She'd been transported to a place; a frightening place that smelled of smoke and fire and gasoline. People were yelling, but she didn't know what they were saying. And the loud pops—gunfire, she guessed, although she'd only ever heard that sound on television shows. Then she saw him, Carl Boyd, only he was young, like before.

Riley watched from behind a tree as men in uniforms crept around, whispering and pointing, and she didn't know what to do until Carl knelt down. He was looking down at something, but she had no idea what it was.

She waited until the area cleared and then ran to him, came up behind him, and reached to help him off the ground. He'd fallen backwards and she wanted to help him. As soon as she touched him, he started screaming; a horrible, terrifying scream and then she screamed too. Then she woke up, here, at home in her bed.

Riley looked at her hands and arms. She grazed her fingertips on her left arm and turned her palm upward to look at her fingers. They felt greasy. Her skin felt like she'd just applied sunscreen, but this didn't smell like sunscreen.

She wanted to rush into her parents' room and tell them what happened. But Riley was afraid. Afraid they'd send her to some hospital or a place for crazy people. Something had happened to her and she couldn't explain it. Her eyes began to pool with tears. She was frightened more than ever and had no one to turn to. *Dillon.*

Riley took to her feet and moved quietly to the door. With sweaty hair and skin reeking of gasoline, how on earth could she explain this to anyone, when she didn't know what was going on herself. Dillon would help. He was her big brother and he would help, just like he said he would last night.

The hall floor creaked under her feet. She cringed each time, praying no one would wake. At the end of the hall was Dillon's room. Riley slowly turned the handle, pushing it open as quietly as possible.

Dillon was asleep, sprawled across the double bed, his dark, unruly hair covering his face.

Riley approached him. "Dillon?" she whispered. "Dillon, please wake up. I need help."

He began to shift, his eyes fluttered, and in a gravelly tone, he spoke. "What? What's wrong, Riley?" She didn't need to answer. Dillon's nose crinkled. "What's that smell?"

Her worry was too much to endure now. Riley began to cry and held out her arms. "I don't know. I don't know what's wrong with me."

Dillon sat up and took in Riley's appearance. "Oh my God. What happened to you? Are you okay?" He pushed the hair away from her face.

She tried to speak, her voice weak and full of fear. "I had a dream. I was in a horrible place and I woke up with this smell. And look." She ran her hand along her right forearm. "I'm all greasy. Dillon, I'm so scared."

"Okay, okay. Just hang on. I gotta think." He scanned her quickly and glanced at the door. "Look, you need to get in the shower. Wash whatever this is off, okay? Before Mom and Dad wake up."

"But it's so loud, I'll wake them."

"I'd rather they wake up from the shower than find you like this. Riley, just do what I say. We'll figure this out, I promise, but right now, you gotta get cleaned up. Then you can tell me exactly what happened, okay?"

She shook her head and turned to leave. Riley would do what he asked and then everything would be fine. It was just a dream. That was all. Her lips quivered again because it had been more than just a dream and the idea terrified her.

The steam from the shower offered some relief and Riley began to feel better. Her tender skin had almost been rubbed raw by the soap and washcloth, but at least that greasy feeling was gone now and so was the smell. She wanted nothing more than to crawl back into her bed and pretend she was sick so she wouldn't have to go to school today. But that would be a mistake because her mom wouldn't let her out of the house this afternoon with Dillon if she believed her to be sick. So she would have to find a way to make it through until later, when the opportunity to talk to Carl would arise. Maybe he had it too, the dream.

Gracie was already in the kitchen, eating a bowl of cereal by the time Riley made it down the stairs, dressed and ready for school.

"Good morning, sweetheart. You were up awfully early this morning," Ellen said.

Riley didn't want to even attempt an explanation, fearing her lies would be transparent, so she smiled and grabbed the box of Fruit-Os and made her breakfast.

"Well, you should at least wait to get in the shower once everyone else has gotten up. You know how loud those pipes can be. Your father wasn't too happy about being awakened so early."

A moment later, Dillon leapt down the stairs and appeared in the foyer, leaning into the kitchen. "I have to go now. I told Matt that I'd meet him in the library before school. He needs some help on an assignment."

Riley knew that had to be a lie. She knew Matt and was well

aware of the fact that he was one of those kids who hung out in the abandoned houses. She didn't like him much and figured that it was Dillon's way of getting out before Jack came down.

"I'll see you after school, right?" He looked to Riley for confirmation.

"Yeah. Thanks, Dillon," she replied. There hadn't been much time to give him the full story, but he got the gist of what had happened. Riley wondered if his abrupt exit might have been due to his own fear of what she'd experienced. It was enough to scare anyone away, but there was no escape for her.

"What was that all about?" Ellen asked.

"Oh, I asked Dillon if I could go watch his practice after school today. That's okay, right?"

"Of course it is. So long as you get your homework done, I'm fine with that."

Riley hated lying to her mother. There were enough lies to go around in this house. But there were so many things she couldn't tell her. Like how scared she felt every time Ellen and Jack got into a fight. Or how often she could see the hurt in her mom's eyes and could feel it in her heart.

Riley knew that trying to explain her feelings, telling her mom that she knew what it felt like for her; those were things that would only make Ellen feel worse and that wouldn't help anyone.

"Gracie, are you ready? We better get to the bus stop," Riley said, hardly having eaten any of her breakfast. The smell still lingered in her nose and between that and the dream, well, she didn't have much of an appetite anyway.

"You girls have a good day. And have fun at Dillon's practice, Riley."

The girls walked into the foyer and pulled their coats off the hangers. Riley turned to see Jack coming down the stairs. He didn't look good. He looked like he had a hangover. Most kids her age probably didn't know what that was, but Riley did. She could feel it too.

"You mind not getting in the damn shower so early next time, Riley?" Jack started as he carefully stepped down the stairs. "You woke up the whole damn house."

"I'm sorry, Dad. Me and Gracie gotta go now. Bye."

There were times in Riley's life when all she wanted was someone to talk to. Someone who understood what she went through on a daily basis. Kaitlyn was a good friend, her best friend, but even she didn't know everything. Riley wondered if she could tell her about the dream, about what happened when she woke up. But would Kaitlyn understand or would she just be afraid for her or *of* her?

[14]

The clouds hung low and threatened to unleash a deluge at any moment, but Riley waited just outside the school grounds where Dillon promised he would pick her up. She checked the time on her wristwatch. School had let out almost ten minutes ago and he still wasn't there. The bus had already left too, so if he didn't show, she would have to hoof it all the way back home, an undesirable prospect, especially if the skies opened up on her.

Just as she was about to begin the trek home, Riley spotted him. Dillon was pedaling fast in the distance. She knew it was him because of the Hoosiers windbreaker he always wore. He hadn't let her down.

He slammed on his brakes, skidding to a stop right in front of her. "Sorry I'm late. Hop on."

Riley jumped onto the handlebars of the bike. It took Dillon a minute to adjust to the extra weight, including the hefty backpack, but he eventually regained his balance and pedaled on toward the main part of town.

Neither one of them knew what to expect. Riley only knew that she had to see Carl Boyd, especially after this morning. Whatever was happening to her, he was a part of; she just didn't know how yet.

"I see his car up ahead. He's parked in front of the diner." Riley almost lost her balance as she turned to Dillon, her legs wobbling against the front wheel.

"Okay. Okay. Just don't fall off." Dillon pulled up to the sidewalk just in front of the restaurant.

Riley jumped off. "I see him inside, but he's with people."

"Do you know who they are?"

"No. Should we just go back home? I don't know, Dillon. Maybe this was a mistake."

"Look, I'm here and you'll be fine. We're going inside a public place. Everything will be all right, Riley. After what happened this morning, something's going on and maybe he can help. But we won't know unless we go inside." Dillon held out his hand.

Riley looked into his eyes for a moment. She felt safe and loved. This was what needed to be done and Dillon would protect her. She gladly slipped her hand inside his and followed her brother inside.

The diner was quiet; only a few people sitting around sipping on their afternoon coffees, mostly elderly folk who were waiting out their retirement. Carl Boyd would have easily blended in among them except for the fact that he had two others in his company; a younger man sitting next to him and a woman opposite.

Riley poked her head out from behind her much taller brother and when she caught sight of Carl Boyd, an instant recognition surged between them. In that moment, she knew he had experienced something along the lines of what she had, to what extent remained to be seen, but she began to feel a little less alone, a little less like a freak.

"Hello, Riley." Carl smiled, nodding his head and casting his eyes upwards to the lanky kid holding her hand. "I see you brought your brother with you. Where's your mom?"

"Um, she couldn't come. She had to stay home with my little sister." Riley figured he could see beyond her lie. He'd seen them that Sunday morning, after church. She suspected he knew a great deal about the Thompsons already.

"Riley, this is my son, CJ and his lady-friend, Melissa."

"Pleased to meet you, Riley." Melissa moved as far as she could to allow the two kids to slip inside the booth.

Riley got in first and Dillon followed, his legs jutting out the side, as they were simply too long to fit into the already tight space. She examined CJ's face. He looked very much like the Carl Boyd she had seen in her dream, the one who had screamed at the sight of her. His hair was short and wavy, his cheeks were high and sloped down to his thick lips. Riley supposed if she was older, maybe a teenager, she might think he was cute. But then, he was at least as old as her dad, so that thought was kind of gross.

"Riley, I think we should talk about what happened last night," Carl began.

Dillon seemed to be the only other one besides Riley who knew what he was talking about. "She already told you?" he asked.

"No, son. She doesn't need to."

Riley looked down, as if embarrassed. "I don't know, Mr. Boyd, but I can't get rid of the smell in my nose. It was on my skin and in my hair."

"What is she talking about?" CJ asked.

"That's napalm and it takes a bit of getting used to. I smelled it too."

"Dad—what's going on here? I thought you had to see this girl because she said you needed some kind of help?"

Carl looked to CJ. "Yes, I suppose you're right. Maybe this all ties together in some cosmic way. I don't know." He returned his attention to the kids. "My son and Melissa came over late last night and I think you might know why, Riley."

She tried to focus in on the idea and push aside what had happened in the dream. Something was changing inside her and she had no idea what it was, but Mr. Boyd seemed to understand. He would believe her now, just as Dillon had.

"I guess I should start at the beginning." Riley paused. "I can read people, see what they see. Their past, their present, anything that has been important in their lives. I don't know how or why, but I can. And a week or so ago, I saw inside Mr. Boyd." She turned to CJ. "I saw that he lost a family before you."

CJ's manner altered from what looked to be curiosity to something along the lines of stunned.

"I don't mean to upset you, any of you." Riley started to tear up.

"It's okay. You're trying to help, that's all." Dillon squeezed her hand.

"I saw that Mr. Boyd could be getting into some kind of trouble. It was the first time I was able to get a sense of what might happen, instead of what has already happened." She paused for a moment. "And now that you're here, I see that it's you who has brought it."

It was clear that Carl's son felt uncomfortable at what Riley had to say, although he seemed to realize that all of this was actually his fault.

"I don't know who they are, but there are people coming for you, and Mr. Boyd."

The diner door flew open and Jack stormed inside. "What the hell is this?" He headed straight for their booth.

Riley whipped around to see her father. "Daddy."

"What the hell are you two doing here with this crazy son of a bitch?"

"It's okay, Dad," Dillon began.

"The hell it is! You two, go on, get the hell out of here and get back home. I'll deal with you later." Jack turned his attention to Carl. "What the hell are you doing with my kids?"

Riley and Dillon hustled out of the booth, but stood just behind Jack.

"Hey, now, I don't know who you are, but this is my father and..."

"Hey, buddy, I don't know who you are either, but this is between me and the old man. You know he came to my house and harassed my little girl? Did he tell you that?"

Jack returned to Carl. "Now, I'm only going to say this once. You'd better stay the hell away from my family. You got me?"

"What, you gonna hit me like you do your wife?" Carl replied, rising to his feet. "You think no one notices all the make-up she wears to cover up them bruises you put on her face?"

Dillon moved toward Jack and reached out for his arm. "Come on, Dad. It's okay; we'll go home now."

Jack yanked his arm away and turned to Dillon, raising it and ready to strike. Dillon flinched.

"Hey, hey. Hold up now!" CJ raised his voice to a level on par with Jack's and everyone in the diner had their eyes fixed on the scene. "Look, my dad meant no harm to your family, sir. Why don't you just take your kids out of here now?"

Jack seemed to realize the attention he'd drawn and lowered his arm. "Go on." He nudged Dillon. "Let's get the hell out of here. Put your bike in the back of the truck. I'm taking you home."

Riley looked back one last time at Carl. "You have to get help, Mr. Boyd. They're coming."

Carl looked at the girl, whose face was full of anxiety. He watched as her father's arms flailed in anger once they got outside. The man was yelling at his children to get into the truck. He noticed Riley peer into the window in search of him. Carl raised his hand in a slight wave, concerned she might suffer further should her dad notice the gesture. It occurred to him to call the cops. The man's temper was out of control, as he saw it. But he began to feel a most peculiar sensation, as though he was being impelled not to act on the idea. He continued to watch them outside and it started to cross his mind. It was Riley; she was telling him she would be fine, they would be fine. She never spoke a word, only looked out of the windshield of the truck directly into Carl's eyes.

Jack tore out of the parking lot and disappeared down the road.

Carl turned to CJ, astounded by this feeling she had implanted into his mind. "I don't know how that girl knows what she does, but I have every confidence that she's right and whoever is after you either knows you're here, or is about to find out."

"I can't go to the cops, Dad. I took part in the robbery—sort of, anyway. But, I don't know how they could possibly find out that I'm here. No one knows. No one."

"Well, I'm telling you now, Riley Thompson has a formidable gift, and I think we ought to listen to her."

JACK SLAMMED THE TRUCK INTO PARK IN FRONT OF THE garage. Riley could smell the liquor in the cab all the way home and she knew Dillon could smell it too.

"Get the hell inside!" Jack pushed the driver's side door open with a shove of his shoulder.

Dillon opened the passenger door and stepped out, lending a hand to Riley. "Come on; let's go."

"I'm sorry I got you in trouble," she whispered.

"There's nothing to be sorry for. Just go on before he yells at you again."

Riley did as her brother asked and scurried inside. Ellen was in the living room, looking through the front window when she opened the door. "Mom?"

"What happened?" Ellen rushed to Riley's side. "I thought you were at Dillon's basketball practice." She began to tremble.

Riley sensed her fear. The fear that her husband would lash out in anger against her or Dillon or maybe both. It was a terrible sensation. Adrenaline coursed through Riley's veins at a frightening pace. Her heart pounded against her chest, forcing her to cough. Riley's eyes widened as if she should run and take shelter from the pain that was coming. "Mom, you're scaring me."

"What did you two do?" Ellen grabbed Riley's shoulders and pulled her forward.

"Nothing. We just went to go see Mr. Boyd at the diner. I didn't know Dad was going to be there."

"You went to see that crazy old man? Why, honey? Why would you do that?" Ellen's face grew pale and her eyes reddened with the threat of tears. "Dillon was with you?"

Riley nodded.

"Go. Go upstairs now and keep quiet." Ellen looked at Gracie, who was sitting in front of the TV, watching cartoons. "You too, Gracie. Go upstairs with your sister and both of you stay quiet. You understand?"

Gracie quickly rose to her feet. "Okay." She ran upstairs without waiting for Riley.

"Mom. I'm sorry. We didn't mean to upset Dad."

"I don't want to hear anymore; just get your bottom upstairs now!"

Just as Riley reached the stairs, Jack pushed in through the front door with Dillon trailing behind. "Hold up. Where do you think you're going?" He turned to Ellen, who quickly made her way into the foyer. "Do you know where your kids were just now?" Jack pulled off his jacket and laid it over the coat hooks on the wall. "I mean, do you even keep one goddamn eye on your children, Ellen?"

"Of course I do. Riley went to Dillon's practice and then they went to the diner for a pop. That's all."

Riley still felt Ellen's fear, but her voice did not convey any. She was protecting them. In her own way, Ellen was doing what she could to protect her children.

"That's all? And do you know who was there? That psycho

bastard who practically banged down our door the other night. I was just driving by and noticed Dillon's bike outside the diner. So I parked up and headed toward the entrance. Well, what a surprise to see these two sitting with Carl Boyd and some other people; God knows who. His son or some shit like that."

"He wanted to apologize to us. That's all it was, Dad," Dillon began.

"Then, the son of a bitch starts telling me how you been trying to hide bruises, that he could still see them on your face." Jack held Ellen's gaze. "Why do you suppose he'd say something like that, Ellie? You been talking to people about our private affairs?"

"No, Jack. I would never—"

"Dad, please. It was nothing, I promise," Dillon pleaded and cast a glance to Riley.

She knew what that look meant, but her feet stood firm. She couldn't let them suffer for her mistake.

Ellen began to walk into the kitchen. "I'm sure this was just some misunderstanding, Jack. Come on now. It'll be dinner soon."

The idea that she was working to diffuse the situation wasn't lost on Riley or, apparently, Dillon, but it was too late. She felt the anger welling up inside of her father. He didn't like it when Ellen walked away. He took it to be disrespectful.

Riley sensed the hate spreading inside her, reaching out like tentacles through her entire body. It wasn't just that either. His head was swimming in alcohol and she felt that too. Riley was dizzy and wanted to throw up, swallowing hard the bile that threatened to rise. This was much stronger than anything she'd experienced before.

Riley gripped the stair railing. The action caught the attention of Dillon. "Riley, are you okay?"

Jack discounted Dillon's concerns, instead heading into the kitchen because he wasn't done with Ellen yet, despite what she might believe.

"I feel sick." Riley began to waver and Dillon rushed to her side. "Just sit down for a minute. You'll be all right." He helped her to the first step.

Immediately, it began. Dillon and Riley exchanged an alarming look as Jack started to shout at Ellen.

"Oh no. This is all my fault." Riley threw her hands over her face.

"Don't you dare say that! This is no one's fault but his." Dillon pointed toward the kitchen. "I'm so sick of this shit!" He turned his head in the direction of Jack's voice. "This has to stop, Riley. We did nothing wrong. Mom did nothing wrong. What the hell was Dad even doing there? I thought he was interviewing or got another job or something. I mean, the truck reeked of booze. He was just out drinking and probably telling Mom stories about looking for a job. He's nothing but a liar!"

"Dillon, please calm down." Riley's chest was tightening and her breaths were shallow. Something terrible was happening to her and she couldn't stop it. "I need help. I need to go to the doctor." She clutched her stomach and wretched over the side of the stair railing.

"Mom, come quick! Riley's sick!"

[15]

The **incident at** the diner left a lingering impression as the three made their way back to Carl's home. No one spoke a word about it; in fact, no one spoke at all. The radio played softly and helped to absorb the silence in the car. Carl's heart went out to those kids. For a moment, he'd reconsidered his earlier thought, wanting to turn around and drive straight to the Thompson house to confront Jack himself, but then he knew it would only escalate an already tense situation and Riley had made her wishes clear.

Her warning had been vague, but she was certain people were coming and CJ probably had a good idea as to their identities, although he hadn't shared the information just yet. It seemed he was still reeling from both the argument at the diner and the fact that the girl knew things about Carl that caught him by surprise.

Carl glanced to his son, who'd been staring out of the

passenger window since he had gotten in the car. He then looked into the rear view mirror to see this young woman who looked as though she might be regretting an earlier decision.

"When I woke you this morning," CJ began, looking to Carl, "when you were having that dream. It was about the war, wasn't it? And that girl—she was there with you?"

"Yes."

"Jesus, Dad." CJ turned away again. "How the hell is that even possible? And she knows what happened to Rosalyn and Mary? I'm guessing you didn't tell her."

"No, I didn't. I don't know how it's possible, CJ. I honestly don't. It scares the hell out of me, though, I'll tell you that much," Carl replied.

He hadn't been much of a father to CJ, partly due to his undiagnosed illness and partly due to the baggage he'd carried into that marriage. He knew the boy's mother always tried to live up to Rosalyn and that she felt like a consolation prize. Maybe she had been, but CJ deserved better than the father he'd been given. Now with everything that was happening, he figured CJ was ready to have him locked up in some mental institution. An inadvertent chuckle escaped him as he considered the idea, but he quickly cleared his throat to cover up the blunder. No one was prepared to consider this situation as anything other than grave, but the image of himself in a strait-jacket was inescapably comical.

"I suppose we ought to keep moving, Dad," CJ said. "I'll take your word for it that this girl knows those assholes are coming, so the only way for you to stay safe is if we leave." CJ turned to the backseat to confirm the plan with Melissa. She nodded.

"You two aren't going anywhere, you hear? We'll figure this out one way or another. And I'm gonna make it right with the

Thompson family. I don't want that little girl to get into any more trouble because of me. I don't know how yet, but I'll find a way to smooth things over with the dad. I think he's a piece of shit, but I sure as hell don't want those kids to suffer any more than they already have."

The door to Riley's room opened, and her eyes flickered at the sound of the squeaky hinges. She noticed Ellen's cautious approach. "What time is it?"

"It's nine o'clock. How are you feeling?" Ellen sat down next to her and placed a hand over Riley's forehead. "No fever. That's good."

She'd been given a welcomed reprieve from school. It had been a difficult night, one that saw Riley sicker than she'd ever recalled. She wondered if that was how Jack felt all the time and thought it must be a terrible way to live.

Ellen insisted she be allowed to stay home and rest. Even through all of it, Riley knew her mother meant well and tried to care for them as best she could.

"I feel better now." Explaining the sudden onset of her illness would prove impossible to a woman who wouldn't be receptive to it in the first place. "Maybe I'll come downstairs in a while and try to eat some breakfast."

"Okay, honey." Ellen rose from the bed and turned toward the door.

"Mom?"

"Yes?" She looked over her shoulder to Riley.

"Is Dillon okay?"

The look that followed on Ellen's face, Riley knew well. It was a strange blend of indignation and shame. It hadn't been Riley's intention to point out the elephant in the room; she just needed to know if her brother had suffered for her mistake.

"Yes, honey. He's fine. He's at school and you father's gone to help a friend." Ellen closed the door behind her.

This had all started the moment Carl Boyd crossed Riley's path. Her visions had grown more intense; dreams had become so real that what she had always called leftovers, random images, had now turned into physical remnants. Last night was just another example that Riley's abilities were becoming increasingly powerful. An influence far beyond the ten-year-old's understanding was driving these changes. Now, not only did Riley fear for Mr. Boyd's safety, she feared for her own and possibly that of her family's.

Riley needed to get out of this bed. She had to work toward a solution before things grew worse, which she was becoming convinced would happen. It wasn't something she could do without at least some assistance and enlisting Kaitlyn to help craft a cover story was the first step.

She rolled out of bed and padded along the floor quietly so as not to alert Ellen of any movement from her room. Retrieving clothes from her closet, Riley dressed in record time. She ran a comb through her fine hair and brushed her teeth. Her nerves grew unsteady as she slipped on her shoes. The question remained as to whether or not Ellen would allow her to leave the house at all.

On her way down the stairs, she maintained secrecy, although at this point, the reason seemed futile. She would be asking to leave, not sneaking out. Riley now stood at the entrance to the living room and wrinkled her brow at the sight before her.

Ellen seemed to be carefully studying a photo album that lay in her lap as she sat perched on the edge of the couch. She must have sensed Riley's presence and turned to see her.

Her face was wet with tears and this caught Riley off her guard. So often, she saw the mother who appeared unaffected by the reality of their situation, pretending as though everything was fine, when it was so clearly not.

"Um—Mom? I'm feeling better and I was wondering if I could take my bike and go to school? It's just that we have a test today and I don't want to miss it." Riley wasn't sure if her tone conveyed the proper amount of both concern for her grades and honesty. Luckily, she was a good student, and so it wasn't out of character for her to make the request.

Ellen quickly wiped the tears from her cheeks and cleared her throat. "Are you sure you want to go? I think you could use some rest, sweetheart."

"I'd like to go, Mom. Really. I feel fine now."

"Okay, if that's what you want. I'd prefer it if we walk there together. I could use a change of scenery."

"I think that might take too long. I can be there in fifteen minutes if I ride my bike. I don't want to miss out on the test." Riley pulled her backpack from the floor beneath the coat hooks.

"If you're sure." Ellen rose from the couch, setting the photo album down. "You come straight home after school today. You hear me?"

"Yes. I will." Riley wrapped her arms around Ellen's waist. "I love you, Mom."

Ellen kissed the top of her head. "I love you too, baby. You get to the nurse if you start to feel bad again and I'll come get you."

Riley nodded and opened the front door. "Bye." As she

stepped outside, closing the door behind her, Riley felt the cool air on her face and, for just a moment, she felt free. Inhaling the clean air, the burden of her worries lifted from her shoulders.

Not wanting to underestimate the timing of her arrival at school, Riley ensured plenty of it would be left before the lunch bell. Her intention was to find Kaitlyn.

The bike lay against the old wood siding next to their garage. Its once bright pink hue now was faded to almost white. It had become too small and her knees rose uncomfortably high as she peddled down the narrow driveway to the sidewalk, her backpack virtually rubbing against the rear tire.

The day was clear and bright and, as Riley rode down her street, she noticed buds of flowers ready to bloom. They were simple and beautiful, nothing like the thorny life she'd come to know in recent years. For a moment, she thought about riding all the way out of town. Forget school, forget home; just go.

Instead, reality prevailed and the school soon appeared in the distance. Riley kept to her plan and turned into the entrance. It was a little too early for the lunch bell, so she would wait behind a nearby tree so a passing teacher might not see her and inquire as to why she wasn't in class. She wished she had a cell phone, if for nothing else than to text Dillon and let him know she was okay. A few kids in her class already had phones, including Kaitlyn and Jacob. But then, Jacob's family was a little better off than most in the town. They owned a couple of the shops: a drug store and a Hallmark gift card store. She smiled at the thought of the dark-haired, dimple-cheeked boy. Some of the girls in her class liked him, but he, for reasons Riley couldn't understand, seemed to like her the best. The pudgy girl with old clothes and stringy blonde hair.

The bell rang in the distance. Its echo reached Riley's ears and she was pulled back into the moment. Her backpack rested against the tree along with her bike and she walked toward the cafeteria as if she'd been at school all day, blending in with the other students. Kaitlyn would be along in a couple of minutes and she strolled nearer, waiting.

"Kaitlyn?" Riley walked up behind her, tapping her shoulder.

"Hey! I thought you were home sick today?"

"I need your help." Riley's glance shifted about as though she was involved in some covert operation; maybe she was. "I've got some things to take care of and if I run late, I'm gonna say that I was at your house, okay?" Of course, Ellen had already insisted that she head straight home today, but Riley was fairly confident she would be home in time. This was only intended to be a backup plan.

"What's going on, Riley?" Kaitlyn placed her hands on her hips. "What kind of things?"

"Look, you know how I get those feelings sometimes, right?"

Kaitlyn nodded.

"Well, something's been happening lately. Like in the last couple of weeks, and I don't know how to explain it, but it's—worse, you know?"

"Not really. What do you mean 'worse'?" Kaitlyn spotted a teacher approaching. "Come over here." She led Riley over to a bench against the corridor outside.

"Kaitlyn, something's happening to me. It all started after Carl Boyd came into the shelter that day. That's why I think he's the only one who can help me and I know I can help him. But after yesterday, there's no way my dad will let me anywhere near him again." Riley held up a preemptive hand, realizing

Kaitlyn would want an explanation. "You don't want to know, trust me.

"Anyway, I just need you and me to have the same story. I don't know how long I'll be, probably not past school letting out, but just in case, okay? If my mom calls your house, just tell her I'm in the bathroom or something. I just need you to make up something. Please?"

"Okay, okay."

"Thank you. You know you're my best friend, right?" Riley smiled, knowing Kaitlyn could be trusted to help.

"I know. But you better not be too late. Your mom might buy an excuse the first time, but if she calls again, you know she'll send your brother over."

"I know, I know. It won't be like that, I promise. Thank you, Kaitlyn. I'd better go now and you gotta eat lunch." She began to walk away. "Tell Jacob I said hi."

Kaitlyn rolled her eyes. "You need to eat too."

"I packed a snack; don't worry." Riley waved goodbye and disappeared behind the oak tree, emerging only a moment later mounted on her bike, heading south of the school.

The ride to Mr. Boyd's house took less time than she recalled having walked it last week. Maybe it was the sense that she had purpose this time. There was no question that he and his son were in danger and she might be the only one who could help. It was no longer some obscure feeling she had. Men were coming; that was a fact. CJ had confirmed as much with nothing more than what she'd seen behind his eyes. She also needed help and that was a fact too.

The sun was almost directly overhead now. Riley figured it must be close to noon. It had occurred to her that Mr. Boyd might not be home. She was able to perceive certain things, but knowing one's whereabouts wasn't one of them. At least, not yet. But as she turned into the dirt lot of the trailer park, a smile appeared on her face because she'd seen his old Ford Taurus and a smaller car next to it. He was home and it seemed his company was still there as well. Good, because this involved all of them.

Her bike had no kickstand, so Riley leaned it against the metal sheeting that formed the side of the trailer. Tossing her backpack over one shoulder, she approached the steps of the front door, but she didn't need to knock.

"Riley? What on earth are you doing here? Shouldn't you be in school?" Carl Boyd scanned left, then right, seemingly to ensure she either hadn't been followed or that her father was nowhere to be found. It appeared neither was the case. "Come on in."

Riley entered the home and spotted Carl's son, CJ, on the couch next to his girlfriend, although she couldn't remember her name. Melanie? Madison? No, it was Melissa; that was right. "Hi." She regretted her sheepish tone. No one would believe her if she couldn't sound believable.

"Hi, Riley. It's nice to see you again," Melissa said.

"How are you?" CJ asked.

He seemed uncomfortable, perhaps because Riley could read people and maybe he didn't want to be read. "I'm fine, thank you."

Carl closed the door and moved to the recliner, gripping the back of it to support his weight. "I'm so sorry about yesterday, Riley. I didn't know—well."

"It's okay, Mr. Boyd. My dad just gets upset sometimes." She looked down at her feet, having grown embarrassed from making feeble excuses.

"So, you've come here knowing he doesn't want you around me. Won't that cause problems for you?" Carl replied.

"No. I mean, yes, if he knew, but he doesn't. Look, Mr. Boyd, I think you know why I'm here. I believe that I can help you and you can help me. For some reason, since I met you, I've been able to—feel things differently, as if they were just as real as you are standing in front of me now. Can you explain that to me?"

"I don't think I can, Riley." Carl lowered himself carefully into the chair. "I can't explain it any more than I can explain seeing you in my dream. This is just as frightening for me as it is for you, young lady."

"I'm not scared." She pushed her shoulders back and raised her chin. "I just don't want to feel like this anymore and maybe if we find whoever it is that's coming for them," she pointed toward the couch, "then maybe this will all go away and things will get back to normal."

Riley held his gaze for as long as she could. He was trying to figure out what she was really thinking; she could feel him prying away at her brain.

"How did you know about my wife and child?" Carl finally asked.

CJ shifted awkwardly in the background.

"I saw your boss or someone like that hand you the telegram. I read it, same as you did. I told you, Mr. Boyd. I can see things and now they're real to me. I know there are men coming for your son." She turned to look at CJ. "I'm sorry, but they know you're here. I've never been able to see into the future, and I can't really say that's what's happening now. It's just that something in your mind is telling me that they know you're here. It became more—definite, I guess—when I saw you at the diner."

"Do you know who they are? The men that are coming?" Melissa asked.

"He looks like a regular guy, kinda tall, I guess, but normal sized, mostly. Kinda balding, and the other one." Riley stopped for a minute as she studied CJ. "He's your friend."

"Johnny," CJ said, glancing to Melissa. "Son of a bitch. I thought it'd be those other guys, not my friend. Although, I guess he already proved to me that he's no friend."

"But how would they know you're here?" she asked.

CJ rubbed his hands together. "I told him where Dad lived once and that I lived here with him a while back. Johnny must've mentioned that. I know that Ray was told to find me and bring me to the men we were stealing from that night. Some kind of bullshit." He looked at the girl. "Sorry, Riley. Some kind of territory grab and these people I was involved with wanted to stake their claim, make a point to the others who were moving in from up north. Hell, I don't know. It's so screwed up. I had no idea what I was getting myself into."

Riley looked at CJ. He knew what he was getting into, but chose to ignore the consequences. She felt the slightest twinge of anger toward him because he was the one who caused this. Not Mr. Boyd and certainly not her, yet here she was paying for it. How many times would she have to pay for what the grown-ups did? But, Riley kept her mouth shut. CJ was a decent person, she could see that, but that didn't change what his dad already knew. That he was kind of a screw-up.

Carl shook his head. "So what are we supposed to do now? These men know you're here in town. It won't be long before they show up at my door same as you two did the other night. Riley, can you see anything else? Do they have a plan or do you know when they'll be here?"

She squeezed her eyes shut, thinking maybe that would help, but that wasn't how it worked for her. Information came to her when it was ready, not when she was. "I don't know. I can't see anything else."

"That's okay, honey. This isn't on you," Melissa said. "There's obviously a bond between you and Mr. Boyd and you've been a great help to us, but there's no need for you to be involved any further. It's not safe and I think Mr. Boyd would agree. We'll have to figure out on our own what to do next. It's probably best if you go back home."

"Melissa's right," CJ started. "I think we need to leave to be sure you and my father stay safe. You can't know how big a help you've been, Riley. If we hadn't known they were coming, well, I hate to think what might have happened."

"You two aren't going anywhere. If they're coming, then we'll get the authorities here and sort this out. I can't have you running for the rest of your life, CJ," Carl said. "But Melissa's right about you staying out of harm's way, Riley. You should go home. I'm sure your parents will be wondering where you are."

"They think I'm at school; well, my mom does, anyway."

"I'll give you a lift back," Carl said, rising to his feet. "Come on; get your backpack, kiddo." He opened the door and ushered her outside, then looked to CJ. "I'll be back soon. She doesn't live far."

He swiped his keys off the edge of the kitchen counter and followed her outside. Riley walked toward her bike and began to wheel it to the car.

"Damn it," Carl said. "Hang on, Riley. Looks like my battery's dead." Carl jumped out of the front seat before she could get in. "Let me go around back to the shed and get the jumper cables. CJ's gonna have to give me a jump."

"Okay." Riley waited near the car while Carl disappeared around back. It wasn't long before the sound of tires on the dirt road caught her attention and a big pick-up truck slowly made its way toward her. An overwhelming sense of alarm took hold of her. She looked around, but Mr. Boyd hadn't yet returned.

It was them. The ones looking for CJ. They were here. She recognized the friend, Johnny. As soon as CJ had mentioned his name, the man's face appeared in his mind and Riley saw it too. It looked like the driver didn't know which trailer belonged to Carl as the two men inside scanned the area.

Riley's feet wouldn't budge. She'd wanted to run inside and warn CJ, but couldn't find the courage. The truck moved in closer and their eyes locked. Johnny stared right at her. It must have been the look on her face that gave it away because he motioned for the driver to stop. The two men jumped out of the truck.

"Mr. Boyd, where are you?" she whispered. He had to have heard the truck coming. Her heart pounded and she got that fuzzy feeling in her head again. She needed to warn CJ and Melissa, but it was too late. Johnny approached her.

"You live here, little girl?"

She shook her head.

"Do you know who does?"

Riley shook her head again. In that moment, CJ opened the front door. *Please, go back inside.* Her head was growing lighter. Her own fear mixed with his and it nearly made her knees buckle.

"There you are, man. What the fuck, CJ? You just take off like that?" Johnny said. Another man appeared from the driver's side and stood next to him.

"Doug. Johnny. Hey, thanks for leaving me to hang out to dry the other night," CJ said.

He was trying to be strong, but she felt his anxiety. His heart raced in time with hers. Now, all she could do was pray that Mr. Boyd hadn't heard the truck, or the men talking, and that he would stay exactly where he was. Trouble wasn't coming. It was here.

[16]

It was the feeling of someone's hand on his shoulder that caught his attention, except that no one else was with him. Carl remained buried at the back of the storage shed in search of the jumper cables. He finally had them in his hands when it happened.

"Riley." She was warning him to stay where he was, that it was too late and the men were here. "No." Carl dropped the cables and scrambled to get out of the clutter that lay before him. He climbed over the old lawn chairs and pushed the deteriorating boxes from his path, nearly tripping himself up in the process. Moving fast was rarely required of him these days and he cursed his ineptitude.

Once he stepped outside of the shed, he heard voices. It was CJ and another man. There was no indication of any raised tones, so maybe this would all work out. He had to hold out hope that they were reasonable men. Carl took a few steps, now standing at the front of the trailer, but unable to see to the side where they were talking. He caught just a glimpse of Riley holding her bike in front of her as if for protection. First and foremost, she needed to be removed from this situation and Carl had to figure out the best way to safely accomplish that.

"I'm sorry it worked out like this, man. I had no idea they were coming or that they knew we were there."

Carl didn't know who was doing the talking and he prepared to carefully make his presence known so as not to infuse any panic in an already tense situation. Calm and quiet, no sudden movements.

The wind kicked up and the shed door slammed shut in its wake. The aluminum frame rattled hard and sounded like a clap of thunder. The noise startled all of them and Carl had appeared from the front of trailer in that precise moment.

Johnny yanked a gun out from the back of his pants and, without hesitation, he fired. The bullet whizzed by Riley's head and struck Carl in the shoulder.

"No!" CJ yelled and leapt to the bottom of the stairs, sprinting toward his father.

"What the fuck are you doing?" Doug shouted, ducking instinctively from the gunfire.

"Oh shit, oh shit." Johnny held the gun out; his hand trembled.

"You son of a bitch." CJ charged toward him as his father dropped to the ground. He rushed past Riley.

She reached out and tried to stop him. "No. Don't!" Riley screamed as her bike fell.

The gun fired again and again, hitting CJ in the chest and neck. The door of the trailer swung open and Melissa ran down the steps. Johnny turned the gun on her, but Doug wrestled it from his hand.

"Get in the goddam truck!" Doug ran to the driver's side and jumped in, starting the engine.

Carl was on the ground, but pushed himself up on his elbow. He looked at Johnny and watched as the man locked eyes with Riley.

"He's going to take me, Mr. Boyd. Don't get up. Please, don't get up."

Riley's words exploded in his mind. He struggled and moaned, both at his own pain and at the sight of his son, who lay still on the ground. He looked to Riley, fearful she would be snatched away as she warned.

"Get in the truck, Johnny!" Doug shouted again, revving the engine.

"We need leverage, man." Johnny gripped the passenger door handle and yelled over the grumbling. "I can't have the old man and this girl going to the cops, and we need to know what CJ told this bitch. Can't risk it, man."

"It's over, Johnny. If you don't get in now, I'm leaving your ass behind." Doug shoved the gear stick into reverse with his foot still on the brake.

"I'm sorry, lady, but you're going to have to come with me." Johnny pulled Melissa from the ground where she was tending to CJ. "Either of you go to the cops and she's dead; you got it?"

Melissa fought, but she was much smaller than the man whose grip on her arm tightened. "I don't know anything, I swear." She stumbled over her feet.

Riley's mouth opened, but no sounds emerged. Her throat tightened and only a whimper made its way out. She thought for sure they were going to take her, not Melissa. With wide eyes, she cast a look to Mr. Boyd. *"We have to help her."*

Carl pushed himself to his feet, clutching his shoulder as he cringed in pain. "Don't you touch her!"

"Stay down, old man, or I'm gonna have to take care of you and the kid. This doesn't concern you. Your boy should've stayed put. We could've helped him." Johnny shoved Melissa into the truck.

Sirens wailed in the distance. One of the neighbors must have called the cops.

Johnny had just managed to get his feet inside when the truck's tires spun, kicking up dust and dirt as it reversed out of the lot and slammed into gear on the main road.

"Stop!" Riley's voice screeched as she tried to yell.

Carl was unsteady on his feet and Riley heard his steps behind her. She rushed to his side, trying to help prop up his weak frame with her tiny body.

"My boy! My boy!"

Carl's face was flushed and wet with tears and Riley continued to help him to his son. She didn't know if CJ was alive or dead and the pool of blood beneath his chest grew around him.

Two patrol cars roared onto the lot, sirens still blaring. Carl turned to see them skid to a halt near the front of his trailer. He recognized one of them as Officer Ward, but didn't know the second policeman.

Both drew their guns, but as they observed the scene, holstered them quickly. Officer Ward rushed to Carl while the other moved quickly to CJ.

"What happened?" He leaned over and swung Carl's good arm over his shoulder.

Riley crumbled into tears as soon as Carl's weight was lifted from her. "They took her. Those men took Melissa and shot CJ."

"He's alive," the other officer shouted. He pressed the radio strapped to his shoulder. "We need an ambulance at 756 Hickory Way. The Shady Acres Trailer Park."

"Who did they take, Riley?" It seemed the incident at Riley's home left an impression on the officer, who immediately recalled her name.

"Melissa. She's his girlfriend. I don't know her last name." Riley walked with them to the patrol car and watched as Officer Ward helped Carl into the passenger seat.

"Is he all right? Is my son all right?" Carl winced as he worked to find some comfort in the seat.

"We're going to get him to the hospital, Mr. Boyd. Help is on the way," the officer began. "Can you tell me what happened here and who took Melissa?"

A barely audible groan sounded from CJ. The other officer placed his jacket beneath his head and pressed on the wounds. He was losing blood at a swift rate. "Johnny Denton and Doug Newman."

The officer leaned in. "What was that?"

CJ tried to move so that he could be heard. "Johnny Denton and Doug Newman. They took Melissa." His eyes closed.

"What did you do, man? What the hell did you do?" Doug pounded his fists against the truck's steering wheel.

"I did what we had to, Doug! What else could I do?"

"How about *not* taking a goddamn hostage, for a start? Why the fuck did you shoot the old man and CJ? Jesus! We were just supposed to pick him up. That's all! And you fucking killed him!"

Melissa knew CJ wasn't dead; she'd felt his pulse and had seen his eyes flutter. The fact that they believed him to be could prove an advantage.

"What's done is done. I can't do nothing about that. I took her because we need to know what he told her about the operation. We can't have her going to the cops and you know it. Those other two back there, the old man and the girl, they don't know who we are. They don't know nothing about what we do."

"Well, they sure as shit know what I'm driving. You think they won't tell the goddamn cops? You shot two people! Shit, you stupid son of a bitch! And now we gotta deal with her?" He glared at Melissa through the rear view.

"Calm down, Doug. You're gonna give yourself a damn heart attack. Ray'll know what to do. He'll want to talk to her."

"And then what? You think he'll just let her go? Who the hell do you think we're dealing with here? You might as well have shot her too! First thing we need to do is dump the truck. Call Bennett and have him arrange to bring your car and meet us as soon as he can." Doug continued to drive along the quiet stretch of road, shaking his head in disbelief at Johnny Denton's colossal fuck up. For a moment, he considered pulling over to the side of the road and throwing the idiot out of the truck. Then again, Doug had his own problems to contend with and getting rid of Johnny would only compound them.

Getting across state lines was top priority. It would only be a matter of time before Indiana law enforcement sent out a BOLO, or "be on the lookout." Johnny's threat to kill the woman wouldn't stop the two witnesses they'd left behind from calling the cops. Hell, they didn't need to call. He'd heard the approaching sirens. They'd already been heading that way. Neither of them would have any trouble describing Doug's Ford F250 either. This whole situation had become a debacle and someone would pay the price for it when word reached Ray. They'd been under orders to bring Carl in as a gesture of good faith to the boys they'd attempted to rob. Hand him over and all would be forgiven. Somehow, Doug didn't believe that would be the end of it, though.

"We need to make it over the border and Bennett's gonna meet us in Sheffield, just a few miles inside the Ohio border. We'll run the truck down an embankment."

"Goddammit. None of this was supposed to happen, Johnny. You were the one who brought CJ in on our deal. His blood is on *your* hands, not mine."

"Is that right?" Johnny shook his head. "Then why the hell didn't you stay with him that night, huh? You're just as much a part of this as I am."

Doug didn't reply, instead casting his eyes into the rear view mirror to see a frightened young woman huddled in a ball and quietly sobbing. He returned his attention to the road and said nothing further.

RILEY SAT IN THE BACK OF THE PATROL CAR, WAITING TO BE taken home by Officer Ward. Other policemen had arrived and started putting yellow tape around everything. The EMTs loaded Mr. Boyd and CJ inside the ambulance and it made its way out of the park and toward the hospital in town. It wasn't much of a hospital; really more like a clinic. It was all they had unless the situation turned even more dismal and the paramedics decided it was better to continue on to the next town over, whose facility was only slightly better than in Owensville.

Riley could feel a burning in her shoulder and pressed it hard with her hand. The pain seared inside her like some kind of hot poker from a fireplace. It took everything she had to stave off the tears. This was Carl's pain she was feeling, the bullet that pierced his shoulder. It felt like she was the one who'd been shot.

Riley believed she was going crazy. It was too much for her, or anyone for that matter, to grasp. There would be no easy explanation for this. Why she was at Carl Boyd's home in the first place when she was supposed to be at school. She'd already been warned about being anywhere near the man. Now there were men and guns and people in the hospital.

Officer Ward opened the driver's door and slid into the seat. He turned back to Riley. "I'm going to take you home now, okay? We're going to have to tell your mom and dad everything. You understand?"

The look in her eyes seemed to be enough for the officer to understand what this would do and how it would go down. He turned back and started the engine.

Riley watched as the trailer slowly disappeared from view and the tires landed on the pavement. Carl Boyd was the only person who shared this unique connection with her. She didn't know where Melissa had been taken or if she was all right. Nor could she feel or sense if CJ had arrived at the hospital or if he was even still alive. It was just Mr. Boyd she could feel. His pain, his fear for CJ and the girlfriend he didn't know. Riley tried to be strong, but she was afraid and the emotions were taking over.

The final turn onto her street and her stomach tightened. Riley took a deep breath as the car pulled alongside her front yard. She closed her eyes and prepared for the worst. The only good thing was that the pain in her shoulder was subsiding and that meant that Mr. Boyd was being cared for. She was grateful for the relief, but now focused on what lay ahead.

"Okay, Riley. Let's get you inside." Officer Ward stepped out of the vehicle and opened Riley's door.

No sooner had he pulled it open did Riley see her mother rushing down the concrete path and Jack appear in the doorway with his hands on his hips.

"Oh my God, what happened?" Ellen asked as she threw her arms around Riley, now standing outside the patrol car.

"I'm okay, Mom. I promise. I'm okay." She wasn't, not by a long shot. Riley wrapped her arms around Ellen's waist and buried her head in her mother's bosom.

"Mrs. Thompson, we need to talk about what happened today and why I'm here. Can we please go inside so I can speak with you and Mr. Thompson in private?"

"Of course."

Ellen led Riley toward the door where Jack still stood, seemingly unmoved by the emotions of his wife and daughter. Officer Ward trailed behind, keeping his eyes fixed on Jack.

"Mr. Thompson, I'm afraid we need to talk. Riley was involved in an incident today at Carl Boyd's residence. May I come inside?"

Jack moved to the side. "Come in."

Ellen and Riley walked into the living room and sat down on the sofa. She continued to stroke Riley's hair, appearing to offer as much comfort as she could to the frightened girl. "I thought you were at school?" she whispered.

"I'm sorry, Mom. I'm so sorry for lying to you." Riley buried her head once again as the men made their way to their seats.

"Mr. and Mrs. Thompson, I'm afraid Riley's been involved in a shooting at the home of Carl Boyd this afternoon."

Ellen raised her hands to her mouth in attempt to muffle the gasp that had escaped.

The officer raised his own to preempt any comments from either of the parents. "Riley is uninjured, I assure you. We will need to get her down to the station to make a statement as soon as possible. She witnessed the incident and can help identify the suspects. I have to tell you that Riley is very lucky to be here right now. These men." He shook his head. "They shot Mr. Boyd and his son and kidnapped his son's girlfriend. This is very bad, Mr. and Mrs. Thompson, and isn't something I usually see happen here in our town. Riley and Carl Boyd Sr., are our primary witnesses. Carl Boyd Jr, at this time, is about to be or is already on the operating table. He was able to give us the names of the men who shot him and I've already called it in and the state police have issued an APB."

"Oh my God." Ellen's voice trembled as she squeezed Riley's hand.

"However," Ward continued, "I am concerned for Riley's safety. Mr. Boyd is in the hospital and I've stationed an officer there for protection. I'd like to do the same for you all. Until we catch these guys, I really don't want to take any chances."

"I don't understand what the hell is going on here." Jack looked to Ellen, who seemed to offer no consolation for his concerns. "My daughter was sick this morning, then felt well enough to go to school. Now you're here telling me she's a goddamn witness to a crime?" Jack raised to his feet and started to pace the room.

"Yes, sir. That's exactly what I'm telling you."

"For God's sake, she's just a kid. Ellen, why the hell did you let her leave in the first place?"

"Dad, this isn't Mom's fault," Riley began.

"Where were you today, sir?" Officer Ward asked.

Riley shot him a look, knowing his words would only make matters worse. "It's my fault, officer. I went to see Mr. Boyd today. I thought I could help him."

"I can't believe this shit." Jack picked up his pace. "No." He shook his head. "No, you're not gonna talk to my daughter anymore. No statements, nothing; you understand me? She's ten goddamn years old! Whatever that old man and his son are involved with hasn't got nothing to do with my Riley. We don't need any damn protection either. I can take care of my own damn family. I think it's best if you leave now, Officer Ward."

The man took to his feet and spotted a teenaged boy standing on the steps in the foyer. Dillon was listening in on the conversation. Officer Ward returned his eyes to Jack. "It seems like your family might need protection and I'm not just talking about from the men your daughter saw today."

Jack moved closer to Ward. "I'm sorry? What exactly are you trying to say to me?"

The policeman stood firm, placing his hand on his revolver. "I think you know what I'm saying."

The two locked eyes for a moment before Ellen finally spoke up. "I think Officer Ward is right and if Riley can help and they can still keep her safe, then we ought to consider it, Jack."

This was clearly the wrong thing to say, but Jack didn't erupt as Riley had expected. Instead, he backed off and released the hold on Officer Ward's stare. "I'd like to discuss this with my family. I'm sure Riley has been through enough today."

"I understand. Yes, I think you should speak to your daughter. She's been through something very traumatic. In fact, I would suggest that you seek counseling for her in the short term." Officer Ward turned on his heel, and headed toward the front door, but not before looking to Dillon, who stood frozen on the steps. The officer nodded and opened the door. "When you figure out what it is you need to do for your family, Mr. and Mrs. Thompson, you be sure and give me a call. In the meantime, I will be stepping up patrols in your area. The last thing I want is for your little girl not to feel safe."

[17]

The probability that Carl would be allowed to go home tonight was pretty slim. The bullet had only grazed his shoulder and diverged without much damage to the tissue and muscle. Still, the doctor insisted that he stay overnight for "observation," mostly due to his age rather than the extent of his wound.

On the one hand, it would offer an opportunity for him to keep an eye on CJ and make sure he came out of surgery all right; on the other, he wouldn't be able to check up on Riley and make sure she was okay. The idea that she'd been witness to what happened upset Carl greatly. She was just a young girl and had already been through enough in her few short years on Earth.

Jack wouldn't allow him anywhere near her, in all likelihood, but at least he'd have gotten a chance to get confirmation from the mother that she was all right—and safe.

What would happen to them now was uncertain. Both had

been witness to the shooting and kidnapping. Good God, the thought of such a thing made his head spin. It was either that or the drugs they had him on. Either way, it was troubling.

The girl had been right on all counts. CJ had gotten himself involved in something that brought danger to Carl, just as she said it would. But he figured she hadn't believed herself to be in danger as a result, and until those men were caught, they were now both at risk. Perhaps another good reason why he shouldn't be allowed to go home tonight. What if they came back? The hospital offered security, although he wondered if Riley would be offered something similar. Surely Officer Ward would want the girl and her family to be safe.

And what about CJ? Did those men know that he was still alive? Would they come back for all of them?

"Evening, Carl. I brought you some chicken broth. Doc says you can't eat solid foods for a while, but this and the Jell-O should help abate the hunger pangs a little." The nurse carried a tray containing a small bowl covered in plastic and a pot of strawberry Jell-O.

Carl had gone some nights with less, so he didn't mind it. "Thank you, Maggie. Any word on my boy? Has he come out of surgery yet?"

"I'll have to check with the doctor. I haven't heard anything, but I'm sure everything's going just fine. Now you try and get some food in you so you can rest."

"All right. I will." Carl grinned at the woman, who was trying to be helpful, but whose tone verged on indifference. "Thank you." He picked up the bowl of broth and removed the plastic film, taking a sip so that she could see it. Seeming to be satisfied, the woman left and Carl was once again alone.

The facility was small, barely a hospital at all, and Carl was in one of the five rooms that currently held two patients; himself and a woman who'd just given birth down the hall.

As he sipped again on the broth, the door opened and he heard heavy footfalls on the vinyl floor, but he couldn't see the person as the curtains hadn't been pushed back all the way. "Hello?"

The steps moved closer and so did the person to whom they belonged.

"Mr. Boyd, how are you feeling?"

"Officer Ward." A fleeting moment of relief passed through him. "Better, thank you. They got me hooked up with some pretty good drugs now." He didn't like the look on the officer's face and carefully set the cup down, keeping his eyes on him the entire time. "What is it? Is everything okay? My son?"

"I'm sorry, I don't have any updates on your son's condition. I'm actually here to talk about Riley Thompson and why she was at your house today." The man pulled up a chair next to Carl's bed. "I have a feeling there's something you're not telling me about your relationship with this little girl. Maybe you should fill me in." He sat down, resting his forearms on his thighs, leaning in so that Carl knew he had the man's attention.

Carl leaned his head back against the pillow. "You wouldn't believe me if I told you."

"Try me."

He looked to the officer again. "I can tell you for certain that I haven't touched that girl, if that's what you're thinking. I'm not some damn child molester."

"I didn't say you were, Carl, and I don't believe it's anything like that at all. Look, you've lived in this town a long time and I've been a cop here for a long time. I know what people say about you and I also know the truth."

"What is it that you think you know about me?" Carl was beginning to feel defensive, although he had no cause to be and wasn't sure why, but the feeling was there nonetheless. Maybe it was because he knew what the people in this town said about him too.

"I know you've been diagnosed with Paranoid Personality Disorder on top of the PTSD you suffered coming back from Nam. I know you keep to yourself as much as possible and I know that your son moved out of your house about three or four years ago."

"Well, if you know all that, then I guess we don't have much to say to one another."

"Carl, in the ten years I've been a cop here, I've never seen anything like what happened at your place today. And frankly, I'm not ashamed to say I'm a little bit afraid those fellas might come back here and try to harm you or Riley." He rubbed his hands together. "Look, I know Riley's dad is a son of a bitch, everybody does, and I think maybe she might have turned to you for help, for whatever reason."

"You're wrong. You got it all wrong. Like I said, you wouldn't believe me. Why don't you just go and catch those bastards who shot my kid and took that poor young woman, assuming she's still alive. I can tell you they ain't messin' around." He pointed to his shoulder.

"No. I don't believe they are, but Carl, you gotta let me in on this. Why was Riley Thompson at your house and why were you at hers the other night?"

Carl looked into the man's eyes. He was pretty good at reading people himself, and figured the cop was being honest. Maybe he could tell him and maybe, in some small way, it would help Riley too.

"Riley can sense things. She knew something bad was going to happen to me within a few days of our meeting at St. Vincent's. She tried to offer warnings, but didn't have much to go on. I attempted to get her to tell her mom, knowing her dad wouldn't help matters, but she didn't trust telling her mom either. But she told her brother, Dillon. He came with her yesterday to meet me and CJ at the diner. Then, of course, Jack showed up. He was probably at the bar down the street and was heading back to his truck to go home. I don't know. But he saw his kids talking to me and CJ and Melissa. As you might have guessed, that didn't go over well with him.

"Anyway, I'd had a bad dream the night before and I swear," Carl paused, "and this is the part you're gonna have a hard time swallowing, cause I sure as hell do, but Riley was in that dream too. Not like she was a part of my imagination. No. She was in my head, talking to me." Officer Ward's face quickly masked in disbelief. "I told you, you wouldn't believe me."

"No, please go on. I'm listening."

Carl went on to tell him about the dream and what Riley had said about the napalm on her skin and in her nose. Then he told him that Riley said there were men coming.

The officer leaned back in his chair, stroking his bristly chin.

Carl rested his good arm over this stomach. "See? I told you." He leaned back again, waiting to see what Officer Ward might have to say about all this.

"And she'll corroborate this?"

"I don't see why not. She's the one who came to me. Not the other way around."

"Well, I have to say that I don't think this was exactly what I was expecting to hear, but it sure as hell seems like she was right; about those men, anyway."

"You don't have to believe me about the other stuff. I know what's true and what isn't. All I want to know now is, what do you plan on doing to find those men and get Melissa back. And how are you gonna protect that little girl?"

JACK PUSHED OFF THE COUCH AND MOVED TOWARD THE kitchen. Ellen watched as he passed her by, still sitting on the side chair in the living room. They'd been talking for the past hour. Well, maybe talking wasn't the right word for it. She listened, he talked.

He had wanted no part in any of this situation and certainly didn't want a cop posted at his front door for an unspecified length of time. Jack was frustrated and, when that happened, his first inclination was to reach for a bottle, which was exactly what he had gone into the kitchen to do.

Jack pulled open the upper cabinet, above the range hood, and grabbed the bottle of bourbon. It was a 1.75L off-label brand that set him back all of about ten bucks. Even that was a stretch, given their current situation. He still hadn't found a job. In fact, he'd only had a single interview, although he'd told Ellen he'd had three to date. That hadn't been his intention; it just worked out that way.

He'd get up in the morning, shower, and dress in halfway

respectable business attire and start pounding the pavement. But sometime around eleven, twelve o'clock, discouraged and turning bitter, Jack would find himself in the local bar, waiting out the rest of the day. Their finances had gone from bad to worse and now he had to deal with Riley tangled up in this mess. And the idea that she'd seen what she had and was lucky to be alive made Jack feel all the more like taking a drink.

They only owned three hi-ball glasses and he set one in front of him, dropping in a few cubes of ice and pouring the bourbon freely over the top. He tipped it back and it flowed down his throat with ease. Jack closed his eyes, the pleasure of the drink soothing his nerves.

His hands braced against the countertop and he lowered his head. Any more discussions with Ellen about this would only bring him to a boiling point and he hated himself when that happened. He couldn't help it; at least, that was what he told himself, even if the voice in his head disagreed.

He hadn't always been that way and Jack often longed for the days when he had a good job and a happy home. But things spiraled pretty quickly after the plant closed. People moved away in search of jobs; his friends, coworkers. They all left him behind. Even his best friend turned on him. The days when the Rosses would come over made him feel whole, like he was a part of the community. He knew what the town thought of him now: low-life loser who couldn't keep a job.

The Thompson name used to mean something in this town. His mother and father were well-respected, upstanding citizens. Jack was on the varsity basketball team, just like Dillon aspired to be. Those were good days.

But they didn't last either. Ellen got pregnant and they got married, forgoing any hopes of college for either of them. When she lost that baby, Jack did what he thought was best: stay with Ellen and work through it. Eventually, they had Dillon. He loved her, but he always wanted more. And he suspected she did too.

"What are we going to do about Riley, Jack?"

He looked over his shoulder. Ellen was standing in the kitchen, arms folded and looking at him as if he had all the answers. He exhaled a breath he hadn't realized he'd been holding. "All of this is because she feels things, isn't it?" He turned to face her now, leaning against the countertop.

They both knew, but never spoke about it.

"I think so, yes. She's just like your dad, isn't she?"

"Yeah. Fat lot of good it did him. He went off and killed himself." Jack poured a double this time.

"He did that because your mother was gone and he was alone." Ellen moved to the kitchen table and pulled out a chair to sit down.

"What were we, then? He had a son and grandkids. No, he killed himself because he couldn't stand seeing her in his dreams anymore. He couldn't stand feeling the sadness in people every time he walked into a restaurant or shop. They all pitied him. That's why he put the gun in his mouth and splattered his brains all over the bathroom."

"Stop, Jack." Ellen turned away.

"What? You know it's the truth. He leaves us this house. The house that I grew up in. The house that my mother succumbed to her cancer in and Leonard Thompson took his own life in. Jesus. No wonder why I drink." He tossed the double bourbon down, swallowing hard this time.

"I don't want Riley to end up like my dad, okay?" Jack pressed the back of his hand to his eyes and wiped away the pooling tears before they spilled.

"I know you're scared." Ellen took to her feet and walked over to him. "So am I, but Riley could be in a lot of danger right now and we need to think about Dillon and Gracie too. What all this is going to do to them. I think we should accept Officer Ward's help until these men are caught." She reached out for Jack's arm.

He slammed down the glass; the ice cubes rattled inside. He could feel rage burning in his stomach. Jack hated being scared, he hated it when Ellen tried to calm him down. She only made things worse. He hated himself for feeling this way. "Just go on up to bed now. I'll be up in a while. I need to sort through everything and try to figure this out."

The tone of his voice seemed enough for her to get the hint that she'd be better off doing as he said. Ellen released his arm and turned away from him. Her steps quietly carried her out and the only sound of her departure came from the treads squeaking as she walked up to their bedroom.

Jack poured another drink.

The weight of her body grew heavier as Riley sank deeper into her bed and sleep began to take hold. The voices she'd heard downstairs faded and the footsteps past her door were long gone.

Her mind had been replaying the images with great detail, as if the event was happening at this very moment. The gun, the white light and smoke that emerged from it when the man called Johnny pulled the trigger. She could still feel the shot of wind that whistled by her ear when the bullet flew past her. And the way CJ doubled over as he was struck. That was the worst part. Riley wasn't allowed to watch much in the way of cop shows on TV, but she had seen people get shot on some shows. It was nothing like real life: the way he yelled out. She could still smell the pooled blood that lay beneath him. The odor reminded her of the jar of pennies they kept on the bookcase in the living room.

The pain she felt, Carl's pain, was gone now and, for a moment, her body didn't ache and the images subsided. But that didn't last long.

Riley stood in front of the large green door. A plaque next to it showed the numbers "103." It was a room number. It took a moment to register, but she soon realized she was at the hospital and this had to be Carl's room. No one else was there. It was as if the place had been deserted. As she cast her gaze around, the black-speckled vinyl floor gleamed beneath the florescent lighting and the worn maroon chairs in the lobby were empty. She looked behind her at the small reception desk; no one was there either.

She placed her hands on the rectangular metal panel, just below the sticker indicating to push. The door was heavier than she had expected and stubborn too, fighting back the pressure she'd applied.

Reluctantly, it opened and inside was a sterile room with two beds. The first bed was empty and the second had an occupant. Riley could just catch a glimpse of feet tenting the cover over them. Light from a television flashed too. She glanced up to see that it was some kind of talk show, although she didn't know who the host was, but did recognize the celebrity guest. A smile appeared when she noticed that it had been the girl from that movie she liked so much; the one about the kids having to fight other kids in a game.

Riley returned her attention to the person beneath the covers and moved forward slowly. It occurred to her only briefly that she might not really be here at all and this was just a dream, but it sure didn't feel like a dream. Her skin raised with bumps in the cool room and, when she looked down, her feet were bare and she was wearing her favorite nightshirt with Hello Kitty on the front. If this wasn't a dream, she would be extremely embarrassed.

A foot shifted and Riley froze for a moment, then started again. A few more steps and she could see legs, a hand at the side of the bed, and eventually a face. "Mr. Boyd? Mr. Boyd, are you awake?"

The old man's eyes fluttered open and he turned his head to see the girl standing before him. "Riley? What are you doing here? It's so late."

"I think this is another dream, Mr. Boyd. Look." Riley pointed to his injured shoulder, except it wasn't injured anymore.

"Oh. I—I don't understand. Please tell me what's going on, Riley?"

"I'm not sure exactly, Mr. Boyd. Last I checked, I was in my bed, then I started seeing all the bad stuff that happened today and now I'm here. Is CJ okay?"

"He came out of surgery and they think he'll be fine, but they'll know more in the morning."

"Oh, I'm so glad to hear that." Riley reached for his hand, gently squeezing his index and middle finger.

Carl smiled wide and his eyes glistened. It had been so long since a child had held his hand. Her skin was soft, smooth. Nothing at all like his calloused, wrinkled hands with knuckles that bulged from arthritis.

"That police officer came to see me earlier. I told him about what you can do." Carl paused for a moment, ensuring she wouldn't become upset at the news. "He believes me, sort of. Enough that I think he'll be open to talking to you more about it. I hope you're not mad."

"No. I'm not mad, Mr. Boyd. I've tried to tell people before. Like my teacher and my mom, but no one really understands. They think I'm just 'sensitive.'"

"I'm sorry to hear that, Riley. You must feel terribly alone."

"Sometimes." Riley released her grip and lowered her arm to her side. "We have to find Melissa. We have to save her."

"How can we do that? We don't know where she is."

"I bet once CJ comes around, he'll be able to tell us where those men live. Maybe Officer Ward can go there."

"Maybe. I think he's more concerned that they might come here. Come after you and CJ again."

"I could feel his fear."

"What's that?"

"CJ's. I could feel that he was afraid when that man named Johnny pointed the gun at him."

"I'm sure he was terrified." Carl's voice cracked with sentiment.

"What I mean to say is that maybe if I can see him again, maybe I can learn something about where they have Melissa. I mean, if he doesn't already know, that is."

"He might; I don't know. Officer Ward didn't say anything, but then CJ's been in surgery. He might not recall everything exactly until he recovers a bit. But, you think you could do that? You think you could help him to find her?"

"I can try, Mr. Boyd."

"Do you think you would know if they were coming back here?"

"I don't know, but I guess so. I knew they were coming before; I just didn't know when."

"How does this thing work with you, Riley? Like you being here now, in my dream. How is that possible? You were there with me at the prison camp too." His lips began to quiver and he tried to blink away the mounting tears.

"I wish I knew. It's only ever happened with you, Mr. Boyd. Before, I could just sense things inside people, you know, like how they were feeling and stuff like that. I'm pretty scared of it too. Like maybe I won't wake up."

[18]

T**he tingling of** pins and needles attacked her arm. Riley reached to take hold of her right shoulder to soothe the pain, but when she looked back to Mr. Boyd, he was gone and, in a haze, Riley's eyes clicked open. She was back in her own bed and the tingling sensation was coming from Gracie, who'd snuck in beside her and was nestled against the arm that had fallen asleep as a result.

She tried to regain focus and let her eyes adjust to the darkness of her room. The window became clear first and was the only source of muted light from the full moon that was right on schedule.

Gracie shifted slightly against Riley's arm and she cringed in pain. Why had she moved in next to her? Had the dream caused her to be restless and awakened her little sister?

Riley never underestimated Gracie. She was smart and she

knew, in some small part, what had happened today. That was probably the real reason.

The arm, however, had to be freed, unless she wanted to lose it altogether, which felt entirely possible at this moment. Riley wriggled it from beneath Gracie's head, working hard not to pull her long hair. Gracie's hair was thick and luxurious, nothing at all like Riley's. Maybe she'd been adopted.

A hint of a grin played on her face at the idea as she continued to free the trapped limb without tumbling her sister to the floor. A moment later, the arm was free and Riley tossed her legs over the side of the bed and raised upright.

She moved to the bedroom window and pulled back the curtain just enough to peek through. Out of her second floor room, she looked down at the street and squinted. Was that...? She blinked and looked again. Yes, it was Officer Ward's car parked out front and it appeared as though he was inside it.

Riley wanted to go outside and talk to him. He was there, protecting her and her family. It was four o'clock in the morning and not a hint of daybreak was visible yet. She would have to be quiet and, in this old house, that wouldn't be easy.

Her robe hung on the closet door handle and she wrapped it around herself, sliding on her ballet-style slippers. It was still cold outside and she didn't want to freeze. Quietly, her bedroom door opened, although still squeaking a little on old hinges. She made her way down the stairs, stepping on the inside of each tread because they didn't make as much noise that way. It wasn't the first time she'd had to sneak around her house.

The deadbolt turned easily and Riley twisted the handle, opening the front door to a blast of cold air. It had to be below freezing, which was pretty normal for March. It was brighter outside than she'd expected. The moon looked enormous and bathed the street in its glow. He must have seen her coming because, in the distance, Riley saw movement inside the car.

She peered through the window and waved. Officer Ward rolled it down.

"What on earth are you doing up? And why are you out here? It's freezing!"

"I just wanted to say thank you for staying here and protecting my family, sir."

"Open the door, Riley, and sit down before you catch your death out there."

She did as the officer instructed. It was the second time she'd seen the inside of a police car now. It was kind of exciting and, for a moment, she'd forgotten why she was there. "Officer Ward, I just talked to Mr. Boyd. He seems to be doing better."

Riley knew exactly what she had said and waited for a response. Carl had already told him about what she could do. She was testing him to see if he was on her side or if he was just another grown-up who thought she had an overactive imagination.

"You just talked to him? On the phone?" he asked.

"No, sir. I saw him, just now, in my dream."

"I see." He turned away, seeming to contemplate her response.

"Well, Carl mentioned you were special. I guess I can see that now."

Her big brown eyes squinted when her round cheeks raised in a smile. He did believe her and it felt wonderful. "Are they looking for those men?"

"Yes, they are and, until they find them, I'm going to make sure your family stays safe. Is that all right with you?"

She nodded. "Do you think you could take me to the hospital

to see Mr. Boyd's son? I think I can help find his girlfriend. She seems really nice and I want to help her."

"Now?"

"Sure. Why not?"

"Because it's four in the morning and I don't think your folks would be too happy with me if I just drove off with you to the hospital."

Riley looked through the windshield at the night sky. Stars appeared in abundance. No city lights to scare them away. "You know my dad doesn't want me to help. I heard him talking to my mom before." She turned back to the officer. "He's scared. He's been scared for a long time, only I can't help him not to feel that way."

"Is he mean to your mom sometimes?"

She nodded. "Sometimes."

"You know, we can help you and your mom. Your brother and sister too. It doesn't have to be this way."

"Officer Ward, will you take me to the hospital or not? 'Cause if not, then I should probably go back to bed."

"I don't think that's a good idea, Riley. Not right now, but maybe in the morning, if you really think you can help."

Riley opened the passenger door. "You think they're coming back and you're not sure what to do. Captain Sinclair doesn't know you're here and neither do any of the other officers. Why didn't you tell anyone, sir?" She looked over her shoulder at the man with powder blue eyes and a baby face that he tried to disguise by wearing a five o'clock shadow.

"I'm not sure, Riley, but by the sounds of it, you already know."

"You're confused by me, maybe even a little scared. There's no reason to be, sir. I don't know why I'm like this, but I do know that I can help CJ and that lady. Mr. Boyd can't do much right now, even if they let him out of the hospital. Everyone thinks he's crazy anyway and that makes me sad. He's not crazy; his brain just gets jumbled up. Mr. Boyd has gone through a lot of hurt and I want to help his son so that Mr. Boyd doesn't lose him too. Will you help me, Officer Ward?"

She'd put him in his place, that much was evident, but he seemed to genuinely consider her request.

"I'll talk to your folks in the morning." He glanced through the windshield. "Well, in a couple of hours, by the looks of it. If they agree, then you and me will go down there and see what we can do. Will that be all right with you, Riley?"

"Yes, sir. Thank you." She stepped outside and closed the door and, as she walked back to her house, Riley turned a final time to wave at the officer. He nodded and she went inside.

It was Doug's turn to keep watch on the girl. He'd managed an hour or so of sleep, although it hadn't been a good rest. His mind revolved around what had transpired and the situation in which they now found themselves. Things would have gone just fine if Johnny hadn't screwed everything up.

The cops were after them and probably the FBI too because they'd crossed the border into Ohio. His truck ended up nose first in an embankment still inside Indiana state lines. He loved that truck.

As Doug sat on the metal folding chair, only a thin layer of padding on the seat, he considered his next move. It was almost dawn and the girl had finally fallen asleep on the mass of blankets they'd put down for her on the floor of the loft. He peered out of the window that overlooked nothing but farm fields, some of them returning to life as the spring approached. This old barn where they held their meetings was fairly secluded and even if the girl managed to escape, there wasn't anything within a five-mile radius. They would likely catch up to her before she reached the nearest building.

Doug, however, had bigger problems, if that was possible. He'd been undercover with these men for almost a year. The case was nearing the end and that end would bring about the successful prosecution of Raymond McAllister and his counterparts, the men from which they'd attempted to steal. A special agent out of the Columbus ATF field office, Doug was ready to put this to bed. That was, until today.

The supervisors weren't going to be happy about this. Doug couldn't risk being exposed because he knew Ray, and Ray would kill him without hesitation. Somehow, he would need to get word to his field office to contact the Owensville police and let them know that they had a man on the inside. Right now, he figured the state police and FBI would be looking for both him and Johnny.

His cover was rock solid. The department transferred ownership of the hardware store to him, had given him a family history, and built an impenetrable persona that would stand up to the harshest scrutiny. And he'd passed with flying colors, entering the world of a radical militia group purporting to be in support and defense of the United States. However, they were nothing more than gunrunning thugs who waved the American flag as they sold their illegally obtained weapons to other criminals.

A year. A damn year and now, as he watched the girl sleep, he thought about how best to get word to the local authorities. He owned two cell phones. One for "Doug Newman" and the other for Special Agent Phil Crayton. That other cell was locked up in a hidden safe in his home about ten miles from here. Next watch wasn't until six, so he would have to stew in his own mess until then.

Riley had been awake since talking to the police officer, who had stayed up all night ensuring that she and her family were protected. She looked at the digital clock on the nightstand. Six a.m. Time to get up. She hadn't had the heart to wake her sister and put her back into her own bed. This was partly the reason for her inability to return to sleep. Even now, as she looked at Gracie, her little face was peaceful, even if she snorted every now and again. Probably a cold coming on.

Before Riley could reach for her robe, Ellen opened her door. "Good morning, honey. I wasn't sure if you'd be awake yet." She walked inside and pushed the door closed against the jamb. "I think it's a good idea if you stay home from school today."

Riley half expected this conversation. She'd heard Ellen and Jack speaking in the kitchen. Both were afraid for her and maybe she was afraid too. She wondered now, though, would Ellen believe her? "Okay, Mom. Did you see that policeman outside our house last night?"

Curious, Ellen walked over to Riley's bedroom window. "No. I didn't."

"He's already gone. I heard him leave about an hour ago."

"How did you know he was there?"

"Something woke me up in the night and I looked out of my window and saw him. I went outside to talk to him too. He's a very nice man."

"I'm sure he is, sweetheart."

"Mom, I know what I did was wrong. I mean, going over to Mr. Boyd's house and all. It's just that I felt that something was going to happen and I tried to warn him. But I guess I was too late."

Ellen moved toward Riley and pulled her into an embrace. "I know you were trying to help but, Riley, it could have turned out so much worse. What if something had happened to you? What would I have done then?"

She gently pushed Riley back to look into the little girl's eyes. "I know you feel things and I'm so sorry we haven't talked about it before. I guess I always suspected it, but I was scared."

"I know, Mom, but this isn't over. Officer Ward thinks those men will come back and I don't know that for sure just yet, but I guess it might come to me when I see Mr. Boyd or CJ again. And if they do, they'll hurt him and his son." It would only frighten her mother if she'd mentioned the danger in which she believed herself to be. Ellen might just lock her inside her room until it was all over and then how could she help Mr. Boyd?

Riley began to sense that there was something Ellen wasn't saying. The conversation she and Jack had had last night. There was something there, but Riley couldn't quite see it fully. But before she could ask, the phone began to ring.

"I'd better get that. Your dad is still asleep." Ellen made her way down the stairs and into the kitchen.

Riley scooted to the top of the stairs to listen in.

"Yes, this is Ellen Thompson."

"I think that would be a good idea. Thank you, officer. We'll be there by eight o'clock. Goodbye."

Riley heard Ellen's footfalls moving toward her and so she tiptoed back to her room. Gracie had begun to stir.

"Is it time to get up already?" Gracie sat up and began rubbing her eyes.

"Yes. You need to start getting ready for school."

"Aren't you gonna get ready too?"

"I think I'm staying home again today. Mom says I'm still not over my fever."

"You better not get me sick." Gracie rose to her feet and shuffled to the bathroom.

Riley moved back out onto the landing, expecting Ellen to return and give her some sort of news. It sounded as though she would be going somewhere, and soon.

Dillon's bedroom door opened and the tired boy lumbered toward her. "What's going on?" No one had given him the full story yet, not even Riley. Jack and Ellen hadn't given her the chance.

"I think I have to go soon. I don't know where yet. Maybe the police station."

"Geez, Riley. I can't believe what happened yesterday. I can't believe you saw somebody get shot. Are you okay? I mean, really okay?"

"I'm okay. I told you something bad was going to happen. You're the only one in this family who believes me." She looked over her shoulder toward the staircase. "I guess they believe me now, though."

"Well, I'm staying with you today. I don't care what Mom and Dad say. No way am I leaving you alone again."

"Thanks, Dillon." She loved him so much and wished things were different. She wished he wasn't always gone. Sometimes, Riley felt as though she had to bear the brunt of her family's dysfunction and Dillon was just biding his time until he finished high school. Then he would abandon her and Gracie. Maybe this would change things for their family. Maybe it would somehow make it better.

[19]

The **final word** came from the head of the family this morning. After some persuasion on the part of Ellen, Jack had agreed to let Riley make a statement for the police. According to Officer Ward, the choice would likely have been taken out of his hands anyway, considering this had become a federal investigation.

Now, as the sun continued to rise in the morning sky, the family waited in the lobby of the police station in town. It was scarcely a ten by ten space that flowed directly into the rest of the building and was not cordoned off. It allowed anyone to watch the comings and goings of the staff, although, in this small town, not many occupied it right now and Riley suspected this was the usual course of business.

The window opposite reflected the rays directly onto Riley's face and so she moved to the other side of Dillon. His tall frame would help shield her from the light. This wasn't where she wanted to be, though. The hospital was her priority. She needed to see CJ and talk to him about where he thought the men might have Melissa. If she could just be face to face with him, it would help. Riley might be able to see where the woman was being held and maybe know for sure if those men were coming back.

"I'm sorry to keep you waiting." Officer Ward approached. "I've asked Captain Sinclair to join us. He's working in conjunction with the federal agents and he'll be required to forward Riley's statement to them. We thought it best if they let us handle this part and they've agreed."

"That's fine," Jack replied.

"Please, if you'll follow me. We have a small conference room in the back where we can begin." He looked to Riley. "You okay with this?"

"Yeah, I guess so."

"Okay then." The officer pressed his hand against Riley's shoulder and gently nudged her along. "Did you manage to get back to sleep this morning?" he whispered.

"No, sir. I tried, though."

He patted her on the back and grinned.

They were greeted at the entrance by the police captain. He held the door open and introduced himself to the family as they entered. "And you must be Riley?"

"Yes, sir."

"Please come in and have a seat. This won't take long."

The room was ordinary and painted in a lackluster beige hue. A dry erase board on one wall; a filing cabinet and bookshelf on another. The window that faced out into the parking lot was covered with metal venetian blinds, and the only indication that it was, in fact, the twenty-first century was the small flat panel TV affixed to the wall in front of them.

Riley took her seat at the middle of the table, swiveling back and forth in the chair. Officer Ward sat opposite her. She ran her fingers along the smooth cherry-stained top that had a high-gloss finish.

"First of all, I want to tell you that CJ Boyd is doing well this morning," the captain began. "I got a call from the doctor first thing and he said CJ will remain in recovery for another day or two before being transferred to a regular room until he's well enough to go home. Carl senior is doing well and will be released later today."

"Can I go and see him? CJ, I mean?" Riley began.

Officer Ward nodded to his captain.

"I think we can arrange that," he replied. "Now, as you may know, CJ was able to give us the names of the men who shot him and kidnapped Melissa Simmons. Our department has been working with the Indiana state police as well as the Ohio state police. Both are also coordinating with the FBI, since this has crossed state borders. So, as I'm sure you can see, this has grown to be much larger than what our small department is accustomed to handling."

The room started to fall out of focus as Riley squinted to clear her vision. She'd eaten this morning, so it couldn't be that she'd become light-headed with hunger. Something else was taking place and as she looked at the faces around the table, they began to appear distorted and blurred. Riley was on the verge of fainting.

"I—I don't feel well." Riley's voice was soft and had almost gone unnoticed until Officer Ward picked up on it.

"Riley. Are you okay?" He pushed up from the table.

She shook her head and looked to Ellen. "I think I'm gonna be sick again, Mom."

"Oh no." Ellen searched the room. "Dillon, bring me that garbage can next to the filing cabinet."

Dillon retrieved the can and placed it in front of Riley.

"Is she all right?" Captain Sinclair asked, appearing highly concerned.

"She hasn't been feeling well lately. I think with that happened yesterday, it probably set her recovery back." Ellen pulled Riley's hair away from her face. "It's okay, sweetheart."

Jack looked at her, appearing to anticipate the worst. He'd been through this sort of thing before.

Riley's eyes rolled into the back of her head and she slumped over the chair.

"Jesus!" Jack rushed to her side. "Honey?" He shook her gently. "Sweetheart, wake up." Jack turned to Officer Ward. "She's out cold. We need to get her to the hospital."

Just as they began to mobilize, Riley came to. Her eyes flickered as her focus returned.

"Riley? Riley, are you okay?" Ellen asked. "Jack, she's awake."

"I'm okay." She paused and her eyes lowered. Her lips quivered as she turned her gaze to the officer of whom she'd grown fond. "CJ is dead."

The uniformed men exchanged an uncertain and perplexing look.

"He was fine," Ward began. "The doctor said he was going to be fine."

Captain Sinclair retrieved his cell phone. "I need to speak with Dr. Roberts regarding Carl Boyd Jr. immediately, please. This is Captain Sinclair."

He seemed to be listening to someone on the other end of the line. "I see. When did this happen?" Another pause. "Thank you." The captain appeared completely nonplussed as he ended the call.

"CJ's dead, isn't he?" Riley asked through a crackling voice and on the verge of tears.

"Yes. He died about twenty minutes ago. Some internal bleeding that they couldn't stop. Riley, how did you know this?"

She looked at Officer Ward and then at her parents. Jack shook his head almost imperceptibly to all except Riley. It was this gesture that seemed to make it perfectly clear that Riley should not answer. "I don't know exactly." That was a lie, because she'd seen it happening. "I just felt a terrible pain coming from Mr. Boyd. He knows too." It was much more than that, but they would not understand. She was beginning to lose control of this ability, this gift that was transforming into a curse. Riley was terrified that it would only worsen and that she might never escape it.

The captain looked at Ward, seemingly more confused than ever. All the officer could do was shrug his shoulders. He was as much at a loss by this as anyone else was.

"I'd like to see Mr. Boyd now, please," Riley said.

Jack ignored her request and slammed his fist on the filing cabinet. "I need to know what you're going to do to protect my little girl and the rest of my family, for that matter. A man is dead, shot and killed, and my daughter was witness to it. And from what you've said, you know the names of the men who did this. Why the hell aren't you people going after them?"

"Please calm down, Mr. Thompson," Officer Ward said. "You're right. We do have the names of the suspects and we are working with the FBI, state police, and Ohio authorities as well. The reason I requested that you come down here was so Riley could make her statement. That's all. And as far as offering protection, I have already requested stepping up patrols in your area. If you'll recall, I also offered to post one of our officers at your house and you refused."

The captain's cell phone rang again. "Please excuse me. I need to take this." He stepped out of the room.

"Riley, I'm not sure it's a good idea for you to see Mr. Boyd right now. I'm sure he must be feeling terrible after hearing the news," Ellen said.

"That's why I want to go, Mom. I want to tell him how sorry I am that I couldn't stop it from happening." Riley began to tear up again, her cheeks growing flush with emotion.

"Oh, sweetheart, none of this is your fault. You have to know that." Ellen pulled her closer in an embrace.

The room fell quiet for a moment. It seemed the idea that all of this had transpired so quickly was not lost on those present. Nothing ever happened in Owensville and now they were dealing with a homicide and a kidnapping.

Captain Sinclair returned as all eyes landed on him. "Ward, can I see you for a moment?"

"Sure."

"Hey." The man with the heavy beard nodded a brief greeting. "Boss says you can take off. He wants you to open up your shop and keep things as normal as possible."

"That's probably best." Doug cast a glance to Melissa, who was now sitting up, sipping on water. "She's been awake for a while and I gave her something to eat. Let's go downstairs."

They made their way down the unsteady wooden ladder to the ground floor of the old building.

"Did Ray say what we're supposed to do next? I mean, we can't just keep her here forever. I'm sure she's got family and someone's gonna come looking for her sooner or later."

"He knows that, Doug. He said he'd come by a little later this morning, after he took care of some things. This whole thing is effed up and we both know it. Ray wanted to send a message to those other boys and all it did was screw us over. Now we got no guns, no CJ, and some woman we're holding hostage. Look, you just get on out of here. Go do what you gotta do. I'll keep an eye on her until Ray gets here."

Doug began to move toward the exit.

"Oh, Ray wants to see you back here by three. Can you swing that?"

"Yeah. I'll be back at three," Doug replied as he opened the big barn doors.

This was what he'd been waiting for. Now he could get home and call his supervisor because, by all accounts, every law enforcement officer in Ohio would be looking for a man matching his description.

Doug waited outside as he no longer had a truck; he needed a lift home and Johnny had offered his services. He leaned against the exterior, raising a foot behind him for support.

The call to his boss wouldn't be an easy one and, in all likelihood, he'd be pulled from cover and they'd swoop in and arrest Johnny. But Johnny was a small fish. He'd wanted Ray and it had taken him eleven months to build a case against him. His best chance to put the nail in the coffin had been that night at the warehouse.

The plan had been to wait until the crates were in Ray's possession. He knew where the stash was kept and he needed enough in the cache to warrant a raid. But the deal had gone south and now he had little evidence to warrant much of anything against either Ray or the other group of men wanting to move in on their territory.

The best that Special Agent Phil Crayton had was evidence that Raymond was selling guns to shop owners who otherwise wouldn't be able to obtain them legally. Sometimes, the contraband would end up in the hands of the gun show vendors as well. It was good, but not good enough. The warehouse would have given him what he needed and the raid could have been in the works by now.

So, the FBI would come in and arrest Johnny, Ray would go into hiding until it all blew over, and ATF Agent Crayton would be no closer to finalizing his case against him.

He hadn't wanted to recruit CJ, but Johnny had already been working to get the man inside. Crayton didn't have a choice as Ray said he "needed a favor." People didn't usually say no to him.

Johnny arrived in his usual fashion, driving too fast and kicking up the damn dirt everywhere. Doug pushed off the wall and walked toward him. "'Bout time you got here."

"Just get in. I got shit to do."

Doug noticed Bennett in the back seat. "What's going on?" He didn't like seeing the Denton brothers together. It usually meant something unpleasant.

"Ray wants to see you now," Johnny said.

"Yeah? Steve already told me, except that he said Ray wanted me back here at three. Wanted me to open the shop for a while and keep things on an even keel. What's changed?"

"Don't know, man. He just said I needed to bring you to him. Now."

Doug stepped into the car and didn't inquire further. Johnny was a man of few words, but his curt tone suggested things might be turning bad for Doug Newman, and maybe for ATF Agent Phil Crayton too.

OFFICER DANIEL WARD WAITED OUTSIDE THE CONFERENCE room with the captain. With his arms folded, he examined the man's face. It appeared that whomever had called, had called with disturbing news.

"That was ASAC Kent Parker of the Columbus ATF field office. We seem to be looking for one of their men," the captain said.

"One of *their* men? Who? Which one?"

"Doug Newman. That's his cover name. Apparently, when the call went out for this guy, the description and the name raised a red flag in the system. His name is Phil Crayton and he's undercover with a group that calls themselves the Liberty Bell Rangers. A group that Johnny Denton also belongs to."

"Shit. Let me guess; they want us to back off until they get their man out of there?"

"That's the thing. They want us to back off, period."

"Are you kidding me? We've got a man who was shot and has just died. This man gave us the name of his killer and we're just supposed to ignore it?" Ward turned away and started to pace the small corridor. "I don't believe this." He returned his attention to the captain. "We got a little girl in there who was witness to a murder and a kidnapping and we can't do a damn thing about it? What about the woman who was taken? Are they going to just let her get killed?"

"Look, just calm down. They haven't heard from their man yet. Once they do, they'll evaluate the situation further and let us know how to proceed. In the meantime, we wait. We take Riley Thompson's statement and wait."

"What the hell good is her statement going to do us now? We know what happened and we can't do shit about it, by the sounds of it."

"Because we still gotta get our ducks in a row."

Ward inhaled a deep breath to slow his aggravated pulse. "Riley isn't like anyone I've ever met before."

"Meaning?"

"That little girl—like she said, she can sense things. I was keeping an eye out at her house until early this morning. She came outside and talked to me. Riley asked to see Carl's son because she thought it would help her find Melissa Simmons. She said she could see inside people, understand their feelings, and know what they've been through. I know how this sounds. Just bear with me here. By going to see Carl's son, she thought the whereabouts of that woman would come to her. He knew where that group hung out, where they work; all of it. She thought something inside him would give away Melissa's position." Ward thought he might be losing the captain. "I know this doesn't make any sense, especially now that we've lost CJ, but I think we ought to let Riley see Carl Sr. They've got some sort of link that I honestly have no idea how to explain."

The captain seemed to consider the request. "Hell, we can't do anything else until we hear back from the feds. Might as well see what we can do on our own until then."

RAYMOND MCALLISTER WAS WEDGED INSIDE THE CRIMSON-colored booth of the small diner outside of Wellington, a few miles away from where they held their meetings. It was still morning, but it seemed the breakfast crowd might have already finished. Either that, or the place didn't do much business and this was just a typical Wednesday morning.

Johnny shoved the gearshift into park and killed the engine. "Let's go." He stepped out of the car. Doug opened the passenger door, standing outside, and raised his seat so Bennett could climb out of the back.

His mind had been replaying every word he'd said in the last two days. Was there something in his remarks that would have been cause for concern? Why would Ray call this meeting when he was already due to meet with the man later today? It wasn't making sense. Doug had been banking on the hours in between to get home and make the call to his field office. They'd have to implement an extraction protocol and that would take time. The longer he stayed undercover, the more opportunity there was for something to go wrong if he believed Ray had grown suspicious.

Doug followed Johnny and Bennett inside the restaurant, where there were only a handful of other customers dotting the area. Ray was in the corner booth; no one else around him.

"Morning, Doug. How was your night? I trust all went as planned?" Ray remained seated, extending a handshake to him.

Doug slid inside the booth, Johnny and Bennett flanking either side of him. He was beginning to feel trapped. "Yeah, everything went off without a hitch. She's doing well and has eaten a little. She's scared, but I suppose that's normal."

"Yep, she's one scared little bitch." Bennett laughed. No one else did.

"You know, Doug, what happened the other night—it was pretty fucked up," Ray said.

Doug only nodded a reply.

"I've been racking my brain, trying to figure out who could have tipped off those other boys. They've got some powerful backing. Own most of the territory from here north up to Columbus. It should've all worked out to plan, but then we got the call they were coming. Shit, if we hadn't had Steve keeping an eye on their movements, well, I hate to think what would've happened if they caught us with our hands in their cookie jar."

"So what is it you're trying to say here, Ray?" Doug asked.

Ray shot a look to the Denton boys and returned his attention to Doug. "I trust you, Doug. You're loyal; always have been for as long as you been a part of our team. So I'm asking, do you think anyone in our group is playing us?"

The easy thing for Doug to do would be to blame CJ. The man was presumably dead. The problem was, Ray seemed to be considering the idea that he was the one spouting off his mouth and working for those other men.

Until he could reach his ASAC, Doug needed to come up with something viable. He needed out of this situation and the only way might be to lay blame on the dead guy, in the interim at least. He felt bad for CJ. He'd liked the man, but right now, Doug's case didn't seem to be the only thing at stake here. His life might be too.

"Well, Ray, my first inclination is to say that you made the right call leaving CJ there that night. He was new, he might've been scared; you know? Those boys paid a visit to my store a few days before we hit the warehouse and gave him the flash drive with the prints for the building. Hell, I don't know, I don't wanna blame a man who isn't here to defend himself, but it sure is coincidental that they happened to know we were gonna show up ahead of the prearranged meeting. Like maybe they put some pressure on CJ to look out for their interests instead of ours."

Ray took a sip of his black coffee; slurped it, more like. He set it back down and looked directly into Doug's eyes. "You know what, Doug? I don't believe in coincidences."

[20]

The Thompsons remained in the conference room, but no words were exchanged, with the exception of Gracie. It was approaching snack time and she was getting hungry and didn't mind complaining about it.

Dillon kept his eyes down and his mouth shut. That was generally his direct response whenever he was in the same room with Jack, but he briefly glanced to Ellen and noticed that she still had her arm around Riley, stroking her hair so much so that it had begun to cling to her fingers with static.

Jack just stared out of the window and onto the parking lot, where the sun had begun to reflect off of the roof of his truck.

It seemed that time had moved at a snail's pace, but eventually, they heard the conference room door open and Officer Ward and Captain Sinclair returned to their seats.

"Are we done here yet?" Jack asked.

The officer looked at Jack, ignoring his impatience, then

returned his eyes to Riley. "You said you wanted to see Mr. Boyd. I've been able to arrange that. Would you like to go and see him now?"

Riley lit up at the news. She'd wanted so badly to comfort him. It was her fault she couldn't save his son and now Mr. Boyd was left with no children at all. "Yes." She looked to her parents. "Can we please go?"

Jack pushed up from the table. "Look, I haven't heard either one of you tell me what you're gonna do for my family. You think I can just sit around and wait for you to make a decision? In case you didn't know, I gotta make a living to keep a roof over my family's head. I don't have time for any of this. I just want you to protect Riley and keep those sons of bitches from finding her. Can you do that?"

"Mr. Thompson, I am sorry to inconvenience you," Captain Sinclair said. "We just want to be sure we know what we're dealing with here. Your daughter has been witness to something terrible and so yes, to answer your question, we can keep her safe as well as your family, but we will need your cooperation. I understand times are difficult right now and, from what Officer Ward has told me, you've been spending much of your time out looking for work."

Dillon rolled his eyes, but it seemed Riley was the only one to notice.

"Please, Dad," Riley said. "I know how hard this is for you to accept. I didn't ask for this; it just happened and I know you understand why. Please don't be mad at the police officers. They're trying to help." She looked to Ward. "But I think maybe they can't help as much as they want to."

The officer's brow creased, working to understand just how it was she knew that.

"You don't have to go to the hospital. I can go with Officer Ward and you guys can go back home. I know how hard this is for you, Dad." Riley rolled her chair back and walked toward Jack. She reached out for his hand. "It's okay. I won't end up like Grandpa." Her voice dropped to a whisper.

Jack turned away for just a moment. It seemed he understood what she was saying. He searched her eyes. She could feel him as he looked for meaning and what it was exactly that she knew about her grandfather.

There was a surge of hope in her, but it was quickly extinguished when Jack's face turned hard again.

"You all can waste your time talking to the old man instead of finding the people who killed his son and could have killed my daughter. But I have to go figure out a way to keep a roof over my kids' heads." Jack brushed past Riley and Ellen.

It looked as though Ellen might attempt to stop him, but she lowered her arm and let him pass. He slammed the door on his way out.

"Figures," Dillon said. "Mom, why don't you take Gracie home? I'll stay with Riley and they can take her to see Mr. Boyd."

Riley wasn't at all surprised that as soon as her dad left the room, Dillon stood to take his place, acting as the man in the family. She was grateful to him, but knew it would not be the end of their troubles. In fact, this was only the beginning.

They'd arrived at the hospital in Officer Ward's SUV.

Dillon took Riley's hand and led her inside the lobby where Ward and Sinclair approached the nurse behind the counter.

She seemed to recognize the men. "I suppose you're here to see Carl Boyd Sr.?" She shook her head. "What a terrible thing what happened to his boy."

"Yes, ma'am. That's why we're here," the captain replied.

"He's in room 103, although I believe the doctor will be letting him out later this afternoon. He seems to be doing better, physically at least."

"Thank you." Ward tipped his head and took the lead heading back to Riley. "He's back here. Are you sure you want to do this?"

Riley, still holding Dillon's hand, nodded.

"Okay, then. Follow me."

Riley walked down the wide corridor. The walls looked to have once been the color of the sky in summer, but now appeared more like the grey skies of winter. She expected to feel nervous, but as they moved closer to Carl's room, she felt a calming sensation surround her.

"This is it," Officer Ward said. "Now remember, he's going to be upset, Riley."

"I know, sir."

He tapped his knuckles on the door. No reply. "Mr. Boyd? It's Officer Ward. I'm here with Riley. She'd like to talk to you."

The silence continued, but soon a faint voice sounded.

"He wants us to come in," Riley said. She was the first to enter the room. She'd recognized it from her dream last night. The blanket, his feet sticking out, even the television on the wall. "Hi, Mr. Boyd." She placed her hand on over his.

"Hello, Riley."

She could see he'd been crying and the sight of him made her very sad. It was his grief, yes, but it blended with her own. "I'm sorry about CJ, Mr. Boyd. I didn't know it was going to happen when I saw you last night."

Sinclair unveiled a look of concern about the comment. It appeared that this prior visit had been news to him. Officer Ward returned the look with upturned palms and a shrug.

"It's okay. It's not your fault at all, Riley. I just want you to know that. None of this is your fault."

Seemed everyone kept telling her that, but she was having a hard time believing it. "It's just, well, I thought if I could talk to him, I'd be able to get a feel for where Melissa was at, and now what are we going to do?"

"You're gonna help me find the people who took away my son and we're gonna get that girl back too," Carl replied with renewed vigor.

"We may already have an idea as to the location of one of the men," Officer Ward started, looking back to his captain to be sure it was safe to continue. "Looks like the driver is a federal agent. Undercover ATF."

"So you know where he is?" Carl asked.

"Sir, we're waiting for the agency to get in contact with their man. They haven't heard from him and they're concerned, but have asked us not to pursue any further action until they make contact," Captain Sinclair replied.

Doug waited for Ray to continue. Clearly, the man was circling him and believed he was the person responsible for the botched robbery. "Like I said, the man was new. Sure, he'd worked for me for a while, but it was Johnny's call to bring him into the fold. I'm not saying he was spying for them. I'm just saying he might've inadvertently said something to those men when they came into the shop. I don't know. Unfortunately, Johnny took it upon himself to draw down on the man and now we'll never know what happened. What I see as our biggest problem is what the hell we're gonna do with this girl."

Ray seemed to consider Doug's words. He raised the cup of coffee to his lips again. Steam rose from the cup as he tilted it against his mouth and slurped. It was like nails on a chalkboard and Doug figured he was only doing it for dramatic flair, building tension. As if he was waiting for Doug to flinch first, but of course, if he did, he'd be as good as dead.

"Here's the thing, Doug." Ray set the cup down and laced his fingers, resting his hands on the table. "We can't keep this girl. You know that as well as I do. And yet, letting her go doesn't seem to be a feasible option either. And the other problem we're facing is the fact that we've still got two other witnesses."

"Right; that little girl and that old man Johnny grazed with a bullet," Bennett said.

Johnny turned sharply and leered at his brother. "He surprised me." Johnny shook his head. "How the hell did I know he was hiding around back?"

"Point being," Ray slowly blinked and returned his eyes to Doug, "is we got a helluva big problem. Everyone's looking for you and Johnny, and that young woman we're keeping hold of. That old man and the girl probably gave a good description of both you two. A' course, I'm assuming they saw the plates on the truck, so even though we ditched it, they're gonna know you're in Ohio."

Doug was starting to get the sense that he was going to be sent on a mission. A mission that would likely end in the death of the old man, the little girl, and probably himself too, assuming Ray wanted all loose ends tied up nicely.

"You want us to take care of the witnesses, boss?" Johnny asked.

"It's only a matter of time before they find you, Doug. Plates are registered to you. If they're not already at your store, they will be soon. That's when the real problems will begin." Ray paused for a moment. "Doug, you gotta clear out your shop *today*. Anything and everything you got tying you to us—destroy it. Any surveillance video showing those boys paying you a visit, get rid of that too."

It seemed Ray hadn't worked out that Doug was the player. That he'd assumed maybe it had been CJ that was working for the opposition. He just needed to find a way to get the hell out of this restaurant and call in for support.

"Then what? You want us to go find the witnesses and take care of them too?" Johnny asked.

"I need to placate those boys and the only way to do that is to make them feel like we got this under control. And that means no witnesses, no loose ends. Doug will clean out his shop, then you two will take care of the loose ends. *Before* the feds show up at his door."

"What about the woman?" Doug asked.

"I'll trust you to handle that one, Dougie."

The doctor entered Carl's hospital room, nodding to

the captain as he walked by. "Hello Carl. How are you feeling? I see you've got company."

"Ready to get the hell out of here, doc. I need to see to the arrangements for my son."

"Yes, of course." The doctor turned solemn for a moment, casting his eyes toward the officers and finally toward Riley.

"Mr. Boyd, I'm afraid as this is a murder investigation, an autopsy will be required and any burial arrangements will have to be postponed until the case is closed," the captain said.

Carl released Riley's hand. "You're telling me that I can't bury my son?"

"I'm sorry, sir, but not until the investigation is over. Especially now that we've got the feds involved, they got their procedures too."

"Well, doesn't that just figure?"

Riley had an idea spark, but was concerned about how Carl would feel about it. She looked to Dillon, who remained silent, his arms folded in a protective stance. She could sense he believed this was all too much for her, maybe even for him and it was, but there was still something she could do to help.

"Would it be okay, Mr. Boyd, if maybe I could see your son?" The idea terrified her. She'd never seen a dead body before and certainly not one that was lying in a morgue. Her grandfather's funeral had been a closed casket and so was her grandmother's before, although it was a struggle to recall the details of that one.

It was then, she remembered, at her grandpa's funeral, that the first feelings came to her. She was young and it was difficult to understand what it meant at the time. The grief Jack felt, even a sense of the pain her granddad had felt. Riley remembered placing her hands on the shiny black casket and feeling a twinge of what she would eventually be able to identify as regret pass through her. It was his regret. And perhaps, by looking at CJ, Riley might sense something in him. It might only be subtle if it existed at all, but she believed there could be something there that might help and she had to try.

There was an understanding that appeared in Carl. As if he knew and that he believed she could help. "It won't be easy, Riley. He won't look like you remember."

Dillon raised an eyebrow. "Riley, I don't think that's a good idea."

"It's okay. It'll only be for a short while, just a few minutes. That's all; I promise." Riley's eyes pleaded. He was the only one in her family who truly understood her. Jack and Ellen were afraid for her or what she might become, but that would have to be considered another time. Right now, finding Melissa was all Riley wanted.

Dillon looked to the captain and Officer Ward. "Is it okay for her to see him? I mean, is there like a law or anything against it?"

"No. Not at all. If Mr. Boyd doesn't object, I certainly won't," the officer replied.

Captain Sinclair seemed unclear about the reasoning behind the request and when he looked at his officer, Ward tilted his head in a nod, indicating that he had the situation under control.

Riley believed that Officer Daniel Ward was now officially an ally and she needed all the allies she could get. A ten-year-old couldn't do much in this world without the help of adults, particularly those who held faith in her.

The doctor interrupted. "I'd like to be sure you're in good enough shape to get out of here this morning. I'm sure you'd like to go with them to see your son." He looked to the others. "If you could give us a few minutes, I'll check him out and he can get out of here."

"Of course. Thank you, doctor," the captain replied.

Riley took Dillon's hand once again and they followed the policeman outside while the doctor finished up with Mr. Boyd.

Captain Sinclair continued on down the hall, signaling Ward to follow him.

Riley watched as the two engaged in a private conversation. "He doesn't think I should see CJ," she said to Dillon.

"Why not?"

"Because he doesn't know or doesn't believe that I can help them." She watched the captain's lips move and his eyes shift toward her as he spoke to Ward. "He's confused and afraid for my safety and for Mr. Boyd's."

"Should I be afraid too?" Dillon knelt down to her level.

"I really think we can find her, Dillon. I think Mr. Boyd does too. Maybe we'll know if they're coming back too. Do you remember Grandpa's funeral?"

"Yeah."

"I remember touching his casket. It was smooth and shiny and I could see Dad's reflection in it because he was standing behind me," she said.

Dillon didn't speak, only arranged his feet to keep from falling backwards.

"When I touched it, I could sense just a little bit of Grandpa's presence. It wasn't much, but I could feel that he wished he hadn't done it; killed himself, I mean. It's just that he couldn't stand the pain anymore." Riley's eyes dampened with tears. "That was when it all started, I think, when Grandpa died."

"I didn't know you knew what happened to Grandpa," Dillon

started. "You think you'll be able to get a feel for something that Mr. Boyd's son left behind?"

"I think so. I'm not sure, but I think so." Riley looked at the two men still talking. "I just need Officer Ward to convince him that I'm not crazy."

"You're not crazy, Riley." Dillon gripped her shoulders gently.

"I know that, I guess, but thank you for saying it." She reached around his neck and hugged him.

She heard the footsteps of the uniformed men walking toward them. Dillon rose back to his full height and pulled Riley close to his hip.

"You can have five minutes, okay?" the captain said. "I'm trusting Officer Ward with this and he's given me his word not to let you stay any longer. It's not a place for a young girl, you understand?"

"Yes, sir. Thank you," Riley replied, squeezing Dillon's hand in triumph.

"Let's be sure Mr. Boyd is ready to go first." Officer Ward headed back down the hall where the doctor emerged. "Is he all right to be released?"

"Yes. I think so. He's getting dressed now. Please understand that he's just lost his son. He's injured and on pain medication and I'm sure you're aware of the other issues he faces."

"Yes. I'm aware."

"Good. I'm slowly getting him back on his meds so that he can stabilize. In the meantime, you'll be responsible for his well-being."

"Understood. Thank you, doctor."

[21]

Ellen finished making the peanut butter and jelly sandwich that Gracie insisted on having for lunch. It was a rare day when the girl would volunteer to eat anything besides her favorite noontime meal. Still, Ellen almost never refused her youngest daughter's wishes and acquiesced this time as well.

As she set the plate in front of her, along with a glass of milk, Ellen peeked through the foyer and into the family room where Jack remained, sulking, as he had since their return from the police station.

She hesitated to approach him. The time was nearing when the local bar would open and Ellen was confident he would be out the door, only to return sometime around dinner, working hard to disguise his drunkenness and slurred speech. She would do as always: ignore his behavior. It was easier that way.

Nearly five years it had been like this. It had grown worse over the past year, but this started for Jack a while ago. The plant closed, then Leo died only a year after Fiona. Ellen tried to understand and she did, for a while. It was a lot for anyone to endure. But after the first time he struck her, he became a different man to her. She saw him stripped down and bare, hardly a man at all. He'd fallen far from that pedestal she'd placed him on years before.

Jack laid off the kids mostly, except a few times when Dillon had pushed him too far. But he was a teenaged boy and that was to be expected. The back of his hand across her son's face wasn't, of course, but it'd happened nonetheless. That was the first time she'd considered leaving him. There had been plenty of times since then too, but she never could do it. Money, jobs. How the hell was she supposed to support her family? Maybe it was an excuse, maybe not. She'd seen plenty of women suffer worse than she did and maybe that was an excuse too. But now with this Riley situation, knowing for certain that she suffered the same affliction as Leo had; well, Ellen couldn't just stand back and watch Riley go through it alone. Maybe it was time to do something because Ellen wondered if the husband she'd known before would ever return.

Right now, her main concern was for Riley, whom she felt was safe for the moment with the kind policeman. She'd authorized Officer Ward to take Riley to see the man who'd been killed. It had been a difficult decision, one in which she did not share with or include Jack. But Ellen was confident it had been the correct one.

The situation would need to be addressed with her husband in time, however. Ellen was sure all that had happened with his family had been the catalyst for his change in behavior. *Another excuse.*

There were times when she blamed her father-in-law for doing what he'd done to his son and grandchildren. She'd believed it had been a selfish decision, one she could not understand. But there were things that Jack knew, things he never shared with her, about his father.

Now, as Jack remained silent, staring at a television flashing images that appeared to matter little, she considered a new approach. "I'll be right back, sweetie." She wiped her hands on the dishtowel, setting it back onto the counter, and moved to the family room.

"Are you hungry? Would you like me to make you some lunch, Jack?" She waited patiently for a moment and was concerned he'd not heard her, but then he turned his head in her direction.

"She's just like him, isn't she, Ellie?"

He appeared to be sincere, if not afraid for Riley. It was the first time Ellen had seen that look in his eyes in quite some time. She moved toward him, sitting on the small sofa angled opposite the couch. "I think she may be experiencing some of the same symptoms."

Jack snorted. "Symptoms? That's one word for it." He looked again to the television. "You know he knew Carl Boyd. They went to school together, before the war."

"No, I didn't know that."

"That was before your family moved here, I think. I only remember that because he mentioned to my mom one day, when I was younger, that he'd seen Carl in town and was surprised he was back. I didn't ask anything about it. What did I care? I didn't know the guy. Of course, I knew that he'd lost his wife and daughter in an accident when he was serving. Some people said that was why he left, moved to some other state or something. I don't know."

"So, were they friends?"

"I think so. Not real close, but I think they hung out once in a while. Honestly, I never asked about the guy." Jack looked at Ellen again. "I wish I had now."

"I can't imagine what it must be like for him. All the loss he's suffered and now this? He's got no one left," Ellen said.

"And he's bat-shit crazy. That's why I don't want Riley around him. He's unstable, Ellen. The man takes anti-psychotics."

"But they have a bond," she began. "I don't understand it, but maybe it's not something we're supposed to understand. Jack, what if she can help find that kidnapped woman? What if she can help find the men who killed his son?"

"Christ, Ellen." He shook his head. "What if she turns out just like Dad? He killed himself because of whatever it was he sensed or could see in people. He sat in our bathroom and put a gun in his mouth because he couldn't bear to feel Mom's pain anymore. She was already gone and he could still feel it."

His candor was something she hadn't seen in him in a very long time. He was overwhelmed, so much so that his eyes welled with tears, but didn't spill. He'd wiped them away before that happened.

Jack stood up from the sofa. "I gotta get out of here."

Ellen lowered her head, disappointed that he'd closed himself off once again and was about to bury his feelings inside a bottle.

He stood next to her and placed a hand on her shoulder. "I'm sorry I'm not the man you married. I don't know who I am anymore. I can't even protect my own family." Jack continued toward the foyer.

Ellen flinched at the sound of the door closing. A moment later, the engine of the truck roared and the sound faded as he drove off into the distance.

THE DOUBLE DOORS STOOD CLOSED AS THEY APPROACHED THE small room that housed CJ Boyd. Officer Ward pressed the button and they began to swing open. Dillon prodded Riley behind him as if protecting her from something neither understood.

The doctor followed them inside and signed a sheet of paper that lay on an unattended desk. "He's in number three." The man walked toward the steel cabinet and pulled the lever open, sliding the body out into view.

Carl looked to the doctor. "May I?" He moved toward his son, looking at the man as if it had been the first time he'd ever seen a lifeless body. Of course it wasn't. He'd seen a great deal during his tenure in the war, but this was his son. This was his only son, lying on a table, grey and motionless.

The trauma proved to be too much and Carl grew disoriented. The others in the room became misshapen. Except for Riley. In that moment, Carl's mind jerked him back to that dreaded place.

"Medic! Medic! I need help over here!" The thick greenery obscured his vision and Carl had difficulty seeing more than a few feet in front of him. The rancid, smoky air from the landmine that had just detonated hung low, further obstructing the world around him.

This part of the jungle was thick with landmines, but the intelligence he'd received indicated safe passage so long as they didn't veer off the path. But an injured woman caught his eye. Her leg had been cut severely and she was just off to the left about ten yards. PFC Hudson began to move toward her to offer assistance.

Carl yelled at him to get back in line, but it was too late. He'd stepped on the trigger and as the man looked to Carl, both knew exactly what the sound was.

The blast ripped the soldier apart. His right leg was severed from his body and what remained was a shredded, bloody mass with a head attached. Carl raised his hand. "No!" he yelled to his men behind him. It was too risky for any of them to help. There was no way of knowing if other mines were in the vicinity.

Carl watched as the injured woman in the distance stood on her feet and trailed off into the jungle. It had been a trap.

A girl appeared in front of him, a young girl he instantly recognized. "Riley? What are you doing here? You'll be hurt. Go back."

"Come with me, Mr. Boyd. This isn't happening. It's only in your head." Riley reached out to take his hand.

"Riley!" Dillon turned in time to see her crumple to the ground.

Both she and Carl seemed to lose consciousness simultaneously, although the doctor managed to take hold of Carl before his knees gave out from beneath him.

Dillon placed his hand behind his sister's head. "Riley? Riley, are you okay?"

Her eyes began to blink as she regained awareness. "Mr. Boyd? Is he okay?"

There was no denying the notion that these two people, an old man and a little girl, shared a unique bond. It was that moment that triggered an undeniable understanding in the others that were witness.

"I can't explain it any more than I could explain how to build a computer, but it's there. You see it now?" Ward pleaded to the captain.

Sinclair looked to the doctor, still cradling Carl Boyd, who had begun to rouse again. "I—yes. I see it."

Riley, with Dillon's help, took to her feet again. "I have to see him." She continued to walk on shaky legs toward the table. More determined than ever, it was as though Riley felt justified by the experience that a strength was present and this would be the only chance she'd have to connect with CJ.

"Mr. Boyd, are you okay?" She approached him as he stood on his own, next to CJ.

He stroked her hair, leaning over to kiss the top of her head. Carl's voice wavered. "I don't know if I'm going crazy, or if we both are."

The corners of Riley's mouth lifted slightly. She turned to see the body that belonged to CJ Boyd.

Dillon moved in closer to her and she could sense the protection he felt for her. "I'm okay. Just give me a second." She turned her eyes to Carl. "Is it okay if I touch him?"

He nodded.

CJ's chilled body had been unexpected. Her hand recoiled at the touch, but only for a moment. "He's so cold."

The doctor stepped toward them. "He's been in here for a few hours and these are refrigerated."

Riley returned her small hand to his forearm, which lay next to his side. Flickers of arbitrary images appeared in her mind, but their meaning was lost. With narrowed eyes, she waited, hoping something recognizable would surface.

A brief, but discernable sight emerged and Riley quickly reddened. It had been CJ lying in bed with Melissa, but it soon passed and she was thankful. More images, this time of people she came to recognize. Her demeanor shifted and a measurable excitement grew.

A barn, or a building that resembled one, came to the forefront. Inside were several men sitting at round tables, and there was a leader. A large, red-faced man with white hair. Anxiety soon passed through her. CJ had been afraid of the men, of what and who they were. He seemed to know immediately that they were not good people. But he stayed, as if compelled to or dreading backlash.

She was seeing through his eyes, only the background was blurred, but Riley could make out certain things. The guns lined up along the back wall, the giant flag hanging between the rafters.

Riley pulled away quickly when the images turned red. It was the moment CJ had been shot. A white-hot light quickly burned through her and now all she could see was red and, for a brief moment, Johnny Denton's face. CJ had seen the stunned look on him as he fired the weapon.

Nothing more appeared and the images were gone. Riley released her hand and turned to Carl. "He showed me a barn. I think she's there, and I know those men are coming back. The man with the white hair told them to."

"Did you see where this barn was?" Officer Ward approached.

"No. It was some place far away and off by itself. I couldn't see anything around it. I think Melissa is there and that she's still alive."

"We know the truck was registered to the undercover ATF agent," Ward began. "Ohio plates, and we know approximately where he was located. We need to contact his office and let them know that we have at least some sort of description of where she might be. I don't know how hard it'd be to get a satellite map of the area. How many secluded barns could there be, especially near the area their man was located?"

"But we have to assume that once the agent has made contact, he'll be able to give them the exact location. He must know where they're keeping her," Captain Sinclair replied.

Ward considered the idea. "The agent could be in trouble. His cover could be blown and, if it is, my guess is, if he's been made, they won't give him a chance to call anyone."

At that moment, Doug had two choices. Make contact with his office and get pulled out, or see this through to finish building his case against Raymond McAllister. So far, he had him on trafficking stolen weapons, but if he could get him on murder and kidnapping, well, the man would go away for life and the chances were better than fair a traffics charge against the Columbus faction would follow suit.

It was more than a risky proposition. If he had any sense at all, the moment Ray gave him the okay to leave this shit hole restaurant, he'd get home to retrieve his cell and call for backup. But he believed Ray hadn't been completely forthcoming and there was a distinct possibility the man didn't fully trust Doug. He seemed to be talking out of both sides of his mouth. Ray might have Doug followed and, if that happened, any trip to a place besides his shop would be noted with suspicion.

"If there's nothing else, then I probably should get to the shop and take care of business," Doug said.

"Of course. Johnny, why don't you help Doug out and keep me informed of the progress. Doug, I'd like you to get back to the barn when you're finished and be sure our little friend is doing all right. I'll be in touch with you later today with further instructions. I have some difficult decisions to make and it'll take some time."

Ray hoisted himself up and shifted out of the booth. His face reddened further at the challenging measure. The man probably had a dangerously high cholesterol count along with his oversized frame. If he had a heart attack right now, Doug's problems would be solved.

But no such luck and now it was determined that Doug would be accompanied. It seemed he was down to only one choice. Ray made his way to the exit without further words, leaving the Denton brothers hovering over Doug like vultures.

"We'd better get a move on," Doug said, waiting for Bennett to slide out so he could follow.

The three eventually stepped outside into the afternoon sun, but on the horizon, dark clouds appeared.

"Looks like we might get some rain," Doug said, wanting to lift the awkward silence.

"Yeah, maybe." Johnny continued toward his car and opened the driver's side door. "Get in. We need to get to the hardware store now."

It seemed Doug would have to see this through after all.

[22]

One final glimpse of his son, and CJ was returned to the metal box. Carl said nothing, only patted Riley on the shoulder and carried on toward the exit.

Dillon placed his arm around Riley and walked her back into the corridor. "Come on. We'd better get home now."

They continued through to the front of the hospital and waited for the others. Riley knew Dillon had no idea what would come next. She was beginning to feel lost; in over her head and wanted to crawl under the covers and hide until this was over.

She wished this had never happened to her. She prayed to be normal again and see in others the same things everyone else did. The façade that human beings showed one another was far better than knowing their true feelings. Riley just didn't want to know anymore.

Officer Ward headed toward the two. "Are you sure you're

okay, Riley? The doctor thought maybe you should get checked out before you go home. You did faint, even if only for a minute."

"I'm okay, I promise. I just want to go home."

"You might not realize it, Riley, but you did help. You and Mr. Boyd share a connection I couldn't possibly explain, but wherever it stems from, it means something. And what you discovered means something too. You understand?"

"I guess so. What are we going to do now?"

"*We* aren't going to do anything. You're going home with your brother to get some rest and I'll be working with the ATF. Hopefully, they've heard from their man and we can find out where he is. If we do, this will all go away, Riley. You and Mr. Boyd will be just fine. I'm going to keep the patrolman in your area and Mr. Boyd will be safe too."

"I hope you're right, sir." Riley looked to Dillon. "I want to say goodbye to Mr. Boyd first, okay?"

He nodded.

Carl appeared weak and feeble. His arm was in a sling and he lumbered his way to the lobby, a forced smile on his face. "Thank you for what you did just now, Riley. My boy would have wanted to help in any way he could and you allowed him to do that. I'm just sorry you had to deal with my episode too. You know, you're a very special little girl." He rested his good hand on her shoulder and smiled. "We'll be okay. These good men will make sure of that. You should go on home and rest, knowing you've done everything you could."

"Okay, Mr. Boyd."

Johnny and Bennett strolled around the hardware store while Doug sat in his office, pretending to purge the files from his computer. He thought for a moment if he might get away with using his store phone to make the call. But if Ray suspected him and, by the hangers-on outside, Doug believed he did, the phone could be tapped. Other opportunities would likely present themselves during the course of the next twenty-four hours and so risking a call from here might not be the right course of action. The Denton brothers weren't the smartest in the bunch, but in the off-chance Ray gave them orders to keep a tight leash on Doug, well, he'd have to find another way.

The flash drive containing the blueprints to the warehouse was in the pencil drawer beneath the desk. He inserted it and waited for the files to load. It occurred to him that CJ had been handed this same flash drive and, for a moment, Doug wondered, had the man taken an opportunity to view these files? Was it possible Ray had installed a keylogger or something similar to track everything that was happening on the computer?

Since those boys from up north came into town, Doug had noticed a change in Ray. He had turned cautious, verging on the extreme. At first, he believed this to be a good thing—for his case anyway. The more paranoid Ray became, the easier it would be for him to build on it, but now he thought that might just backfire on him. If Ray believed CJ had taken a look at those prints, the whole situation could have been one big setup. Let CJ take the fall, which was exactly what happened.

Doug removed the drive and shoved it into his pocket. The idea that he could perhaps send an email to the ASAC, letting him know what was happening, vanished in an instant. He had to believe Ray had gone over the edge with paranoia. After becoming

Ray's right hand man and spending the better part of year with him, Doug knew not to underestimate the man, especially if that man thought he had been deceived.

"I think that's everything." Doug emerged from the small office to find the Denton brothers playing with the staple guns. He often wondered how it was that those two idiots managed their way into this little club and why CJ would have ever been friends with them.

Doug recalled the day they'd brought CJ into the store and asked that he discuss the possibility of a job. The store was already taking time from the case he was building and so the help was needed. Now he regretted ever meeting the man. It would be something for which Doug would atone for down the road, no doubt.

"You two ready to get out of here or would you rather keep shooting yourselves in the legs with staple guns?" Doug pulled his keys from his pocket, fumbling with them in his hands.

"Yeah, all right. Put the gun down, dipshit," Johnny said to his brother. "We need to get back to our guest anyway."

Doug stood at the door, waiting for the boys to move along.

"You sure you got everything?" Bennett asked.

"Yeah. I got it all." Doug pushed the door open and let the brothers outside first. The wind nearly ripped the door handle from his hands. "Holy shit! Where'd this wind come from?"

The skies were darker now and it was approaching late afternoon. Doug grew concerned by the threatening weather and hoped they wouldn't have to endure a heavy storm. He would be meeting up with Ray again soon for an update, further delaying his ability to reach out for help. He figured that, by the end of the day, both he and Johnny would be heading back to Owensville to pay the old man a visit. Doug knew one thing for sure. He wouldn't let anyone else die on his watch. Not the old man and certainly not the little blonde girl. Doug locked up the store.

The men made their way back to Johnny's car and stepped inside, shaking away the leaves and misplaced hairs from the strong winds.

"Jesus! You'd think a tornado was coming," Bennett said.

"Ray's gonna meet us back at the barn in an hour. We'd better get back there. It'll take forty minutes and we need to check on our guest," Doug replied.

THE POOR WEATHER CONDITIONS PERSISTED, AS RAIN HAD fallen and made the paved roads slippery and the dirt roads muddy. The winds blew through the trees with enough force to rip the young leaves that had begun to form off of the mostly bare branches.

Doug had grown anxious, not only a result of the ominous weather, but by the predicament in which he'd found himself. They were dangerously close to being late for their appointment with the big man and the more he considered the possibility that Ray had, in fact, turned on him, the more necessary an exit strategy became.

"Finally!" Johnny turned into the gravel drive that offered little grip for his sorely balding tires. "Shit. Looks like Ray is already here." He pulled into the spot next to Ray and the other man who'd been tasked with keeping an eye on the hostage.

"Don't worry about it. He can see the weather's turned to shit. Let's just get inside." Doug stepped outside and pulled his light jacket across his body, but it didn't do much to keep him warm. He had enough meat on his bones, but not so much as to offer the kind of protection those extra layers offered a man like Ray McAllister.

Doug had managed to concoct a plan in the event things headed south and wouldn't hesitate to implement it should the need arise. His safety and the safety of the hostage were his top priorities. If he could make it out of here alive in the next few hours, he believed, with the information on the flash drive, the shooting of CJ Boyd, and kidnapping of Melissa Simmons, Doug had a case, tightly sealed, against Ray McAllister, the Denton brothers, and a few of the men from the northern territory. He just needed the chance to make contact with his people.

"I wondered when the hell y'all would get here." Ray headed toward them.

Doug knew where they kept the guns. Not the ones on display against the back wall, but the ones they traded. A large cache of them were stored in a room at the back of the building. It had been added on in recent months and was well secured. He was the only other person who knew the combination to enter, apart from Ray.

Of course, if he needed to get there in a hurry, that might pose a problem, one he hadn't yet figured out and hoped not to have to. "Weather out there has turned to shit. Got delayed on the wet and muddy roads heading out." Doug approached Ray and shook hands with him. "How's she doing?" He cast his eyes upwards to the loft.

"Fine. I don't think she's knows shit. By the sounds of it, she was just his fuck buddy and nothing more. Nice piece of ass, though. Young too. CJ did all right for himself. Still wish things hadn't gone the way they did, though. It wasn't how I wanted it, Dougie. You gotta know that."

Doug eyed the man's body language; feet, shoulder-length apart, arms hanging by his side. By all accounts, he was behaving just as he always had, with one exception. The position of his feet. His right foot was about six inches behind his left, as if he was ready to sprint at a moment's notice, not that he believed the man could sprint anywhere. But the fact remained that he was about to bolt, or he was compensating for his balance, like maybe he was carrying a weapon.

No guns were allowed on any person when they entered the building. But as Doug examined him, the shifting of Ray's balance from one leg to the other, he considered the possibility that he was packing and the weight of the .40 caliber gun added just enough to offset his left from his right.

Doug was used to carrying weapons and was trained as such, but Ray didn't often carry, at least not in the time Doug had been acquainted with him. The implications of this recent development was not sitting well.

"So what are your plans, then?" Doug asked, already knowing the answer.

"Why don't you and I have a seat over here?" Ray placed his arm over Doug's shoulder and led him to one of the tables.

Doug glanced at the others, the Denton boys and Steve Nelson, the man who was usually assigned to do grunt work. None appeared to be placing themselves in such a way as to cause him concern. It seemed they knew nothing of Ray's plans. On the other hand, neither did Doug.

"We got a problem here, Dougie, that I think you might already be aware of." Ray pulled the chair out and lowered onto it.

"I'd say so, Ray. What's the plan?" Doug followed Ray's lead.

"Like I said earlier, I don't think that girl up there knows anything, but after what's happened, I think we'd be up shit creek if we thought we could just let her go and all would be hunky-dory."

"Ray, let me talk to her. She's from around here and she's not stupid. I think I can convince her to keep her mouth shut. Maybe even toss a little cash her way to get herself out of town. The last thing we need is another death on our hands. Those other boys won't hesitate to move in on us if they think we're gonna have the law breathing down our necks. We'll lose everything, Ray."

"Maybe you're right. I've been listening to them badmouth our operation for too long, insisting we wouldn't be in this situation if we'd vetted our men better. I don't need to give them cause to come in here and take over what we've built. Follow me." He hiked up his large, ill-fitting jeans and walked toward the back of the building.

Doug followed closely behind. Ray's comment about his vetting process pressed hard in his mind. He turned to see if anyone might be watching where they were headed, but it seemed no one was paying any attention.

They reached the far end of the building, near the storage area. Ray pressed the code on the keypad and the heavy door clicked open. He proceeded to walk inside and motioned for Doug to follow.

"Close the door."

The voice in Doug's head told him this was bad. He was alone inside a room where they were the only two people who could access it. "What is it?" he asked as casually as he could muster, although the adrenaline was already pumping fast and hard through his body.

"You know, I shoulda dug a little deeper where you were

concerned. But you know, I wanted to trust you. You seemed like a good man. A hard-working man with a hardware store, a house. No family, though. I suppose that raised a red flag for me, but I just pushed it aside. Ignoring the better part of me."

Doug tilted his head as if unsure of where the conversation was headed and why, but exposing no fear in his eyes. "What's this about, Ray? Come on now. We got shit to take care of."

"I know that. And that's what I'm doing now. Taking care of shit I shoulda taken care of a long time ago."

"Ray?"

"I started getting concerned a while ago. Just before ol' CJ came into the picture, but you know, I didn't want to believe it. I'd heard some rumblings that you would off and disappear right after some of our meetings. Like you was in some kind of hurry or something. Of course, I didn't think much of it at first. But then, you hired CJ. He was a good man, I know that now. And I feel damn sorry for what happened to him. Because, as it seems to have turned out, he wasn't the one I shoulda been worrying about. You were." Ray pulled a gun from the back of his belt and raised it to Doug's forehead.

"Now, you gonna tell me how you came to buy a house that was never even on the market for sale? Seems a lot of cash to come up with to offer that old woman. Cash a man like you shouldn't have had."

"What? First of all, I got that money after my dad died. I had to sell his house and used the money to buy mine. So I'm not sure where you're getting your information." Doug searched his mind. Someone had given him up, but who the hell could possibly know? Doug began to consider the possibility that one of those sons of bitches from Columbus had someone in ATF. Someone who was feeding him information.

"You know I got people too, Dougie. And they tell me that Doug Newman doesn't exist. At least, not before about ten years ago. So, tell me. Who the fuck are you?"

Doug was a highly trained agent. A quick thinker. He'd been undercover several times before, but this was the first time he found himself laboring to find a way out. Raymond McAllister was pointing a gun at his head, standing a few feet from him. The door behind him was shut, locked automatically by a keypad. If he was going to get out of there alive, he'd better find a way to convince the man before him to lower his gun.

"You know who I am, Ray," Doug said. "I've been by your side for the past year. Have I ever done anything to make you think I was being less than trustworthy?" Doug studied the man's eyes, searching for signs that he might think to reconsider the notion that Doug was the traitor in the group. "You're listening to someone with an agenda, Ray. I don't know what they told you, but I've been nothing but loyal." He paused for a moment. "You need me to take care of the loose ends? I can do that." His pulse remained elevated, but his body stood unmoved. Doug waited, his eyes locked onto Ray's, his mouth growing dry, but he would not falter, *could not* falter.

The gun began to lower, but Doug still held his gaze. Ray's arm slowly returned to his side as the safety was put back in place. The two were silent for a moment longer, although Doug believed the time to have stopped completely.

"All right," Ray began. "You and me, tonight. We're going to take care of our little problem in Owensville. Johnny can see to the girl upstairs."

In that moment, Doug knew his life would be spared, but for how long he didn't know. For now, his concern was for the woman. Leaving her in Johnny's hands would most certainly mean her demise. "Let me take care of her too." Doug held up a hand as if volunteering to further prove his loyalty. "You leave it up to him and we'll have a much bigger mess on our hands, I can promise you that."

"Maybe you're right." Ray moved toward the door again. "You've got an hour. Then we're going back to Owensville. I'll have the brothers keep an eye out on the hardware store and your house. If they see the feds coming, they'll tell us. Don't fuck around, Dougie. We don't have much time."

[23]

The **fact that** Riley had been expected to sit at the dinner table and put food in her mouth was so absurdly out of place that she could do nothing more than stare at it as though the concept of eating was completely foreign. Yet another example of Ellen's attempt to bring normalcy to her family when they were clearly far removed from any such notion, although Riley supposed that to know how to behave under these circumstances was beyond the reach of any of them.

It wasn't long into their meal when the sound of keys jingling in the lock of the front door signaled a familiar and unmistakable event. Jack was home.

The fierce winds endeavored to rip the door from Jack's unsteady hands as the gust blew through the foyer. A storm was brewing on the horizon. Pushing the door closed, he walked inside to the lingering aroma of roasted chicken.

Jack's erratic approach was confirmation of where he'd spent the majority of his day. Riley could smell the booze before he made it to the kitchen. Any acknowledgement of his arrival on the part of her brother was non-existent. But Gracie, in her blissful ignorance, continued eating and Ellen remained indifferent.

Disillusioned yet again, Riley felt a growing sense of frustration toward her father. After all that she had been through, Jack behaved as always – selfish. So many times, she had tried to empathize with him. She wanted to excuse his behavior, just like Ellen. Riley recognized that, in his heart, he hadn't wanted this, and yet he did nothing to change who he had become. How could he do this to her? She felt so lost, so burdened by this alleged gift that had been passed down to her. Riley wanted her father back and yet, day after day, the possibly seemed to slip further away.

"Am I late for dinner?" Jack's speech was so slurred that it was almost indiscernible.

"There's a plate in the oven for you," Ellen replied, her eyes remaining fixed on her plate.

Riley was sure that her grandfather must be watching over them, and especially Jack. It seemed like a miracle that he made it home without harm to himself, or worse, to others.

She looked at Dillon. His head hung low as he stared at a plate of food that appeared to hold no interest for him. It was her brother who had been there for her today, not Jack. Heat continued to rise in her belly.

A flash of lightning illuminated the kitchen and the clap of thunder that followed was booming and close at hand. Riley flinched at the noise and it distracted her from her thoughts, but only for a moment.

Jack stood at the oven and opened its door to claim his dinner. He moved carefully with the warmed plate and set it down on the table. The chair screeched as he pulled it across the yellow linoleum and carefully sat down as though he might tumble to the floor. Riley watched her father behave as if nothing had happened. As if she hadn't seen a dead body today, or witnessed a man shooting at people, only narrowly escaping herself. The heat within was unrelenting, becoming almost painful in her chest.

That sickening feeling twirled in her stomach too and she tried to keep it at bay with a gulp of water. It was the sickness he brought home. There was no way to regulate her own feelings with what she was experiencing from Jack. The loss of control was overpowering. "Stop!" Riley screamed, her hands pressed hard on her temples to stop the dizziness.

"What's wrong?" Dillon pushed up from the table and rushed to her side.

"I'm sorry Grandpa killed himself!" she shouted. "I'm sorry you don't have a good job any more. But it's no one else's fault. Just yours, Dad. It's yours!" She'd already spent too much of her childhood suffering through other people's pain, feeling their anger and hurt. Now she needed her father more than anything, and his solution was to abandon her and refuse to acknowledge what was happening to himself and his family.

"I can't be around you any more, any of you. There are people coming who want to hurt me because I saw what they did, because this stupid thing inside me knew they were coming in the first place." She turned to Jack. "I just wanted you to understand, but you think I'm a freak just like Grandpa. That's why you get drunk. You can't handle what I am and so you take it out on Mom and Dillon." Her face was flushed and she gasped for breath. "I hate you!" Riley stormed into the foyer and snatched her coat off the hook.

"Where are you going?" Ellen demanded. "Riley, get back here!" She rose to her feet.

Dillon turned to his parents. "You did this. You *both* did this."

"Don't go!" Gracie shouted with tears already streaming. "Don't leave, Riley!"

"You're not going anywhere alone. I'm coming with you." Dillon grabbed his coat. He pulled the door open to the falling rain. Riley drew the hood of her jacket over her head and stepped across the threshold into the downpour. Dillon was only steps behind her.

Doug knew damn well there was no chance Ray was going to let the woman go. He'd instructed her to be "taken care of," which, in Ray's eyes, meant to make her disappear.

He had an hour and then Ray was picking him up to head out to Owensville. Johnny had been instructed to stay with him. This left the distinct impression that Ray might just be playing along to see if Doug would do what needed to be done, final proof as to whether or not he was a loyal partner. This new obstacle would be a problem for Doug. His intention was to let Melissa go and tell her that he was undercover and that she could go to a safe house until this was all over. He knew exactly where to send her, but he couldn't do that with Johnny Denton hanging around.

"You gonna do this or puss out?" Johnny asked.

"I thought you and your brother were supposed to keep an eye out on the shop? Let us know if the feds were coming?"

"Just as soon as you and Ray head off back to Owensville, me and Bennett are heading over there. My instructions were to make sure you dealt with that girl upstairs. Now, you gonna do as Ray says, or do I have to put a call in to let him know you can't handle it?"

Doug moved toward the thin, shorter man. He had a good four inches and thirty pounds on him. No one else was inside the barn, save for the girl. He could hear the storm passing overhead with claps of thunder growing distant, although the rain still pelted hard against the barn's corrugated metal roof.

"Look, Johnny. I don't need you babysitting me, okay? If you wanna handle the situation up there, then, by all means, be my guest. But if not, then back the fuck off and let me do what I need to do. You're the one who put us in this position and I'm the one who Ray has trusted to get us out of it."

"Who the fuck do you think you are, Doug?" Johnny stepped back, clenching his hands into fists.

He wanted to rile him up and he was banking on Johnny's short fuse to blow.

"You got a problem with me? Maybe we should take this outside?"

Johnny snarled his lips and bent down, ready to bum rush him, but Doug was prepared.

He reeled back at the force of the man barreling against him. Eventually, he found his balance and braced his back leg against Johnny's weight. Doug thrust his arm out, knocking Johnny to the ground. The man lay flat on his back and Doug quickly straddled him and knelt down, each knee holding down his arms.

"You shoulda fucking got in the truck, Johnny. All this shit is on you, man." Doug pulled his right arm back, curling his hand into a tight fist. And, like a hammer, it dropped right onto the man's cheek. Blood spewed from his mouth and a tooth dislodged, bouncing to the ground.

Johnny had been knocked out cold. Doug didn't have long before he would come to again and so he worked fast. Getting back to his feet, he stepped behind the unconscious man and dragged him by the arms toward the back room, where the guns were kept.

Melissa must have heard what was happening and began to shout. "Help! Help!"

Doug pressed on, approaching the only room that would contain the man long enough. He entered the number on the keypad. The door opened and he pulled Johnny inside. The possibility existed that Johnny would be able to shoot his way out of the room, but Doug would have enough time to untie Melissa and get her into the car before that happened. He figured he had about fifteen, maybe twenty minutes before Johnny roused and figured out what was happening. He would only need to load one of the guns and shoot the lock. But it was a heavy door with a heavy bolt and even that would take some time to get through.

Doug pulled the door closed and ensured that it re-latched. He rushed up the stairs to the loft. Melissa wasn't in good shape. She looked in desperate need of both sleep and food. It had been thirty-six hours that they'd kept her up there with little nourishment and only moving to get her to the bathroom when she needed it.

"Come on. We're getting you out of here. You'll be safe with me." Doug retrieved a pocketknife and began cutting away at the plastic ties around her wrists and ankles. "I'm with the ATF and once we get out of here, I'll call for help and get you someplace safe. You understand?"

She nodded.

Doug continued to work fast. The ties broke under the knife's blade and Melissa tried to push up from the ground, but she was weak. He took her by the arm and pulled her up with ease – her slight frame could have only totaled to a buck five at best. "We gotta go. Can you walk?"

"Yes, I think so." Melissa rubbed her knees and shook her legs. "I can, yes."

He took the lead back down the steps to the ground floor of the barn and took a quick glance back in the direction of the room. All was still. Johnny must have still been out.

As he began to look on toward the exit, a sudden and defeating thought occurred to him. "Damn it!" Doug's face flushed with anger at his own careless actions. "Stay here. I have to get the keys."

He headed back toward the room to retrieve the car keys from Johnny's pocket. It was the one thing he'd completely forgotten about. The number was again entered into the keypad and the door clicked open. Doug pushed back slowly, carefully. He soon spotted the unconscious man's foot and it remained still. Feeling a little more sure of himself, Doug continued on in attempt to get the keys and get the hell out of there as quickly as he could. Time was running out.

The full length of Johnny's body came into view and when Doug caught sight of the man's face, he closed his eyes, knowing what was coming.

The gun fired from Johnny's hand while he lay on the ground. The sound echoed inside Doug's ears and he waited for the moment it would pierce his body. It took a millisecond and Doug was on the ground. Blood poured from the near point-blank shot to his forehead.

Melissa, hearing the gunfire, covered her mouth as an irrepressible shriek escaped. She had only two choices: run out of the barn and get as far away as she could before he killed her, or stay there and he would likely put a bullet in her the same as he did the undercover ATF man who was trying to help.

It wasn't much of a choice and so Melissa took to a sprint through the main door. She had only the clothes on her back. No identification, no money, but she ran as fast as her legs would take her down the muddy and slick drive and out onto the main road. Cover would be critical and there was plenty of it on either side. But she needed distance and the open road offered that better than the rugged terrain of the woods with rain-soaked soil that would be difficult to traverse.

She had but a moment to decide and her decision was to keep on the main road. For the first time in her life, Melissa was grateful to have been an excellent track and field athlete in high school and she was pleased that some of her abilities remained intact. Her stride returned, the muscle memory instantly recalled. If only she'd been wearing better shoes. Ballerina flats offered little support or traction on the wet asphalt. Still, she sped along, praying for as much distance as possible before Johnny Denton roared along in his beat-up Gran Torino. He'd already shot CJ and now Doug. She doubted, if he did catch up to her, that he'd even bother to pull over and run after her. He'd just point his gun through the passenger window and fire. She'd go down fast.

The idea propelled her to an even quicker pace. Several minutes had passed; ten, maybe fifteen. It was hard to tell. Her world was a blur as the rain assaulted her and she was flying down the highway for her life at a break-neck speed.

It was only when a distant humming reached her ears did

Melissa's senses sharpen. She wiped the water from her eyes and listened carefully to the sound of tires on the road and an engine purring. It was unmistakable. But it sounded nothing like the blown out muffler of Johnny Denton's car. This sound was coming from a small car, probably foreign, with its quiet four-cylinder engine droning along the highway.

Her lungs ached for breath and Melissa hesitated to turn and confirm the approaching vehicle, fearing it might slow her down a pace or two. She could afford neither, but the possibility that someone other than those who'd held her captive might offer assistance, trumped her fears.

Without slowing, her head turned to the pavement she'd already trod. Out of the corner of her eye, Melissa saw a car – a Toyota, to be exact. It wasn't a Gran Torino. She began to slow her pace, turning on her heels and jogging backwards. Her thin arms waved in the air and anyone who could see her face would know the panic it held and that she was in desperate need of help.

Melissa allowed herself a brief smile at the sight of the driver behind the wheel. An older woman, graying, maybe in her fifties or later. Tears fell down her cheeks as the car slowed, its wheels turning in her direction along the side of the road.

"Are you okay, miss?" the woman asked.

"No." With no breath and her adrenaline exhausted, it was the only word she could muster.

"Get in. You're definitely not okay."

Melissa pulled the door open and stepped inside, resting on the grey velour fabric of the passenger seat, her hair and clothes dripping. "Thank you."

The woman pulled back onto the road and continued.

Melissa drew a breath. "Can you take me to the police?"

An abandoned house three blocks away. That was where Dillon took her. The rain was coming down hard. Inside the old house, the winds howled through, thanks to the several broken windows that had been boarded up at one time, but no longer.

"It's okay. We'll be safe here," Dillon said. "For a while." He pulled his cell phone from his pocket and turned on its light, shining it around the area where they now stood. He'd noticed several missed calls from home, but ignored them. The place had been one of the several hangouts for the local high schoolers, sometimes including Dillon. He knew there was a mattress and a couple of blankets in one of the rooms. It had been used more than a few times by other teenagers and it would offer warmth in the otherwise freezing house.

No electricity, no water, and certainly no heat. Riley began to wonder if she'd made the right decision. But her feelings had grown strong; she'd been infuriated by her father's actions. Her gift had become so powerful in recent days, Riley couldn't be sure of the potential it held and knew that in order for her family to stay safe from her and the bad men that were coming, it was the only solution.. And now she'd dragged Dillon into it.

"You should go home. You're not safe here with me." Riley folded her arms around her body, but it didn't keep her warm.

"Upstairs. There's some blankets and a place to sit. Come on." Dillon seemed to ignore her words; instead, he ushered Riley up the stairs in front of him, aiming the light of his phone for illumination.

She stepped into the narrow corridor as Dillon pointed her in the direction of the room that would offer some comfort.

The darkness retreated only a little as he directed the light source inside the small room, exposing the mattress and blankets lying on the floor. "Over there. Go sit down and wrap the blanket around you."

Dillon moved toward the cracked window, its integrity in question. He peered through to the left, then right. "Doesn't look like this storm's gonna stop any time soon. We'll probably be here for the night." He turned back toward her. "But we'll be safe. I promise."

"I'm not so sure, Dillon."

[24]

Maybe the people in this town were right to believe Carl Boyd was crazy. The idea was not lost on him as he sat alone in his trailer. What the hell did he care anymore? His son was dead. The guilt he felt for the child who had tried to help him and had seen far more than a ten-year-old ever should weighed just as heavy.

Carl was baffled by Riley Thompson and her gift of acuity. To be eyewitness to what others had experienced seemed a terrible burden and one he would not wish on his worst enemy. What he regretted most now, however, was his inability to do anything to find his son's killers. The police were hamstrung, the FBI could do nothing, and it seemed red tape was preventing any of them from capturing the sons of bitches.

If they all believed him to be crazy, then so be it, but he couldn't just sit here and do nothing. He was going to get out of this damn trailer, no matter if he was injured. No matter if a storm was approaching. Sitting there and doing nothing wasn't going to help Riley or find justice for his son.

The police – that Officer Ward and Captain Sinclair – assured them they would be safe, but Riley knew better. The patrols they'd promised had slowed when the rains came and Carl was beginning to feel as though it was just him and Riley, unlikely partners in an extraordinary situation.

It was difficult to pinpoint the exact time of day without checking the clock on his wall. The darkened skies alluded to a much later hour, although he confirmed it to be approaching six p.m. The deafening clap of thunder ripped Carl from his ambitious thoughts of vigilantism. But what happened after that shifted his thoughts entirely.

Hail. Nickel-sized hail was coming down, slamming against the trailer's aluminum frame. Carl pushed off the chair with his good arm and moved toward the kitchen window that offered a better view of the main road. "Son of a bitch." He had lived in Indiana long enough to know the signs. It may have only been early spring, but tornadoes came when they wanted to. And one was coming tonight.

The woman kept her eyes on the road and her hands in the ten and two positions. She did not look at nor did she begin to question Melissa. It seemed she was waiting for her to offer up in what kind of trouble she'd found herself.

After catching her breath and attempting to make sense out of what had happened, Melissa was ready to speak. "Thank you so much for stopping." She inhaled deeply, preparing to explain why there was a drenched and frightened woman in the passenger seat of this stranger's car. "I was being held captive. Kidnapped. And I escaped. They would've caught up to me if you hadn't shown up." Melissa turned to the woman. "You saved my life and I don't even know your name."

"Janet Hulstead." The small woman with the slender face and too-large glasses smiled briefly at Melissa. "I'm so sorry. Are you hurt?"

"No." Melissa began to exam her arms and feet and legs. She was not scathed.

"Good. We're heading straight for the police station up ahead about five miles. Do you know where you are?"

Melissa looked to the woman and shook her head. "No."

"We're on the outskirts of Hamilton."

Melissa knew the town. It was about an hour from Cincinnati.

"Should be at the local station in just a few minutes. We'll be sure to get you some help. It looks like you need it."

For the first time in two days, Melissa felt as though she would survive this. Now, help was near and she would make sure the bastards who shot CJ would be found. Melissa wondered if he was okay, if Carl and Riley were okay too. Admitting that she'd grown fond of CJ wasn't something she was ready to do, but the feelings were there and had taken hold. The thought that she would see him again and this terrible event was over raised her spirits, stifling the fear that had consumed her.

Johnny Denton stood in front of a seething Raymond McAllister. Not only had the moron killed one of their own, but he'd also let the girl go. It was all Ray could do to stop himself from pulling his gun on the idiot in front of him and put him out of his misery.

Instead, the bloated ringleader paced the area beneath the rafters of the barn, pondering his next step. The woman would surely go straight to the police, pointing them in the direction of their locale, and the time it would take to dispose of Doug Newman's body properly would ensure the cops had ample time to track them down before they completed the deed.

Considering options now was pointless; action was required and so Ray turned to Johnny. "Take your brother and go back to that shit hole of a town and take care of the girl and the old man. Leave me to get rid of Doug."

It didn't take a genius to understand that there'd be no coming back from this trip. Cops and the FBI would be everywhere, and Ray knew it. Johnny seemed to catch on quickly to the idea that his boss had just worked out a plan for his own escape, leaving his brother and him to take the fall for everything.

"Get Bennett and get the hell out of here. Now!" Ray shoved the man backwards and watched as Johnny sheepishly walked toward the front door. "Call me when you get there."

Ray moved as quickly as he could to the storage room. Doug's body lay on the ground, the blood no longer flowing from the shot to his head. Instead, it circled him on the concrete floor. "Goddammit!" He pushed his hand through his thick white hair and knelt down to empty Doug's pockets. The contents lay beside the dead man. From what Ray could see, nothing appeared out of the ordinary. A wallet, some loose change, and the keys to the hardware store. Ray picked up the wallet and pulled open the pocket where money was usually placed. He retrieved the three twenties and the ten inside, shoving the cash into his own pocket.

Ray continued to sift through the many compartments inside the wallet. Driver's license, a few credit cards, insurance card. Typical stuff. He pulled the driver's license from its holder. It must not have been removed often because it was stuck to the plastic insert. But when he managed to wrangle it out, he spotted something behind it.

A business card. A little mangled, worn down and faded, but it was a business card from the hardware store. Ray turned it over and, on the backside, a name and number were scrawled in ink. His first thought was to dial it. The number could have been a family member, or a friend who might come looking for him.

Ray waited as the line began to ring. Finally, an answer.

"ASAC Parker."

"You have to find them, Officer Ward. We've been looking for her and Dillon for the past hour. The weather's turned bad and they're out there somewhere." Ellen tugged on the sleeve of her shirt as she spoke to the officer on the phone. Jack was only feet from her, trying to listen to the conversation. It didn't take him long to sober up after the kids disappeared. Riley's words appeared to have at least some effect on the man. He knew there were people out there who wanted to hurt Riley because of what she'd seen, even though he'd tried to drown the idea away. Jack had assured Ellen the children would come back, but he was losing confidence. They'd set out briefly to look, but as the hail came down, the assumption was that Riley and Dillon would return, forced to come back by the weather. They, of course, hadn't.

"I don't know where they went. That's what I'm trying to tell you. We can't find them and you have to!" Ellen cried.

"Calm down, Mrs. Thompson. I'll go and look for them now, but you call me immediately if they show up. Do you understand?"

"Yes, yes. Just please find my children." Ellen set the phone down and turned to Jack. "He's going to look for them now."

"You know, I bet they're with that old man. That son of a bitch has caused us more trouble. This is his goddamn fault."

Ellen appeared stunned by Jack's failure to accept any responsibility for the situation. She glared at him and courage somehow found its way to the surface, and she drew her shoulders back and stood tall. "No. This isn't Carl's fault." Although she did not accuse him directly, her meaning was not lost. "And if you think my children are there, then you sure as hell better take me there now."

Jack turned away, out of guilt or shame or maybe both, understanding that it was his actions that drove Riley away. She was risking her own safety out of an anger she'd felt toward him. He hadn't wanted to believe she was like his father, and neither had Ellen, but that was exactly what she was and he would have to face up to it, or lose his daughter forever. "You're right; this isn't Carl Boyd's fault." Jack reached for Ellen's hand. "Our kids are out there alone because of me. I did this to our family." It seemed to take an act of desperation on the part of Riley for him to begin to understand what he'd done. "Let's go find them."

Jack waited for Ellen to put Gracie's coat on. This wasn't over for them. If or when they found the kids; the idea that Jack might just lose his family anyway weighed heavily on his mind. He could see Ellen had been pushed too far, they all had. And there were some things that could never be taken back.

Gracie was terrified and Jack could scarcely handle his own emotions right now, but his instincts took over and he began to evoke the memories of what he had once been – a decent father. He had to try to soothe the girl. "We'll find them, sweetheart. Okay?"

The rain had become relentless as Johnny and Bennett crossed over the border into Indiana. Owensville was another forty-five minutes away, but in these conditions, it might take them twice as long. All depended on the river crossings and rising water levels.

"What the hell are we supposed to do when we get there, Johnny?" Bennett asked. "This whole thing has turned into a giant clusterfuck and I don't see as we're gonna be getting out of there unscathed."

Johnny's look was enough to convey that there would be no way out of this deal. If they returned, Ray would kill them. If they showed up at Carl Boyd Sr.'s house or tracked down the little girl, the cops would take them down. It was a lose-lose situation, except for Ray McAllister.

The thought of just driving on through down to Mexico had occurred to Johnny, but then he feared McAllister would always be on the hunt for them. He was a powerful man with powerful friends. Turning himself in and working with the feds to bring in Ray didn't seem a good option either. Johnny wanted no part in going to prison, even if on a reduced sentence for helping them to find the ringleader.

They were indeed up a creek and maybe the only solution was to take out the witnesses and reduce his chances of being identified, but he still had to contend with the woman who'd escaped. So right now, Johnny was starting to feel down right despondent about finding a way out of this mess.

"I'm here to report a kidnapping." Melissa stood at the front desk of the police station. She was mostly dry now, but looked like she'd been put through one hell of a ringer.

Janet stood beside her, offering whatever support she could. "I found her alongside the highway about ten miles back. I'm Janet Halstead. She said she'd been taken hostage by some men and escaped."

The officer behind the desk seemed to perk up, like this wasn't something she heard on a daily basis. "Can I get your name, please?" she grabbed the telephone receiver.

"Melissa Simmons."

The officer pressed a few buttons and waited. "Detective Lewis, I have a Melissa Simmons here who would like to report a kidnapping." She paused for a moment. "Her own. Thank you." The woman walked around to the front. "Follow me, please. Are you hurt in any way, ma'am?"

"No. I'm not hurt." Melissa looked at Janet. "Thank you so much, but you don't need to stay. I'll be okay from here on out. Please, you should go back to your life. I can't thank you enough."

She wrapped her arms around the woman who was not much bigger than she and kissed her cheek.

Janet returned the embrace and smiled. "I hope everything will be okay for you, Melissa. Goodbye."

The officer turned back as Janet was leaving. "Ms. Halstead, if you wouldn't mind just leaving your contact information on my desk, in case we need to ask you a few questions?"

"Of course."

The two continued along the corridor to an office near the back of the building. As they approached the door, Melissa peered through the glass insert and spotted a man inside behind a desk.

The officer opened the door and allowed Melissa inside first. "Detective Lewis, this is Melissa Simmons. I've inquired as to her condition and she says she's uninjured."

"Thank you, Harris."

The officer nodded and closed the door on her way out.

"Ms. Simmons, please have a seat." The detective motioned for her to sit in the chair opposite his desk. He studied her face and body, appearing to assess the situation. "I'm very sorry this has happened to you. Why don't you start from the beginning?"

After a lengthy explanation, Detective Lewis seemed to consider her account of what had happened. "And so you believe these men are going back to find the witnesses?"

"Yes, sir. I'm sure of it. I heard them talking. They think CJ is dead, but I felt his pulse. I know he's alive. They're coming after CJ's dad and Riley Thompson. And, like I said before, the man named Doug, he was trying to help me. He said he was with the ATF."

"And one of the men shot him?"

"Yes. Johnny Denton shot him just like he shot CJ. Doug's

probably dead. I don't know because I didn't stick around to find out."

Detective Lewis turned to his computer and began typing.

"Can I please call CJ and make sure he's all right? We can warn them. We don't have much time. I know those men will be on their way to Owensville. Please."

The detective watched his screen for some time, and it seemed he'd found something of interest.

"Son of a bitch." He sat up straight, his manner turned sharp and focused. "I'll call the Owensville police and warn them. ATF in Columbus has a bulletin out on Johnny Denton. They'll need to know about their man. In the meantime, you're going to stay here with us. Do you have any family you need to call?"

"No." Melissa thought of her sister, but they hadn't spoken in a long time. Her parents were dead and CJ was really all she had apart from a few friends. No one close. "Can I please just call CJ? I have to know that he's okay."

The detective handed her his desk phone and then continued to enter some sort of information into his computer. Melissa's cell had been taken from her as soon as Johnny had shoved her inside the truck and now, she couldn't recall CJ's number from memory. "Shit."

"What is it?"

"I don't have his number. It's in my phone and my phone is gone." Melissa dropped her head into her hands and cried.

"It's okay. We'll get word to him somehow. Right now, I just want you to relax. You've been through a lot." Detective Lewis took to his feet. "Melissa, I have to leave and take care of a few things. Officer Harris will look after you until we can arrange for you to get to your boyfriend in Owensville. I'm sorry I have to go, but all hell's about to break loose."

THE HAIL POUNDED ON THE ROOF OF THE ALREADY BATTERED truck as Jack drove slowly toward Carl Boyd's home.

Ellen peered through the windshield and into the black sky. The little pellets of white ice fell from the darkness and bounced off the glass. "Oh my God. We have to find them, Jack."

"We will. I'm sure they're at the old man's house. He could've had the decency to call and tell us." Jack turned right toward the glowing "Shady Acres" sign that flickered as though it was about to short out from the rain. "Doesn't matter. We're here anyway."

"Promise me you'll stay calm, Jack. The last thing we need is for those kids to take off again."

Jack turned to Ellen, his look suggesting she need not point out the reason they were there in the first place. She'd had a right to, of course, and he supposed it didn't matter to her if he felt guilty about it or not. He wasn't entitled to anyone's sympathies. "You stay here. I'll get 'em." Jack stepped out of the truck and into the hailstorm. He raised the hood of his coat and walked toward the door of the trailer. But before he had the chance to knock, Carl pulled it open.

"What do you want? Why are you here?" Carl asked, without offering the man shelter.

"I know my kids are here. You better get them or I will."

"What the hell are you talking about? Nobody's here. Just me."

"Don't screw around with me. I am not in the mood." Jack was angry with himself more than with the old man, but he hadn't understood how to control it and so he directed it the only way he knew how. "I know they would've come here first."

"Look, *no one* is here. Okay?" Carl glanced toward the truck and spotted Ellen with the littlest Thompson inside. "Where's Riley?"

Jack stepped onto the first tread of the metal risers and was only inches from Carl's face. The hail felt like coins striking his head. "She's here, goddammit, just like I said. Now either let me in or bring me my son and daughter!"

"Mr. Thompson, I can promise you that if your children were here, I would have brought them back to you, whether you deserved them or not."

Jack stepped closer to meet Carl's eyes with his own. "Where are they?"

Headlights advanced in the distance through the misty air and falling ice. The SUV moved closer toward the home where it seemed a standoff was about to occur.

At first glance, Carl squinted cautiously, appearing to question if it was the men who killed his son. Instead, the telltale red and blue bar of light suddenly flashed on the roof of the approaching vehicle. Another patrol and the timing could not have been more appropriate.

Jack immediately stepped down and turned his attention to the police officer now stepping out of his SUV.

"What's going on, gentlemen?" Officer Ward began to move toward what had grown into a tense situation. He noticed Ellen and Gracie still inside the truck and it didn't seem to take him long to realize what had happened. Jack had taken matters into his own hands and called on Carl Boyd himself.

Jack was the first to speak. "My kids are inside there and this man refuses to let me see them."

"Officer, I assure you that no one else is here besides me. Although I don't blame those kids for running away."

Jack lunged forward.

"Hey, now. Hold up," Ward interjected. "You mind if I have a look inside, Carl?"

"Go right ahead." Carl stepped aside and waved the officer in.

As Ward looked around, he realized that there was virtually no place to hide in this small space. He glanced into Carl's bedroom and narrow bath, eventually returning to the living room where Carl waited. "You haven't heard from Riley or her brother today?"

"No, sir. I haven't, not from the time we left the hospital. I've been here ever since, just as you instructed."

"Dammit. We've got a real problem on our hands here, Carl. Riley and her brother Dillon left the Thompson home about an hour and a half ago and no one's seen them since. Mrs. Thompson called me to find them. Have you—you know—sensed anything?" It seemed Ward was almost embarrassed to make such a statement, but there was no other way to put it.

Carl knew what he was getting at. "Not really, no. I haven't been able to focus much with these painkillers they've got me on and my other meds. I don't think she's tried to reach out to me at all."

"I've got to find those kids." Officer Ward moved back toward the front door. "You see them or hear from them, you call me. Got it?"

Carl nodded, but paused for a moment. "I want to come with you. I want to help you find them. It's just that I've felt so damn helpless. Officer Ward, you know I'm a goddamn Marine and I just can't sit here and do nothing. If those kids are out there, they're in danger because of me—and my boy. It's gotta be up to me to find them."

"That's not a good idea, Carl. You're in no condition to be going anywhere. I'll track them down, I swear. In the meantime, I still have a patrol car coming by to keep an eye on your place." Ward's cell phone buzzed in his pocket. "Excuse me for a minute."

"Ward here."

From the cop's expression, the news was clearly not good.

Officer Ward ended the call. "Carl, we need to get you to a safe place. And if we don't find those kids, I believe they'll both be in a lot of danger."

[25]

The derelict house continued to howl and the hailstorm pummeled it with impressive force. The noise sought to induce a headache in Riley. She stepped away from the window of the bedroom and looked at Dillon with anxious eyes.

"What is it? What's wrong?" Dillon asked. "Get away from the window now and sit down. It's freezing in here and you need to wrap up."

Riley shuffled, returning to the old mattress on the floor. "We can't stay here. We have to go see Mr. Boyd."

"Why? I don't understand." Dillon draped the blanket over her shoulders, forgoing his own comfort.

Her eyes welled with tears. "I'm sorry I did this, Dillon. I'm so sorry." She pulled her knees to her chest and dropped her head.

"Riley, what's happening? Please, you have to tell me. Are Mom and Gracie okay?"

"I—I don't know. It's Mr. Boyd. He's afraid." They were far from Carl's house and the fact that she knew what he was feeling from such a distance further proved that her ability had become stronger. The headache was worsening and everything she felt had grown more intense.

"Afraid of what?"

"He thinks we're going to die. Dillon, we have to go. We have to find him and tell him we're safe. He knows the men are coming."

"They're coming, now? Are you sure? Jeez, have you seen this weather, Riley? We can't go out in this. Besides, don't you think we'll be safer here? No one knows where we are."

"You don't understand. We *have* to. If we can reach Mr. Boyd or even Officer Ward, they won't go out looking for us. That's what they're going to do; go out looking for us. And I can't be sure they'll stay safe."

"And what about you? Will you be safe?"

This was a question to which Riley truly did not have an answer. In the years since she first developed this ability, she'd never once been able to sense what her future would hold. Maybe it was God's way of keeping her sane.

But she had to convince Dillon to track down Mr. Boyd or the policeman before they went all over town searching, although she suspected her parents were already on the lookout. They could go to Mr. Boyd's house, but it was possible that he wouldn't be there. On Dillon's bike, in the harsh winds and pelting hail, it would make the journey both lengthy and dangerous. But Dillon had a cell phone and they could call the police station.

"Your phone." Riley looked to the pocket where he kept the cell. "Can you call the police station? You're right. We can't get to

Mr. Boyd. It might take too long and we'd be too late. But we can call for help. Officer Ward knows. He believes me and he'll get Mr. Boyd to safety. I know he will."

Dillon pulled the cell from his pocket. "He'll tell Mom and Dad where we are. It's his job."

"I don't think that matters anymore." An alarming image surfaced in Riley's mind. One that brought with it death and destruction. "Please, just call."

He'd retrieved the business card from his wallet that Officer Ward gave him when they were at the hospital. The light from Dillon's phone illuminated his face as he dialed the station's number.

The line was filled with static, cutting in and out, a result, no doubt, of the storm. Finally, the line was answered.

"Owensville Police. How may I direct your call?"

Dillon stumbled on his speech before eventually finding his voice, which was already frayed from nerves, and asked for Officer Ward.

"I'll have to radio him. He's out on a call. May I ask if there's a problem?"

"Um, please, if you could just get hold of Officer Ward. It's about my sister, Riley Thompson. He'll know what it's about."

"Okay and what is your number?"

Dillon repeated his phone number and the woman on the other end said she would get the message to him, but it might take some time. "I'm sorry, Riley. I did all I could. They're going to try to contact him, but he's out driving around."

"He's with Mr. Boyd. I saw him."

"When?"

"Just now. They're talking in his living room." Images were

coming at her from every direction now. Most didn't make sense to her, but she had seen the two men, only briefly, and they were standing by the old chair. She looked up at Dillon. "I guess we'll have to try to get there on our own."

Dillon pulled his coat on and helped Riley with hers. "Okay, let's go." He pressed the button on his cell to light their way back down the stairs.

The cold air penetrated the first floor of the old house. Broken windows allowed the air and hail inside and the lack of insulation made it feel as though they had no shelter at all.

"It's freezing out there, Riley."

"I know."

Dillon opened the door and the gusty wind pushed them both backwards a step as the door flew from his hands. The air whistled around them and the freezing rain blew inside where they stood. "Come on!" Dillon shouted as he pushed his bike onto the front porch. "Stay close." His raised voice was barely heard over the gale force that hit their bodies like a punch to the gut.

He climbed on his bike and reached out for Riley's hand to steady her as she lifted her short leg over the bar at the front. It would be a painful and uncomfortable ride, but sitting on the handlebars wasn't an option this time around. It was far too dangerous and she would take the brunt of the weather. This way, Dillon could offer at least some shelter for her with his arms encompassing her small frame.

Dillon led them down the busted concrete path toward the road. Neither one could see more than ten feet in front of them. The bitter cold pierced Riley's body as she squinted her eyes in hopes of offering them some protection while trying to see what lie ahead.

The dirt gutters were filled with little white balls of ice. The road was slick with the mixture of oil and water. Dillon struggled to gain balance. He did his best to pick up the stride as they approached the stop sign at the end of the road. Mr. Boyd's house was a good mile and a half away and it would take them some time to get there in these conditions.

The wind became too strong and so Riley had to close her eyes. And when she did, she could see Mr. Boyd, but he wasn't in his trailer anymore; he was back in the jungle. He was having another flashback and she suddenly found herself right there with him.

Her head fell back onto Dillon's chest. She was lingering somewhere between a state of being awake and asleep, inside a world shared only with Carl Boyd.

"Riley? Riley?" Dillon couldn't stop. He had to keep going and did his best to steady her so she would not fall to the ground.

Riley wandered inside the memories of Carl Boyd. She was standing with him in the hospital again, staring at his son. And just as quickly, the image faded and she was there in the jungle as he shouted orders to "Move! Move! Move!" and pointed his men in the direction of the smoke and explosions.

Her heart pounded and her young mind did not understand why she was here or if she was safe. "Mr. Boyd?" she shouted. "We need to go back! They're coming and we have to go someplace safe!"

The young man, tall and muscular, but with alarm in his eyes, turned to the little girl standing next to him in the middle of the hellish place. "What's happening, Riley? How do we get back? I don't know what to do!"

Riley extended her hand and the young Mr. Boyd reached out

for it. His was rough and calloused, dirty and bloody, but she held on to it as tightly as she could. "Follow me!"

She didn't know where to go, except away from the burning smell and the sounds of men screaming in pain and shouting orders at one another. Riley pulled the man along, leading him somewhere, anywhere but here.

They ran endlessly until they reached an intersection, no longer in the jungle. They were back in their small town and when she looked up at Mr. Boyd, he was still in his uniform and still young.

The sky was blue and the air was warm, but this place looked unfamiliar to her. "Are we home?" she asked him.

"I think so." Carl began to study the surroundings. He seemed just as confused as Riley. "Why are we here?"

"I don't know." She stood with him, still holding his hand, waiting for something that would lend reason as to their presence here.

"Wait. I know this. I know where we are." Carl looked as far left down the road as he could.

In the distance, a car was nearing. It was an old car, Riley thought. A great big old car her dad would have called a "classic." She looked to Carl, but he only stared at the approaching vehicle.

Riley peered along the road that ran perpendicular and saw another car in the distance. Same kind of old car, but she didn't know what it was. She turned her head in the direction that Carl was looking and watched as that car approached. Her eyes shifted back and forth between the two roads and the advancing cars.

Carl remained still, squeezing her hand almost hard enough to hurt, but Riley said nothing. She only watched with him, the speeding cars moving down the road toward one another. She glanced up to the post they were standing near. A stop sign should have been on the end of it. Instead, there was nothing. "Oh no," she whispered.

Riley looked to the other corners of the intersection. There were no stop signs except at one location where a tree slightly obscured its view. "Oh no. Mr. Boyd. They're going to crash."

She cast her eyes up at him, but his face was unmoved. A permanent look of fear fixed on him.

The car that was advancing along the road in front of them began to slow, as if it was about to stop. She began to feel relief when it rolled to the intersection and halted just before it entered.

It soon began to move again; the driver seemed to assume that it was safe to continue.

"No!" Riley screamed.

The first car barreled through the intersection and slammed into the side of the other one that had begun to move forward. The vehicle was pushed sideways and both slid for several feet until finally coming to a stop. The sound the metal made as it was bending and crunching forced Riley to cover her ears. The shrill noise felt like a blade slicing through her brain.

Carl returned his attention and sprinted into the road where the mangled cars billowed smoke from their engines. Riley followed behind him, running as fast as she could.

Carl rushed to the driver of the car that had been t-boned on the passenger side. "Are you okay? Are you hurt?" he asked the man.

The interior of the car had crumpled, but stopped short of the driver's side and the man appeared to be okay, save for perhaps an injury to his leg and forehead, which both trickled with blood.

"Riley. Stay here. Don't move!" Carl said.

She stayed put for a moment, but the need to look inside at the injured driver took hold and she moved anyway. A swell of recognition grew inside her. She'd seen pictures of him and had known him as a much older man. "Grandpa!"

Carl stepped quickly to the other car. The front end was a twisted mess of metal, but it appeared that the interior remained mostly intact. He moved to the driver's side and peered through the broken window. Shattered glass covered the two people inside. The windshield had broken.

The passenger appeared to be a young girl, nine, maybe ten years old. She lay slumped over. Carl pushed the unconscious driver away from the steering wheel. Her head fell against the headrest and Carl reeled backwards at the sight.

His eyes were wide and his chest began to heave. He raised his hands to his head and pressed hard against his temples. Carl squeezed his eyes shut. "Please God, no."

Riley turned away from her grandfather, who was beginning to move. She noticed Carl looking as though he might pass out. "Mr. Boyd." She rushed to his side. "Are you okay? What is it?"

Carl brushed past her and back to the woman in the driver's seat. "Rosalyn! Rosalyn! It's me—Carl. Wake up, sweetheart. Wake up!"

The woman did not budge and Carl looked again at the young girl in the passenger seat. Blonde hair, long and stringy. "Oh no." He rushed to the other side and carefully lifted the girl so that she was sitting up again.

"NO!" he screamed.

Riley covered her ears as the sound of agony arose from the young man in uniform. She began to sob, now understanding who these people were. This was his family, his wife and daughter that had been killed while he was at war.

She gripped her chest from the pain in her heart. Riley was feeling his pain and it throbbed so severely, it could have just as easily been a heart attack. Her head grew light.

Carl wailed as he dropped to his knees. "Why am I here? Why did you show me this?"

Riley's grandfather stepped out of his car on shaky legs and approached the other vehicle. She knew in an instant he could not see either of them. He reached the driver's side and dropped his head into his hands.

Riley watched her grandfather weeping for the two people in the car. A woman and a young girl.

Why were they here? Who brought them here to behold such a horrible scene? Carl remained on his knees, hunched over, crying at the loss of his family, reliving the pain he'd already been through once before. Only now, he had to be eyewitness to the event itself.

"Take me from this place. I'm begging you, take me away from here."

Riley moved away from the car and toward Carl. Her grandfather tried to help the people, but it was too late. She took Carl's hand again. "I'm so sorry, Mr. Boyd."

Riley came round again and found herself on the bike, Dillon's hand across her chest to keep her from falling. It took a moment for the leftovers to subside and her emotions to settle. This had taken a toll on her body and mind as both felt drained. She looked up at him.

Dillon appeared relieved to have her back. "Oh, thank God."

"Dillon, I saw Grandpa. He was in that accident that killed Mr. Boyd's family."

"What?" Dillon still had a raised voice as the weather was worsening and the hail falling harder than before.

"We have to get to Mr. Boyd." She began to take in her surroundings. It looked as though they were getting close now. The flickering sign in the distance indicated as much.

Dillon turned the handlebar of his bike onto the muddy drive of Shady Acres. He slogged through the slick and slimy path toward Carl Boyd's trailer.

They arrived to a darkened metal box. No lights on inside. No cars in the makeshift covered spot.

"No one's here, Riley. What are we going to do now?" Dillon tried to shield his sister from the torrent of hail as he waited for instruction.

She didn't know what to do. Riley believed Carl had been here. The earlier visions seemed to confirm that as well. Maybe they had still been too late.

The sound of a car approaching behind them caught their attention. Headlights shined in their eyes, temporarily blinding them to their surroundings.

"That must be him." Riley said, a smile crossing her face.

The car came nearer, crawling through the mud toward them. Dillon started to dismount from the bike, but Riley stopped him.

"Wait." She held her hand against his chest as they both remained straddling the bike. Her eyesight regained focus and Riley could now see inside the car. It was not Mr. Boyd. It was not the police officer who had been so kind.

"Oh my God. Dillon, it's them."

[26]

The **police station** was inundated with calls from stranded citizens. The storm had knocked the power out over much of the town and the traffic lights were down, causing a few fender benders.

Captain Sinclair ordered the patrol units to offer assistance, with the exception of Officer Ward. He and the captain remained in the small conference room with Carl Boyd and the three members of the Thompson house. All had been arguing as to the whereabouts of Dillon and Riley, no one having accomplished anything.

That changed, however, when Carl's eyes rolled back and his torso fell limp onto the table they had been sitting around. Officer Ward suspected it was Riley's doing. That perhaps she was attempting to reach out to him.

Several minutes passed before Carl returned to them. He was

pale and glistened with sweat as if he'd had a fever and it had just broken. His eyes were red and swollen with tears.

Ellen was the first to approach. "Are you okay, Mr. Boyd? You passed out." She leaned over him, her hands clenched his shoulders.

Carl cast his eyes to her. His vision was hazy and his head still swirled with the sight of his dead wife and child and the man who was there, trying to help, but it had been too late. "Your father," Carl began, looking to Jack. "He tried to save them."

"What are you talking about?" Jack asked.

"The accident that took my first wife and daughter, Mary. The one who looks so much like your Riley." Carl shook his head. "My God. I never knew. I wanted to believe it had been his fault and I never listened to anyone who tried to tell me different."

"I don't know what you're talking about. I don't know of any accident my dad was involved in."

"That's probably because it was before you were born. I'm sure he never mentioned it to you. Why would he?"

"My dad, Riley's grandfather, had the same ability she has. Reading people, feeling what they feel. For my father, it had been a curse that eventually killed him," Jack replied. He'd never admitted it to anyone apart from Ellen before. But so much had happened and so much was at stake, it seemed Jack felt as though he had nothing to lose and that in some small part, admitting it to Carl Boyd would help him to heal.

"That's why she and I share this—connection," Carl began. "When I came back here, after my divorce, I never wanted to see Leo. I knew what had happened and I just assumed it was his fault. I never forgave him for it." Carl lowered his head. "He brought

Riley to me to show me the truth." Turning to Jack, he continued, "But she's done so much more for me than that. You have to know how much she's helped me, even bringing my son back to me."

"But he's dead now too," Jack replied.

"Yes, but I believe it would have come to that no matter what she could have done. He was with me in his last days and I'm grateful for that." Carl began to study Jack. "You're afraid Riley will suffer the same fate as your father?"

Jack looked at Ellen, his own eyes dampened with tears. "Yes."

Carl took to his feet, striving to regain composure. "I think your children are at my home right now. Riley was reaching out to me. I'm sure they're both there and we have to get them."

Sirens wailed in the distance and it wasn't the police cars. These were warning sirens signaling that a tornado was coming.

Officer Daniel Ward looked to his superior, and it seemed the captain had also been caught off guard by this latest development. "We have to go get those kids, Captain. Listen to that."

Sinclair looked to Jack and Ellen. Both appeared desperate. Carl Boyd, who had already been injured, returned the same stare. It seemed the captain would have no choice and the sirens meant they had precious little time. "We have ten, maybe fifteen minutes before that tornado hits. We need to find out where it's going to touch down first." Sinclair hurried out of the room to get a grasp on the situation.

"Jack, we have to go and get them now!" Ellen's voice cracked and trembled with fear.

"You stay here. I'll go and get them." Carl started to leave.

"You're not going out there by yourself. I'm coming with you," Officer Ward replied.

"We're all going. These are *my* children," Jack said.

"We can't take Gracie. It's too dangerous." Ellen had a firm grip on their youngest.

"We've got a shelter here. Whoever's in this building will be heading down there now. I'll see to it she's looked after." Ward took Gracie's hand and led her out into the corridor where staff moved quickly toward the shelter.

The others were only steps behind them as they prepared to leave the safety of the station and attempt to find the children.

"Stay here. I'll be right back," the officer said. "Come on, Gracie; this way, honey."

On his return, the others waited at the entrance. Ellen watched the trees bend against the winds and the traffic lights appeared ready to snap off of their poles.

"We have to leave now!" Her tone was just short of utter panic.

He pulled his jacket closed and placed the hood tightly over his head. Jack pushed the door open and the winds nearly took it off its hinges. "Stay behind me," he shouted to Ellen.

Officer Ward rushed to his SUV and unlocked the doors. Ellen helped Carl inside, sliding in after him while Jack entered the front seat.

"For God's sake, where's it expected to touch ground?" Carl asked the officer.

"From what we know right now, they expect it to hit just outside Terra Haute first, then head this way. We don't have much time. It's an EF3."

Everyone in the car knew what that meant. An EF3 was bad, very bad. Winds reached upwards of two hundred miles per hour, causing roofs to be torn off and cars to be tossed around.

"My God. If they're in that mobile home park..." Ellen trailed off. "Have you tried calling Dillon's cell again?" she asked Jack.

"All services are down," Ward began, "including cell towers."

Ellen pressed her hand over her mouth, working to keep herself from falling apart.

"It's okay, Ellen. We'll get to them in time. I'm sure of it." Carl reached for her shoulder, a trivial gesture, but one that served its purpose.

Riley and Dillon remained still, their faces masked in fear. The sirens sounded in the distance and they both knew what they meant.

The men in the car stared back at them. It seemed they might have been confused by the sight of two young kids standing before them in the torrential hail. They'd expected to find the old man. Instead, Johnny and Bennett Denton were looking into the eyes of two very frightened children, wet and trembling from the cold and fright.

"Shit, Johnny, there's a goddamn tornado coming and we got these kids standing in front of us. Where's the old man?"

"Shh!" Johnny waved a hand in his brother's face. "Just give me a minute to think, dammit!"

"We ain't got a minute. Can't you hear them sirens? We gotta get the hell outta here, man."

Johnny ignored Bennett and stepped out of the car. His jacket offered little protection from the winds, although the hail seemed to be slowing down, a sign that likely meant the tornado was close.

"I know you," he said to Riley. "You both best git inside this car before that tornado comes. You two don't wanna be out here when it hits. All these trailers are gonna get blown right off their jacks. You won't survive."

"Don't," Riley said, sensing that Dillon wanted to move. "He killed CJ. He was the one who took Melissa."

"Riley, we can't stay here. He's right. We'll never survive if we're standing out here. You know that."

"I'd rather die than go with you. You'll only kill us anyway, just like you did with CJ," Riley shouted.

Johnny moved toward them, his boots trudging in the mud and his jeans soaking through. "Now listen here, little girl. No one's gonna hurt you, all right? I just wanna see to it that you and this young man stay safe."

"Stay away from my sister!" Dillon shouted as he stepped off the bike and pulled Riley off with him. The bike fell to the ground and he pushed her behind him.

"Sister?" Johnny smiled. "I see." He turned back for a moment to see that Bennett was still inside the car. He waved for him to get out. With reluctance, the man emerged from the dry warmth of the car.

Dillon stepped back, forcing Riley to lose her footing and almost fall to the ground, but she gripped his arm and remained steady.

"Riley, run!" Dillon turned on his heel and pushed her forward.

They ran to the end of the muddy road. A wooden fence surrounded the park and it was bending and twisting in the winds, ready to break off and fly away at any moment.

The brothers were close behind and so Dillon directed Riley to veer off to the left toward the storage units. They had solid concrete foundations and offered perhaps only slightly better protection than the trailers would.

"Shit!" Dillon pulled on the padlock of one of the units. "It's locked." He tried the others, but they were all secured, probably more so than the trailers themselves.

One of the neighbors must have heard the shouting or at least spotted the headlights on the narrow path between the mobile homes. He emerged from his home. "You all better be getting out of here," he said, heading to his car. "Tornado's in Terra Haute and coming our way! They say another could spring up anywhere."

The man hopped into his car and turned the engine. He spun his tires and squeezed by Johnny's small carjacked Nissan sedan.

"Johnny, get the fuck back here. Screw these damn kids. We gotta find some shelter now!" Bennett began to jog back to their car.

Johnny continued on. He ran toward the storage units, spotting a few footprints that hadn't yet been washed away. The rains were settling down now and it would be easier to catch sight of them.

"Where can we go, Dillon?" Riley asked as they huddled behind one of the storage sheds.

"I don't know." He pulled her in close, covering her with his own body.

They both noticed the small car pulling away, but it only took a few moments before another arrived.

"It's Mom and Dad!" Riley pushed her head out of her brother's protective hold and spotted the police car. "It's the police! They're all here and so is Mr. Boyd!"

Dillon peered around the corner and smiled at the welcome

sight, but then quickly felt the cold barrel of a pistol in the back of his neck.

"You both best come with me."

Riley turned slowly and saw Johnny Denton standing over them, holding a gun to Dillon's head. "Please, please don't hurt my brother." Headlights shined directly at them and debris was noticeably blowing through the shafts of light. Riley squinted and spotted Officer Ward stepping out of his SUV.

He'd moved to the other car and drew his gun on the brother who now sat in the passenger seat. "Let the kids go," he shouted to Johnny.

Johnny looked at Bennett. The man's eyes were wide as they darted between the gun pointed at him through the passenger window and his brother, who was about to shoot a teenaged boy.

A bolt of lightning flashed, striking a large oak tree at the front of the park. The ground shook beneath them as the great oak trembled. A branch was split in two and fell with a heavy thud.

The unexpected show of force from Mother Nature drew the attention of those that remained in dangerous proximity to the fallen wooden shard. Smoke and embers billowed from its now burnt and pointed end.

This was Riley's chance and it wouldn't be squandered. While the man with the gun pointed at her brother looked to the smoldering tree, she locked eyes with Dillon. They connected in a way they never had before. She was able to tell him what to do. And he obeyed.

Dillon raised his elbow and shoved it hard into Johnny's stomach. He might have only been fourteen years old, but he was six feet tall and his long arms offered a reach for which many men would have wished.

Johnny doubled over in both surprise and pain.

"Come on!" Dillon swooped Riley up in his arms and ran toward the patrol car.

Ellen shouted through the raised rear passenger window. "Run! Run!"

Officer Ward turned his gun on Johnny and moved toward the man who was reclaiming the wind that had been knocked from his lungs, a firm grip still on his pistol. "Drop your weapon!"

Johnny stood upright. The winds were gaining strength and it appeared to be a struggle for him to keep both his feet planted on the ground. He looked at the kids who were already in their mother's arms by the time he straightened. She had ushered them inside the vehicle.

"Mom, we have to get out of here. The tornado's coming!" Dillon said.

Jack was in the front passenger seat and noticed the keys were still in the ignition. He turned to Ellen. "We need to go."

"Jack, we can't leave him," Ellen replied.

Riley knew her mother was right. They couldn't just abandon him. "We have to wait, Dad. Please don't leave yet." The previous anger she'd felt toward Jack was evaporating, at least temporarily. So much had already transpired that she hadn't the energy and, if it was possible, she was feeling weaker by the moment.

"Are you okay, Riley?" Carl asked.

"I guess so. I'm so sorry about the accident. I never knew."

"It's not your fault. It wasn't anyone's fault and at least I know that now."

The standoff continued outside, each man pointing his weapon at the other.

"You see what's coming, Denton. If you want to survive, drop your gun." Officer Ward took another step forward against the brutal wind. "You know that your partner is ATF, right? Doug Newman? He's one of us. It's over, Johnny." Ward had to shout over the prevailing storm.

In the distance, a black cloud formed into a funnel. This was it. A vortex was spinning into a tornado as wide as the horizon itself. Even in the darkness, its black swirling mass was discernable.

"You're screwed either way, but if you come with me, at least you'll live," Ward began, "Look behind you, Johnny."

It seemed Johnny just realized that he'd killed a federal agent, but that Officer Ward hadn't known this fact. He looked into the officer's eyes, defeated. Ray had sent him on a mission from which there was no return. Had he known about Doug? Maybe so and that was the reason he'd wanted to send Johnny off on a wild goose chase to find the girl and the old man.

Johnny smirked as he spotted the funnel cloud approaching. There was no way out. He looked to Bennett, still held up inside the car. There was still a chance for him. He hadn't been the one who pulled the trigger, killing now two men.

Riley knew everything Johnny was feeling in that moment. The fear that he would be swept away by the tornado, or be shot by the Owensville policeman. He was contemplating a choice. "Wait! No!" she shouted from inside the running car.

Johnny raised the gun to his head and fired. His body went limp and collapsed to the ground. A yell sounded from inside the car where Bennett Denton remained. He'd watched his brother take his own life.

Ward recoiled at the sight. He looked back to his SUV where Riley screamed in horror. There was no more time to waste.

They had only minutes before the tornado would be on top of them.

He had to think fast and get these people to safety. Johnny Denton had chosen the easy way out and there was nothing more the officer could do. He moved toward the brother, whose head had dropped into his hands, weeping at the loss.

He pulled open the passenger door of the car and ripped the man out. "Come on; we have to get out of here!"

Bennett stumbled to the ground, still sobbing.

"Get up! You're going to die if you stay here!" Ward yanked on his shoulder, trying to pull him up from the muddy ground. Bennett wasn't a tall man, but was stocky. His full frame was difficult to maneuver and he offered little help to the officer trying to save his life.

"Johnny! I can't just leave him," Bennett pleaded.

"I'm sorry. He's gone, but you're not. Look ahead. You see what's coming? If you don't come now, I'll have no choice but to leave you too. There are children in that car and I will protect them."

Bennett looked inside the SUV and spotted the little girl and her brother. The girl seemed to look back, straight through him. He stood up on his own and shook his head.

Ward took the lead again and walked toward his vehicle. There was enough room for one more in the department-issued Tahoe. "Get in!"

The sky was pitch black and Ward looked down the path of trailers, praying that no one was left inside. There was no time to check each one. If they didn't leave now, they might not leave at all.

He jumped into the driver's seat and slammed the running

SUV into reverse. Riley watched as Johnny Denton's body remained still, slowly sinking into the muddy surroundings. Her gaze turned upwards at the looming tornado in the distance. She looked to Carl. "I'm sorry I couldn't find you sooner. I shouldn't have left home in the first place. You wouldn't be here if it weren't for me and maybe that man would still be alive too."

"As much as I don't want to admit this, none of us would be here if my son hadn't been involved with those people. I loved him, and I think he was trying to straighten himself out. He was trying, but got caught up in something he couldn't see his way out of. That's why we're here, Riley. And I have a feeling if it weren't for you, I wouldn't even be alive."

"Hurry! Hurry!" Jack yelled to the officer. "It's coming!"

[27]

The time it would take to drive back to the station for shelter was time Ward knew they did not have. Instead, he veered onto the highway and headed south, just in front of the black cloud.

"Where are you going?" Jack asked.

"To the old factory. They've got a shelter," Ward replied.

Jack knew of the old shelter. He'd been in it several times before. He'd worked at the plant for nearly fifteen years, before it shut down. It'd been his first real job and had paid well at the time, allowing him and Ellen to marry and get a decent place.

It was all so different in those days. Dillon was young and they were happy. Somehow, it all went wrong after that. Jack's mother passed away and a year later, his dad took his life. The plant had already been shut down and he was drinking too much.

Now they were going back to the place where Jack had once been valued and respected. He knew what they all thought of him, even Officer Ward. Jack had become someone he didn't recognize and he'd already hurt the ones he loved too many times. He sat in that passenger seat, ashamed and angry at what he'd become. It hadn't been anyone's fault but his own.

"I know a short cut to get down there," Jack said. "Managers used to use it to get into the shelters first so they could keep everyone under control. Keep them from panicking."

Ward shared no love for this man, but at least he had offered something more useful than moping around as he had been the entire day, offering no help whatsoever. Ward raised the corners of his mouth and tipped his head in acknowledgement.

Riley's brain pounded against her skull, the headache worsening still. She was being overwhelmed by feelings of distress and hurt and rage from everyone in the car. She pressed her palms against the sides of her temples to soothe the ache, but it didn't help.

The idea of jumping out of that SUV and facing the tornado seemed a better alternative than the agony she was feeling in this moment. Her mother's fear, her father's regret. Bennett Denton's pain at the loss of his brother. Mr. Boyd's loss. Dillon was afraid; even Officer Ward was afraid and all these emotions swirled inside her young and fragile mind at the same time. There were no limits to what she could perceive now, and it was terrifying.

Riley's heart was racing and beads of sweat were forming on her brow. The temperature, even inside that car, wasn't warm enough to cause that. No. It was something else.

The old plant appeared in the distance. Just a shadow against the already blackened skies, but it was there, its large, rectangular shape, with smoke stacks standing tall. Broken windows and overgrown shrubs surrounded it.

"That's it, up ahead." Jack pointed in front of him.

"I see it," Ward replied.

The tornado was almost upon them. In the side view mirror, Riley could see it gaining on them. How would they get inside before it hit? A powerful sensation forged its way up from deep in the pit of Riley's stomach. Strong, angry, hateful. Her eyes grew wide when she finally realized what it was. The tornado. And it wanted them.

Ward skidded into the parking lot that was already flooded with water. He shoved open his door and leapt out, yanking the rear door open. His jacket whipped across his chest, flapping around him. "Get out. We don't have much time!"

Jack had already jumped out and was helping Dillon out of the other side. "Come on, son; you have to hurry." He took Dillon's arm and steadied him as he stepped out. "We have to get your mother and Riley to safety."

Ellen stepped out quickly onto Ward's side. "What about Gracie?"

"She'll be fine, Ellen. She's safe. Now we need to make sure your other children stay safe. You have to hurry." Officer Ward looked to Jack, who was rounding the backside of the SUV with his son and Bennett in tow. "You lead."

Their words were carried away by the winds. They each shouted at one another to move on and get inside as quickly as they could.

"Mom! It's coming!" Riley folded her arms around her stomach. The pain was too much and she doubled over.

Carl had slipped out after Ellen and was struggling to keep up with the younger people, but found renewed energy at the sight of Riley's distress.

"Baby!" Ellen bent down to help her.

"I've got her!" Ward gather her up in his arms. "You're okay, you're okay. I've got you."

"We're going to die!" Riley screamed.

"No, we're not!" He picked up his pace to keep up with Jack, who was nearing the main entrance of the building.

"It's locked!" Jack turned to the officer. But rather than wait, he picked up a boulder that was a few feet away and returned. He threw it into the glass window next to the door and watched it shatter and pushed away the remaining shards, stepping inside the opening.

A moment later, he opened the door.

"Hurry! This way!" Jack led them toward the back of the building.

What windows had previously remained intact began to rattle. Riley looked up and saw one of them bending and warping until finally it exploded. "It's here! It's here!" she screamed as Ward continued running with her in his arms.

The building groaned as the winds forced their way inside, lifting broken glass and metal debris that had been left behind and tossing it with ease. The three-story factory shuddered. Metal railings slackened from their posts and sailed like flying daggers. Iron staircases crumbled to the ground, crushed under the weight of the winds.

Machinery left behind began to rattle and their bolts loosened. The entire structure was twisting at the will of the tornado.

"Just ahead!" Jack shouted behind him. "Twenty feet!"

Riley raised her hand to her dripping nose. Her fingers were covered in blood.

Ward looked down at her. "Oh my God! Riley, you're bleeding!"

She trembled and tears streamed down her face. Her stomach felt as though someone was wringing it from the inside and her head continued to pound. "Mommy!" she cried.

Ellen turned to see her daughter's face smeared with blood. Streaks of tears stained pink, making their way down to her neck. She stopped cold and sprinted to Riley's side. "Baby! Baby, what's wrong?"

"Ellen, keep moving!" Ward glanced back at the soaring debris. "We have to get inside the shelter!" He spotted Carl struggling to keep up. "Come on, Carl. We're almost there."

They ran fast, working to catch up to the others who had just arrived at the shelter entrance. A set of steel doors lay just outside the building beneath the overhanging roof. A padlock held the doors together.

Ward gently returned Riley to her feet, ensuring Ellen had a hold on her. She could not stand upright on her own; the pain in her stomach was too strong.

"Step back!" He drew his gun from its holster and pointed it at the padlock. In his desperation that neared panic, he'd forgotten to release the safety. Once he did, he took aim again and fired a shot. The bullet ricocheted off the lock, busting it open in the process.

The large metal doors rattled hard, raising several inches before slamming back down again. Officer Ward and Jack braced their legs against the concrete base of the entry and each pulled on a door, lifting it back against the force of the wind.

Jack raised his side enough so that Dillon could crawl in and he waited for Ellen to lead Riley down so that Dillon could guide his sister the rest of the way inside.

"I got you, Riley." Dillon held out his hands, reaching for her legs and placing them down on the ladder.

A gust of wind ripped the door Ward held in his hands as though it was a mere slip of paper being torn from a notebook. The storm was upon them.

"Get in!" Jack shouted to the officer.

They were the only two left outside now. Ward looked to Jack and back to the storm. The adjacent structure, a small tool shed, had been ripped off of its foundation and was spinning inside the tornado. He had only moments.

"Get in, Ward! I'll be right behind you," Jack repeated.

The shelter was little more than concrete walls with a few shelves and a couple of dilapidated chairs, but it was enough to protect them. Ellen gently sat Riley down on one of chairs. She still suffered and the pain was growing. Nausea swirled inside her just as the tornado had been swirling above them.

"I'm scared, Mom. I feel so sick." Riley leaned her head against Ellen's shoulder.

Dillon held her hand on the other side as he cast a sideways glance to Bennett Denton, a man whom he wished wasn't even alive. He was partly responsible for the danger in which they now found themselves. Carl was nearby, ensuring the man wouldn't try anything stupid.

"It's okay, Dillon," Riley started. "He was only following his brother; he didn't know what else to do." It was one thing to feel what others were feeling, but it was something else entirely to muster any sympathy toward the people who had caused all of this. She looked at the man, Bennett, whom she had not met before today. "Where is Melissa?"

He only glared at her, but she felt the rage inside him. For his brother and for being stuck inside this shelter.

"Dammit, Ward, get the hell inside! I got this!" Jack continued as the officer watched the destruction of the smaller buildings.

It seemed these were the final words Ward needed to move inside. He'd never been this close to an EF3. He was awestruck and quickly nodded his head and began to step inside the opening, placing his foot on the first rung of the ladder. "It's your turn, Jack."

Jack nodded and waited for the officer to descend. He turned his gaze upwards where the roof used to be. The SUV they had arrived in was lifted with ease and spun around in the air above. In that moment, looking into the blackness and witnessing the powerful forces that God could bear down onto whomever he pleased, Jack seemed to discover his own mortality. How selfish he had been to live his life this way and how he'd come to regret the way he'd treated his family. He didn't deserve to survive this.

Inside, Riley felt a shift in the storm. It still writhed with fury around them, but she knew Jack was peering into the depths of this beast, searching for meaning in his actions. The pang of regret pierced her mind. Shame, loathing, fear. All of these emotions she felt so strongly were coming from her father.

"Daddy? Daddy, come inside!" she yelled, cringing with the ache that still resided inside her gut. She knew he was considering giving up; that he thought it was best for the family if he was gone, but she couldn't bear the idea. No matter what he'd done in the past few years, he was still her daddy and she loved him with every ounce of her heart. "Daddy!" she screamed again, trying to push herself up from the chair. Her nose dripped blood again and her head spun.

"Riley, sit down, honey!" Ellen peered up at the opening and spotted the officer coming down, but Jack remained at the surface.

Officer Ward was now at the bottom of the steps, yelling for Jack to come inside, but he only stood there, gazing into the storm.

Jack seemed to hear the distant screams of his daughter. He blinked his eyes and looked inside where Officer Ward waited for him, waving an arm to come down.

"Daddy, please come in. I don't want you to die. Please don't die. I need you, Daddy."

It was Riley's voice that echoed in his head as though she was standing beside him, whispering in his ear. He squeezed his eyes shut, forcing the tears to stream down his face. The sound of the wind and debris flying about was almost deafening, but he could hear his daughter's plea.

Jack stepped inside the opening, descending the ladder. As he moved closer to the bottom, the remaining door was ripped off its hinges. The wind made its way inside the shelter, but it was far less intense. They were safe, cold and afraid, but safe. Jack hurried to Riley, who was propped up against a masonry column, nose bleeding and hand over her stomach.

"I'm here baby. I'm never going to leave you. I swear to God, you'll get your daddy back." He looked to Dillon and Ellen.

Ward stood near Carl and Bennett Denton.

"Are we going to be safe in here?" Carl asked.

"Yes. Just stay back in this corner and I think we'll be safe," Ward replied.

They watched in awe as the tornado fully engulfed the factory. The sound of twisting metal and shattered glass could just as easily have been from an explosion, but it had been the tornado. Soon, the eye of the storm surrounded them.

Inside were still dark skies, but it was peaceful and calm. It would not last.

"Is it over?" Dillon asked.

"No. Not yet. We're in the eye," Carl said.

The pounding in Riley's head subsided just a little, as though the storm was catching its breath. The sentiments of those in the room seemed to recover from the danger they had faced. They felt safe and she could feel it.

Carl appeared weak and in need of medical attention. His eyes were glazed over and his face was pale. "Can you feel it too, Mr. Boyd? Can you feel the storm?"

"What does it feel like to you, Riley?" he asked.

"Like someone's got their hands around my stomach and is twisting it so hard I can barely breathe." She dabbed a tissue under her nose again. The blood had slowed. "I'm not sure what's happening to me, Mr. Boyd. I feel like I'm a part of the storm, like it lives inside me."

Jack listened to Riley speak of the pain. He recalled a similar statement from his father. It was only days later that he had taken his life. "Riley, you have to let it go. It has taken hold of you because it can, because you let it. You have to learn how to block it out, learn how to control it. It's something your grandpa never could figure out. It's something I haven't learned yet either."

"What's happening to me, Daddy?"

"I don't know exactly, baby. I think Grandpa felt this way too. I know he did." Jack looked at Carl. "I'm so sorry about what happened to your family. I had no idea that my father was in the accident that took them. I doubt he ever forgave himself."

The eye of the storm passed and the winds howled again. All conversation stopped as they looked to the skies. If it was possible, it seemed even stronger this time. The chain-link fence that enclosed the abandoned grounds broke free and whipped around. The posts flew over the opening of the shelter.

"Get back!" Ward moved toward the others to get them back a few more feet.

One of the steel poles catapulted through the opening and struck Jack in the back of the head. He collapsed to the ground in an instant.

Riley screamed at the top of her lungs. "Daddy!"

[28]

Daniel Ward had been an officer in the small town of Owensville for the better part of ten years. He'd dropped out of Purdue University while working toward a degree in civil engineering. His scholarship money had run out and he'd begun to grasp that a job would likely not be awaiting him upon graduation.

So rather than pile up the student loan debt, Daniel opted to leave school for another purpose, one that had brought him to this place now, standing over a man, treating a severe injury with what little medical knowledge he had, most of which had been bestowed upon him during his training as a police officer.

The injured man was the father of a little girl who had a special power within her, the likes of which Daniel Ward had never seen before. And as she watched her father get struck down by a piece of debris tossed inside their shelter with the speed of a javelin, he could not let this man die, and certainly not in front of his daughter.

Amidst the screams of the man's wife and children, Daniel Ward worked. Tearing off Jack's shirt, he carefully lifted him to his side to get a better look at the wound, but he needed help.

It only required a look from the officer for Carl Boyd to rush to his aid. The only other adult male in the room was hardly a man at all, merely a puppet whose strings were no longer being pulled and so he remained limp and useless.

The boy, however, the man's son, offered help. Daniel would not deny him and so instructed Dillon to raise his father's head slightly and place his jacket beneath it.

"Carl," Daniel began, "press on his hip to keep him on his side. I can see the cut just beneath his shoulder." Daniel knew it had been a miracle the man wasn't struck directly in the head. If he had been, the officer would be placing the boy's jacket over his father's face instead.

As Daniel fashioned a bandage from Jack's torn clothing, he wondered if the little girl, Riley, had played a part in ensuring the makeshift lance had been redirected from what would have ensured Jack's instantaneous demise. He knew the girl was powerful, but just how powerful he could not possibly know.

A half-moon-shaped gash about four inches wide continued to spill blood. Daniel applied as much pressure as he could, but the rag soaked through. "We have to get him to the hospital," he said to Carl. The aged man had already suffered an injury and could offer only so much assistance.

They both looked to the opening above them. A small shaft of light was growing. The black clouds were passing and the stars were beginning to shine through.

"It's gone. Mom, it's gone!" Riley carefully rose to her feet as the nausea seemed to pass, just as the storm had. She pointed to the clearing skies above. "We can go now and get Daddy to the hospital."

The problem remained for Daniel. How to transport this man without causing further damage. He was unconscious and although not a tall man, he had some girth about him. It would take the help of Bennett Denton to get Jack out of that shelter; a man that would have seen Riley and Dillon dead.

Daniel looked to the remaining Denton brother, and back to Carl. It seemed Carl was thinking the same thing. Get his help or watch Jack die.

"Come on; we need to get Dad out of here." Dillon bent over, placing his hands beneath Jack's arms. "Come on!" he yelled as though no one had heard him the first time.

Perhaps the boy could handle the weight. People in distress were often known to exceed their normal strengths. He was tall and gangly, but the possibility was there and so Daniel opted to accept this haphazard Plan B. "Okay. Are you sure you can do this?"

Dillon nodded.

"Come to this end. I'll take his shoulders. We need to get him up the ladder carefully."

Just as they began to hoist Jack, Bennett approached, placing his hands beneath Jack's back and assisting Daniel.

The three carefully moved toward the ladder. Daniel stepped on the first rung. It was wet and slippery from the rain and just as he placed some weight on his leg, his boot slipped off the wet piece of metal. "Son of a bitch!" But he pressed on.

Ellen drew Riley closer and all began to move toward the shelter's opening. Carl brought up the rear as they waited at the bottom for the three to get Jack safely to the top.

"He'll be okay, Mom. I know he will," Riley said. She believed it too.

Ellen glanced at Carl; both seemed to be praying that the girl was right.

Daniel was the first to emerge at the top. The destruction, even visible in the darkness, almost caused him to stagger back, but he retained his grip on the injured man. The auxiliary buildings around the factory were gone, except for their foundations. The plant itself had neither a roof nor any windows remaining.

As they all reached the top, holding Jack in their hands, they seemed to spot Officer Ward's patrol car simultaneously. It was upside down at the end of the parking lot. They had no way to get Jack to the hospital.

Dillon might have been the first to realize what this could mean; that his father might not survive. "Please, you have to call an ambulance."

"Set him down. Gently!" Daniel said as they knelt down. He quickly returned to his feet and reached for the radio attached to his uniform. "This is Officer Ward. We need an ambulance at the Caterpillar plant on Higgins Road."

Daniel released the button and waited for a response. The radio remained quiet for too long and he wondered if the station had been hit. The youngest of the Thompson family was in the shelter there, but without some sort of reply, it occurred to him that perhaps it was no longer there at all.

Daniel squeezed his eyes shut, praying. Finally, through a static-filled line, the radio burst to life again. "We've got emergency services nearby and are now heading your way. Be aware it may take a while. We've had several reports of debris on the highway and this might cause a backup."

"Ten-four." Daniel released the button, then pressed it again. "Carol, is everyone all right over there?"

A shorter pause this time. "Yes. We're all fine here, Dan. The tornado missed us, but we understand there to be a whole lot of damage and we're rallying services as best we can. Did you find those kids?"

"Yes. But we have an injured man, Jack Thompson. He needs help as soon as possible."

"Ten-four. Help is on the way."

Daniel looked to Dillon and grinned, nodding to the boy as if ensuring that everything would be fine.

Only a moment later, the others emerged. Riley first, Ellen, and then Carl. Riley immediately sprinted toward them.

"Is he going to be okay?" she asked Dillon.

"They're sending help now."

She knelt down beside Jack and placed a hand on his cheek. "It's okay, Dad. You'll be fine." It seemed the pain in her stomach evaporated, just as the tornado had, eventually dissipating in a cloud that floated toward the sky.

Ellen wrapped her arms around Riley as they both remained at Jack's side. Daniel retrieved handcuffs from his belt and placed them on Bennett Denton. He might have offered assistance, but that didn't change the fact that he was going to go to jail for a long time.

"I assume the ATF and FBI will want to have a word with you," Daniel said as he clamped the cuffs.

Bennett said nothing. He appeared to understand the full breadth of what had happened. His brother had seen no way out and chose to end his own life, leaving Bennett to clean up the mess.

In his eyes, Daniel believed he saw vengeance. "I can only hope you do the right thing and help to bring to justice those responsible for taking this man's son," he pointed to Carl, "and endangering these children."

Denton remained stoic, but his eyes flashed with a moment of what Daniel believed was remorse, but he supposed time would tell.

Jack began to moan. His eyes fluttered and he was returning to consciousness. Blood still pooled from the wound, but it seemed the pressure they'd applied to it had helped slow it a small degree.

He reached for Riley's hand. "I'm sorry." His words were barely audible, but she could hear him.

She leaned in and kissed Jack's forehead. "I know, Daddy."

The sound of sirens arose in the distance. This time, it was the kind they welcomed to hear. Help had indeed come for them.

The flashing lights of the ambulance sliced through the darkness as it raced up the long drive toward the parking lot where they all stood waiting.

"They're here!" Riley looked to Jack. "They're here, Dad! You're going to be okay!"

Two EMTs rushed to Jack's side and quickly conferred with Officer Ward as to the circumstances and nature of his injury.

"Sir, can you hear me?" one of them asked.

Jack nodded almost imperceptibly, but Riley could see it and quickly looked to Dillon for confirmation.

A whirlwind, not unlike the tornado that just passed, spun, only this time, it was those working to help Riley's father. They loaded him onto the ambulance and offered all a ride out of there.

Daniel Ward watched what was left of the plant shrink in the distance as they drove away, the destructive remains visible in his side view mirror. He felt lucky that they all survived.

Riley waited with Ellen and Dillon in the lobby of the hospital outside of Owensville, near Terra Haute. Their small clinic had sustained too much damage and so the ambulance continued on for another thirty minutes to reach a place that could treat Jack.

He was rushed inside and they began work to control the bleeding. Fleeting consciousness had returned to him and he'd spoken words to Ellen that Riley could not hear, although she didn't need to know what was exchanged. Ellen appeared indifferent as she turned away from him. It seemed forgiveness could be a distant prospect.

Now, he would be taken into surgery after the discovery of a punctured lung he'd sustained from the impact.

"He'll be okay, won't he?" Riley asked.

"The doctors say he'll be fine, honey," Ellen replied. "Come on; we need to get to Gracie. She must be very scared right about now."

Riley had already figured out what her mom wouldn't say; that although Jack would be fine, it was likely their marriage wouldn't be. As she turned to Dillon, her assumption appeared to match his own. She recalled Jack's contemplation to give up when it would have been so easy for him to be taken away by the storm. The regret he'd felt. But maybe it was still too late, and Ellen had finally reached her breaking point.

There was a conviction in her mom now that Riley hadn't known before. Ellen blamed Jack for putting her and Dillon in harm's way and perhaps this life-threatening event was enough to shake her out of whatever haze she'd been living in for the past few years. But as Riley watched her father nearly die in front of her, she felt a renewed hope, that he would again become the father he once was, just as he promised.

Daniel waited in the lobby for a fellow officer to take Bennett Denton back to Owensville, where the ATF agents awaited him. Another car would take the Thompsons and him back to the station so that Ellen could reunite with Gracie.

Riley walked to Officer Ward. "Did they find Melissa? Is she okay?" It was obvious the officer had been briefed on the situation as she sensed his relief at the mention of the woman's name.

A fresh clarity had begun to descend upon Riley. What she could sense in others now seemed to come to her in a controlled manner. Whether it was the storm that had nearly ripped through her, or showing Mr. Boyd what he needed to see in order to put the past behind him, she was gaining control of her gift rather than the other way around.

"Yes. She's safe. It's over now, Riley." Daniel turned to Ellen. "I spoke with Captain Sinclair and he told me that the ASAC in the Columbus ATF office had received a call earlier in the day from an unknown subject. The call was triangulated for a location, leaving them little doubt that their man had fallen. The man Riley had known as Doug was actually Agent Phil Crayton. This evening, just before the storm hit us, ATF agents converged on the barn Riley saw in one of her visions. They raided it and captured several of the men, including the leader of the group." He turned back to Riley. "Melissa had escaped and was helped by a stranger.

She was taken to a police station and so even if the ATF hadn't received that call, her statement would have been enough. They won't ever come after you again. You understand?"

She nodded.

"What did the doctor say about her?" Daniel asked Ellen as he looked toward Riley.

Ellen began to stroke Riley's hair. "He said she was fine and that the pain in her stomach and the nose bleed was just caused by panic from the storm."

"But you know differently, don't you?" he asked Riley.

"It wasn't panic, Officer Ward. It was the tornado. I could feel it inside me, but I'm doing better now. Mom says I'll have to go see a doctor on a regular basis. I know she's afraid I'll be like my Grandpa, but I won't be. I understand what this is now and I just need to learn how to keep it from hurting me, the way it did Grandpa."

"And what about Mr. Boyd?" Daniel looked beyond Riley for a moment toward Carl, who was resting in one of chairs in the lobby. Already injured, it was clear the impact of recent events would linger in him for quite a while.

Riley glanced back at him. "I don't know. I think I was supposed to help him, but I'm not sure I have."

[29]

Several days passed and the town was still trying to recover from what had begun as an EF3, but turned into an EF4 by the time it landed in Owensville. It had been the worst tornado that part of Indiana had seen in many years.

The schools remained closed, the Red Cross had rolled into town, offering assistance, and everyone seemed to be coming together to help. Donations had been pouring in and would seek to give the Thompsons, among others, what they needed to put their lives back together.

No one knew what had happened to Riley and Dillon that night, before the storm hit. That they'd been chased by a gunrunning militiaman who shot himself in the head when Officer Ward arrived.

No one knew that Riley felt as though she might die when the tornado touched ground, that she could feel every bit of fury it contained. The pain had become so terrible that her nose began to bleed. They didn't know that Jack was about to allow his life to be taken as punishment for his actions, but that Riley pleaded for him not to.

They only knew that they'd managed to find shelter just in time and that her father had been injured. It was probably better that way. Only those close to Riley would ever understand what happened to her not just that night, but what transpired between her and Mr. Boyd.

Now it was the morning of CJ's funeral and Riley was putting on a new dress that Ellen had purchased for her the day before. Jack had been released from the hospital, but wasn't well enough to attend. He had no place else to go and so Ellen reluctantly allowed him to return home, but had made it clear it was a temporary situation.

It had been the first time in years that he'd gone more than a day without a drink. In fact, it had already been four days. He even refused when the doctor prescribed painkillers, insisting that headache pills would suffice.

The details were left out when Gracie received an explanation. She was too young and wouldn't understand all that her family had suffered in the last several days. The last several years, really, and Riley was glad she hadn't known and was glad Gracie had remained at the shelter at the police station. She had been well cared for and, in the end, much safer.

Riley walked down the stairs in her new navy blue dress and her hair pulled back in a bun. She'd figured out how to do it herself.

Jack lay on the sofa in the family room and was the first to catch sight of her. A smile crossed his face and it seemed to push aside his pain. "You look so pretty, sweetheart. Are you sure you want to go?"

"Yes. I'm sure." She continued toward him. "I want to be there for Mr. Boyd. He's going to need me for a while."

"I imagine he will." He reached for Riley's hand, kissing the back of it.

"I'll be okay, Dad."

"I know you will."

Ellen soon emerged from her bedroom, dressed for the funeral. Dillon wasn't far behind as he came down in the only pair of dress pants he owned and an Oxford shirt.

Riley wanted to see Mr. Boyd and had dreamt of him in the night, standing over his son's grave, weeping. But it hadn't been as before; she hadn't been there with him. It was only a dream. Perhaps that part of her gift had passed. Or maybe it just lay dormant until it was needed again.

She wanted to understand it. Why and how it all started. The triggers. And how it was possible to control such a power so that she would not end up like her grandfather. The pain he must have felt from others in addition to his own would have been overwhelming for anyone.

She hoped that this knowledge, this insight into what really happened to Mr. Boyd's family, would help to heal him. Riley didn't like the idea that he was truly alone now. No wife, no children. She feared for him and what he might become.

"Well, don't my children look lovely?" Ellen reached for Riley and pulled her close.

So much healing needed to happen yet, both for her family and Mr. Boyd. She understood why her mother had insisted Jack seek help. Ellen had been forced to face what Jack had become and finally found the courage to confront him and this was not lost on Riley. "We'd better go now, Mom. I see Officer Ward outside. He's waiting."

"Will you be all right on your own for a while?" Ellen peered around the corner into the family room.

"Yes. I'll be fine. Please send my regards to Carl and let him know that I would be there if I could."

"I will. Goodbye." Ellen opened the front door and waited as Riley and Dillon stepped outside into the warm air and calm skies, a much different scene than a few days ago. In fact, it was finally beginning to feel like spring.

Daniel stood next to his SUV and opened the passenger doors. In the front seat was Melissa Simmons.

Riley locked eyes with her for a moment and she instantly understood that Melissa would be fine. She was hurt by the loss of CJ, but in the end, she would be okay. "Hi, Melissa." Riley stepped into the back seat.

"Hi, Riley."

The others stepped in and Daniel drove to the small church on the west side of town. The grounds were large, totaling at least three acres, but the building itself, which had stood there for fifty years, surviving multiple attempts by Mother Nature to tear it down, was demure, humble; a symbol of the humility and faith this small town offered.

A broad smile spread across Riley's face and the others were taken by surprise to see so many people at the church. It looked as though the entire town had shown up to say goodbye to the son of a man none of them really knew.

"Oh my goodness, look at them all," Ellen said.

And, at the front of the church, Riley noticed him. Carl Boyd

Sr., standing in his best suit, looking too thin and frail, with the few strands of hair on his head neatly brushed back. Captain Sinclair had arranged transportation for him and he now seemed to catch sight of Riley too, because a smile she'd never before seen on his face appeared.

His heart was broken, she could feel it, but she could also feel a warmth inside him and this made her happy.

At the end of the service, the people filed out of the church. It had been standing room only with some left outside, only able to listen to the minister speak through a microphone they'd added at the last minute, not expecting the enormous turnout.

Riley stood beneath the large hickory tree with its branches showing signs of new life. Her heart was content, her pain had faded. She cast her eyes toward the crowd and spotted Jacob, the boy who held her young heart in his hands. So much had happened since she'd seen him last. It felt as if it had been years, not days or weeks.

He caught her glance and began walking toward her. He wore light grey pants and a white button-down shirt, and Riley thought he looked handsome. She still wondered where Kaitlyn and her parents had been. She'd tried to find her before the service, but without success.

"Hey, Riley." Jacob twisted a small wild flower in his fingers and cast his gaze down for a moment.

Riley's heart soared at this because she knew he felt as she had. "Hi." An awkward response, but at least she'd managed to speak.

"Are you doing okay?" he asked.

"Yeah, I guess so."

"I hear school will open back up in a week. I guess we got an early Spring Break."

"Yeah, that's cool," Riley replied. "Did your house make it through?"

"The roof got damaged and some broken windows, but we were in our basement," Jacob said.

"Good. Yeah, our house got a little bit too. Could've been worse, I guess." She knew it could have been a whole lot worse. "Have you seen Kaitlyn?"

Jacob looked over the green fields. "No. I haven't."

In that moment, Riley spotted Ellen walking near.

"It's about time to go, sweetheart," she said.

"Okay, Mom." Riley started to walk away, but turned back toward Jacob. "I guess I'll see you later?"

"Sure." He smiled. "Maybe I can come over and help you guys with cleaning up?"

"I'd like that." She turned back to her mother and followed. "Can I say goodbye to Mr. Boyd first?"

"Of course, honey. I'll wait for you by the car," Ellen replied.

Riley continued to the edge of the grounds where Carl stood alone, for the moment, at least. Several had already converged upon him to offer condolences. "Mom says I have to go now and I wanted to say goodbye." She wrapped her arms around his waist, resting her head against his chest. Riley could hear his heart beating. "Are you going to be okay, Mr. Boyd?" She already believed she knew the answer.

"I'll be okay. But that's not to say that I wouldn't mind some company once in a while, if you feel like dropping by."

"I'd love to." And that was the truth. She'd begun to see Mr. Boyd as more than someone she felt compelled to help. He'd become a lot like a grandpa. She needed that and she suspected he did too. "Do you think we'll still see each other in our dreams?"

"I don't know, but maybe it's time I work on letting them go, don't you think?"

She nodded. "I guess I better go now. I'll see you soon, Mr. Boyd."

"You can call me Carl, honey."

Riley continued on to the car where Officer Ward and Melissa waited.

"You ready to go back home?" he asked.

"Yeah." Riley stepped into the waiting car where Dillon and Ellen had already entered. She watched the two of them; Melissa and the policeman who had believed in her. A wave of happiness surged inside. It was their happiness. It seemed that there could be a future for them, but she would not tell Daniel. He would need to figure it out on his own and so would Melissa.

Riley was beginning to understand how to govern the feelings, those of the others with whom she came into contact. It would take time to master the gift, but Riley never backed away from a challenge.

Officer Ward pulled alongside the front of the Thompson home, rolling to a stop. He stepped out to open the rear passenger door and Ellen was the first to emerge.

Riley followed, but rather than continuing toward the house as Ellen and Dillon had after a brief thank you and goodbye, she stood in front of him for a moment. "Thank you for believing me, Officer Ward. I don't think any of us would have survived if you hadn't."

He placed a hand on her shoulder. "You're the bravest girl I have ever met, Riley Thompson. You ever need anything, don't hesitate to come see me, okay?"

She gave him an enthusiastic hug. "Goodbye." She turned to Melissa. "Goodbye, Melissa."

Riley watched from the front porch as the officer's SUV pulled away. As she looked on at the end of the road, another sight caught her eye. Kaitlyn, her mother, and father walked along the pathway. Her mom was holding a casserole dish.

Kaitlyn took to running and hurried to the porch, wrapping her arms around her best friend.

The two didn't exchange words for a moment, only held each other tightly as ten-year-old best friends did. A moment later, and her parents approached. They hadn't been to visit this house in nearly three years and Riley wondered why they were here now.

"Hello, Riley," Mrs. Ross said. "Are your parents inside?"

"Yes."

Mr. Ross followed behind. "How's your dad doing? Okay, I hope?"

"Yeah. Would you like to come inside?"

"That would be wonderful. Thank you." Mrs. Ross waited as Riley pushed open the door.

"Mom, Dad! Mr. and Mrs. Ross are here."

Ellen quickly appeared from the family room, as she'd been checking on Jack when they arrived home. "Mike, Liz, what are you doing here?" It seemed she realized the question might have sounded nothing like she intended. "I mean, I'm so glad you're here. Please come in."

"I'm sorry we didn't make the service. We were having some windows replaced and it took longer than we thought. Was it nice?" Liz asked.

"It was beautiful. I think Carl was taken aback by the turnout."

"I baked this for you this morning. I thought you might need a break from cooking." Liz handed Ellen the casserole dish.

"Thank you so much. It's so good to see you both. It really is."

Mike moved into the living room where Jack remained on the couch. "How you feeling?"

"I've been better, but not too bad. I'd get up, but..."

Mike offered his hand as he approached the couch. "No problem, man." He took hold of Jack's hand and gently shook it. "It's good to see you."

"You too, Mike," Jack replied. "I—um, I know that I haven't been a good friend lately, or a good anything, really, but I just want to say that I'm working on making things right."

"I hope so, Jack. I really do."

Riley took Kaitlyn's hand and the two ran upstairs to play in her room.

It would be a difficult road ahead. Ellen would have to find a way to care for the children on her own; she would have to regain their trust too. But Riley held out hope that what had happened meant something. That the lives lost, the pain she'd suffered, that her family had suffered, hadn't been in vain and that her home would not be broken forever. But that's what little girls do, isn't it? Wish for a happy ending?

THE END

ABOUT THE AUTHOR

Bestselling author Robin Mahle lives in Virginia with her husband and two children. Her Kate Reid mysteries have drawn praise for grabbing hold of the reader and refusing to let go. And the intense, fast-paced style of storytelling led her to create another series, the Lacy Merrick thrillers, which readers have called "believable, and ripped from today's headlines." With powerful leading ladies and action-packed thrill rides, Robin hopes to continue taking readers on roller-coaster adventures that will leave them breathless.

If you enjoyed Ms. Mahle's work, please share your experience by leaving a review on Amazon

Get **Exclusive Previews, and news on upcoming releases by signing up to receive Robin's Newsletter

For more information visit Robin at:

robinmahle.com

ALSO BY ROBIN MAHLE

Behind Her Eyes - A Riley Thompson Thriller (Book 1)

All the Shiny Things - A Kate Reid Novel (Book 1)

Law of Five – A Kate Reid Novel (Book 2)

Gone Unnoticed – A Kate Reid Novel (Book 3)

Blackwaters- A Kate Reid Novel (Book 4)

Endangered - A Kate Reid Novel (Book 5)

The Pretty Ones – A Kate Reid Novel (Book 6)

Last Word – A Kate Reid Novel (Book 7)

Deadly Reckoning – A Kate Reid Novel (Book 8)

Unbound: The Kate Reid Series Box Set (Books 1-3)

Primal Deception - A Lacy Merrick Thriller (Book 1)

Shadow Rising – A Lacy Merrick Thriller (Book 2)

First Target – A Lacy Merrick Thriller (Book 3)

Landslide

Beyond the Clearing

www.ingramcontent.com/pod-product-compliance
Lightning Source LLC
Chambersburg PA
CBHW062114170626
46813CB00002B/446

* 9 7 8 1 7 3 2 6 4 1 3 0 3 *